LOCKDOWN
on
LONDON
LANE

Beth Reekles

LOCKDOWN on LONDON LANE

 by wattpad books

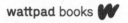

wattpad books

Published in Canada by Wattpad Books, a division of Wattpad Corp.
36 Wellington Street E., Toronto, ON M5E 1C7

www.wattpad.com

First Wattpad Books edition: February 2022
ISBN 978-1-98936-585-4 (Trade Paper original)
ISBN 978-1-98936-586-1 (eBook edition)

Library and Archives Canada Cataloguing in Publication
information is available upon request.

Printed and bound in Canada
1 3 5 7 9 10 8 6 4 2

Cover design and illustration by Elliot Caroll
Cover concept by Ashley Santoro
Typesetting by Neil Erickson

This one's for the Cactus Updates crew. From PowerPoint nights about rom-com meet-cutes to Christmassy murder mysteries, it was fun "not" hanging out with you. Thanks for helping to get me through lockdown.

Sunday

Sunday

<u>*URGENT!!!!!!!*</u>

<u>*DO NOT IGNORE THIS MESSAGE*</u>

<u>*NOTICE TO ALL RESIDENTS OF LONDON LANE,*</u>
<u>*APARTMENT BUILDING C*</u>

Dear Resident,

As you will be aware from our previous missives on the subject, due to the current situation in which we are potentially facing a global pandemic due to a highly contagious virus, building management has made the decision to impose a seven-day quarantine on any apartment building in London Lane where a resident is found to have the virus.*

Unfortunately, someone in BUILDING C has tested positive.

BUILDING C is now in a seven-day lockdown. Please remain calm, remain safe, and wash your hands regularly. We ask that you avoid use of the elevators except for emergencies and avoid contact with other residents. Most importantly, please remain in your apartment.

Have a good week!

With kind regards,

The London Lane Building Management Team

*PLEASE NOTE: If you think you have contracted the virus, you are to inform your building's caretaker immediately. If you do not follow instructions, management reserves the right to serve notice of eviction to any tenant or to impose significant fines for breach of contract. Your caretaker for BUILDING C is MR. ROWAN HARRIS.

Chapter One

It's starting to get light out; the venetian blinds are a pale-gray color that does nothing to keep the sunshine away. The entire window seems to glow, and pale shadows fall across the rest of the room, obscuring the organized cluster of hair products and cologne on the dresser, playing tricks on the hoodie hanging in front of the wardrobe doors. There's a knee digging into my thigh. I rub a hand over my face, feeling last night's mascara congealing around the edges of my eyes, and start to peel myself out of the bed, hissing when I discover an arm is pinning down my hair. I bunch it up into a ponytail, slowly, to ease it free inch by inch.

The mattress creaks when I sit up, but—Nigel? I want to say Nigel—snorts in his sleep, still totally out of it, oblivious to my being in his bed.

I glance over my shoulder at him.

Still cuter than his profile picture, even with a line of drool down his chin.

"This has been fun," I whisper, even though he's fast asleep. I blow him a kiss and creep across the bedroom to silently wriggle into my jeans. I look down at the T-shirt of his I borrowed to sleep in. It's a Ramones shirt, and it feels genuinely vintage, not just some ten-pound H&M version. Actually, it's really goddamn comfortable. And cute, I think, catching a glimpse of myself in the mirror leaning against the far wall. Oversized, but not in a way that makes me look like a little kid playing dress-up. I tuck it into the front of my jeans, admiring the effect.

Oh yeah, that's cute.

Sorry, Neil—Neil? Maybe that's it—this shirt is mine now.

My long brown hair, on the other hand, looks kind of scraggly and definitely not cute. Yesterday evening's curls have dropped out, leaving it limp, full of kinks, and looking pretty sorry for itself. I run my fingers through it, but give up. Hey, at least the smeared mascara is giving me some grunge vibes that totally match the Ramones shirt.

Collecting my own T-shirt and bra from the bedroom floor, I tip-toe into the open-plan living/dining room. Where'd I leave my bag? Wasn't it—a-ha, there it is! And my coat too. I stuff my clothes into my bag, then look around for my shoes.

Come on, Imogen, think, they've got to be around here some-where. I can't have lost them. I wasn't even drunk last night! Where did I leave my damn shoes?

Oh my God, no. I remember. He made me leave them outside, saying they looked muddy. Like it was my fault it rained last night and the pathway up to the apartment block was covered in mud from the flower beds. And I joked that they were Prada and if someone stole them this had better be worth it, even though I'd only bought them on sale from Zara.

I do a final sweep just to make sure I've got everything. Phone—check. House key—yep, in my bag.

I hesitate, then do a quick dash back to the tiny two-seater dining table near the living-room door to nab a slice of leftover pepperoni pizza from our delivery late yesterday evening.

Breakfast of champions.

I step over some junk mail as I sneak out of the front door. It can't be much later than seven o'clock. Who the hell delivers junk mail that early in the morning? Who is *that* dedicated?

My shoes are exactly where I left them.

And, all right, in fairness, they do look like I trekked through a farmyard. I really can't blame him for making me take them off outside the apartment. I'm going to have to clean them up when I get home.

I hold the slice of pizza between my teeth as I wriggle my feet into them—and *ew*, they're soggy—and then I slip my coat on.

Okay, good to go!

I skip down the stairs to the ground floor, munching on my pizza and already on the Uber app to get myself a car home. These shoes are cute, but not really made for a walk of shame.

"Excuse me, miss?"

Despite there being nobody else around, I don't realize the voice is directed at me until it says, "Hey you, Ramones!"

When I turn around, I find a tired, stressed-looking guy with a handful of leaflets. Mr. Junk Mail, I'm assuming. He's wearing a blue surgical mask over his mouth and ugly brown slippers.

"Thanks, mate, but I'm not interested," I tell him, and make for the door.

Except when I push it open, it . . . doesn't.

I grab the big steel handle and yank, and push, and rattle, but the door stays firmly locked.

What the fuck?

Oh my God, this is how I die. A one-night stand and a serial killer peddling leaflets. Please, please don't let anybody put that as cause of death on my gravestone.

"Miss, you can't leave," the man tells me wearily. "Didn't you get the note?"

"What note? What are you talking about?"

I turn to him, my phone clutched in my hand. Should I call the police? My mum? The Uber driver?

The man sighs, exasperated, stepping toward me, but still maintaining a good distance. Like me, there's a rumpled look about him, but he looks more like he rushed out of the house this morning, not like he's just heading home. There's a huge ring of keys hanging from his belt. Then I clock the white latex gloves he's wearing and get a sinking feeling in my stomach.

"We got a confirmed case from one of the residents. The whole building's on lockdown. That door doesn't open except for medical needs and food deliveries."

I stare at him, all too aware that my mouth is hanging open. After a while, he shrugs in that *What can you do?* kind of way.

It's a joke, I realize.

It's got to be a joke.

I let out an awkward laugh, my lips stretching into a smile. "Right. Right, yeah, good one. Look, um, totally get it, real serious, but can you just . . . you know, use one of those keys, let me out of here? Cross my heart, I'll be *super* careful. Look, hey, I'll even cancel my Uber and walk, how about that?"

The guy frowns at me. "Miss, do you realize how serious this is?"

"Absolutely," I reassure him, but instead of sounding sincere, it comes off as fake, like I'm trying too hard. Condescending, even. Shit. I try again. "I get it. I do, but look, the thing is, I was just visiting someone. So I shouldn't really be here right now. And I kind of have to get home?"

There's a flicker of sympathy on his face, and I let myself get excited at having won him over. But then the frown returns, and he tells me sternly, "You know you're not supposed to be traveling unnecessarily, don't you?"

Damn it.

"Well, I mean . . . couldn't you just . . . "

I look longingly over my shoulder at the door. At the muddy path on the other side of the glass, the washed-out flower beds with the droopy rosebushes and brightly colored petunias. Freedom—so close I can almost taste it, and yet . . .

And yet all I can taste is my own morning breath and pepperoni pizza.

Which is not as great now as it was two minutes ago.

What are the odds I can snatch his keys off his belt and unlock the door before he catches me? Hmm, pretty nonexistent. Or what if I just run really hard and really fast at the door? Maybe I could smash the window with one of my heels? Ooh! Could I hypnotize him into letting me out of here? I could definitely give it a go. I've seen a few clips of Derren Brown on YouTube.

"Seven-day quarantine," my jailer tells me. "I've got to deep clean all the communal spaces. Anyone could be infected, and unless you're going to tell me you've got fifty-odd tests for all the residents in that bag of yours, nobody's going anywhere. Believe me, this is no fun for me either. You think I want to be playing security guard all day long just so I don't get fired by management and end up evicted?"

Okay, *fine*, well done. Congrats, Mr. Junk Mail, I officially feel sorry for you.

"But—"

"Listen, all I can suggest is you go back to your friend"—I appreciate that he says *friend* as though we're talking about an actual friend here, when it's so obvious that's not the case—"and see if you can get a grocery delivery slot, and maybe one from Topshop or whatever, see you through the next week. But unless you need to go to a hospital, you're stuck here."

*

I trudge slowly, grudgingly, back up the stairs. My shoes are pinching my toes, so I take them off, slinging the straps over my index finger to carry them. Mr. Junk Mail stays downstairs to scrub down the door I just put my grubby hands all over, almost like he's warding me off, making sure I don't try to leave again.

What the hell am I supposed to do now?

Ugh.

I know exactly what I'm supposed to do now.

But still, I hope for the teeniest bit of luck as I jiggle the handle for Apartment 14.

Locked.

Obviously.

Weighing up my options, I finally sit down on the plain tan doormat, my back against the door, and press my hands over my face.

This is what I get for ignoring all the advice.

Not so much the *stay home* stuff (although that, too) so much as the *You're not in university anymore, Immy, stop acting like it* advice—from my parents, my friends, my boss, hell, even my little brothers.

As I always say, who needs to grow up when you can have fun?

This, however, is decidedly *not* fun.

My only option is to do exactly what I would've done back in university: phone my bestie.

Despite the early hour, Lucy answers with a quiet but curt, "What have you done this time?"

"Heyyy, Luce . . . "

"How much do you need, Immy?"

"What makes you think I need money? What makes you think I've done *anything*?" I ask with mock offense, clutching a hand to my heart for dramatic effect, even though she can't see me. And even though I can't see her, I absolutely know she's rolling her eyes when she gives that long, low sigh. "Although, all right, I am in . . . the *littlest* spot of trouble."

"Did you forget to cancel a free trial?"

Lucy's so used to my shit by now that she knows how melodramatic I can be over something like that—melodramatic enough to warrant an early-morning phone call like this.

But, alas.

I open my mouth to tell her I'm stuck with Honeypot Guy, the guy

I've been messaging for the last week or so, whom she specifically told me not to go see because there's maybe a pandemic, and now I'm stuck quarantined in his building and I only have the one pair of underwear and I didn't even bring a toothbrush with me and . . .

And I *hate* admitting how right Lucy always is.

Even if, technically, this is all *her* fault, because she was too busy with some stupid wedding planning party last night to answer her phone and talk me out of going to see the guy in the first place. So I decided to go, and not tell her about it until I was safely back at home, just to prove a point about how she always makes a big deal out of nothing, how she worries too much.

"Oh Jesus Christ, you went to see him, didn't you? Honeypot?"

I *cannot* tell her the truth.

At least, not yet.

"No! No, no, of course I didn't," I blurt, even though I fully expect her to see right through me. "I, um, I'm just . . . well, look, so, the thing is . . . "

I don't like lying to my best friend—to anybody, really, if I can help it. If anything, I'm a total oversharer. But I decide this is for the greater good. I mean, really, I'm just doing her a favor, right? If she knew, she'd only spend the week worrying and stressing about me. I'm just sparing her that.

Lucy cuts me off with a sigh, understanding that whatever it is, it's a bit more than the usual mischief I get myself into, and she says, "Oh, you're properly fucked this time, aren't you?"

"Thanks, Luce."

Thankfully, she doesn't push me for answers. "How's your overdraft?"

"Not great."

"Did you run up your credit card again this month?"

"A little bit."

We both know that actually means "almost completely."

"Will a hundred quid cover it, Immy?"

"I love you."

"I'll add it to your tab," she tells me, and I know she's smiling. "Are you sure you're all right?"

"Oh, you know me!" I say, laughing. I'm weirdly relieved that being quarantined with a one-night stand isn't the craziest thing that's happened to me in the last month or so. It's definitely not as bad as the night out where I climbed onstage to challenge the headlining drag queen to a lip sync battle, is it? "I'll work it out. Just . . . yeah. Thanks again, Luce. I'll tell you everything when I see you next."

"Don't you always?"

Lucy has a way of ending conversations without having to say good-bye. I know her well enough to recognize that this is one of those moments. I say good-bye and thank her again for the money she'll send me, the way she always does, which I will repay in love and affection and memes until one day in the distant future, when I have miraculously gotten my life together enough to pay off my overdraft *and* have enough left to put a dent in my ever-growing tab at the Bank of Lucy.

Feeling at least a little better, I stand back up, dust myself off, and knock on the door.

It takes a few minutes to open.

He's disconcerted and groggy and wearing only his boxer shorts. The carefully coiffed blond hair I'd admired in his pictures is now matted, sticking up at all angles. The dried line of drool is still there on the side of his mouth.

I give him my biggest, bestest grin, cocking my head to one side and twirling some hair around a finger.

"Hey there, Niall. Um . . . "

He yawns loudly and holds up a finger to shush me before covering his mouth. He shakes his head, blinking a few times, then looks at me, confused and none too impressed.

"I hate to be an imposition, but your building is kind of . . . quarantined."

"It's what?"

I look for the piece of paper I stepped over earlier and bend down to pick it up. It's a printed notice that, at a quick glance, instructs residents to stay indoors for a seven-day period. I hold it out to him, staying silent and swaying side to side, hands clasped in front of me, while he reads it, rubbing his eyes. He has to squint, holding it up close to his face.

"Oh shit."

"There's a guy downstairs, and he won't let me leave," I say. "I'm *really* sorry, but unless you want to take it up with him . . . "

I step back inside the apartment, leaving my shoes outside once more. He's speechless as I put down my bag and coat.

"I'm just going to use your bathroom. You know, wash my hands." I waggle them at him, as if to prove what a responsible grown-up I am.

When I come out he's still standing by the door, still clutching the paper.

"So, Nico, listen—"

"It's Nate."

"What?"

"My name?" He raises his eyebrows at me, looking more pissed off than tired now. "Nate. Nathan, but . . . Nate."

I bite my lip, grimacing. I'd kind of hoped if I ran through enough names, I'd hit on the right one eventually. I'd also kind of hoped if I said them quickly enough, he wouldn't notice.

"Sorry. You're . . . you're saved in my phone contacts as the honey-pot emoji. You know, 'cause you . . . you said that if you were a fictional character, you'd be Winnie-the-Pooh, and you said your mum kept bees and . . . and that your favorite chocolate bar is Crunchie, which has honeycomb in it . . . I thought it was cute at the time, and funny, but then I realized I'd forgotten your name, and you deleted your profile off the dating app, so I couldn't check *that* . . . "

Nate's face has softened.

But then, as I take my coat off, he realizes what I'm wearing and lets out a loud, disbelieving laugh. "You're really something, aren't you? Talking your way over here when everyone's meant to be social distancing—"

"I didn't hear *you* complaining," I mutter, none too quietly.

"Sneaking out without so much as a good-bye, *and* you were planning to make off with my favorite shirt. Wow."

"Maybe it was just going to be a good excuse to see you again."

He laughs, rolling his eyes. "Imogen, believe me when I say I have *never* met anybody like you before."

I curtsy, even though it sounds like an insult, the way he says it. "Thank you."

That, at least, makes him laugh. Nate-Nathan-Nate runs a hand through his hair, taming it only slightly, then tells me, "There are spare towels in the bathroom cabinet if you want to take a shower. I'm going to see if I can get a food delivery slot online. Then, I guess we'll . . . I don't know. Figure this out."

I'm not exactly sure what there is to "figure out" besides maybe ordering some frozen lasagnas and a few pairs of underwear, but I nod. "Right. Totally. You got it, Nate."

So much for my swift exit.

Chapter Two

It's automatic, the way I roll over when I'm not even fully awake yet, my arm out to pull her closer. The empty space beside me startles me for a second before I wake up enough to remember where she is. I turn back over to face my bedside cabinet, rubbing the sleep out of my eyes with one hand and fumbling for my phone with the other. My hand closes on it and I yank out the charger.

There's a notification waiting for me on the screen: a text from Charlotte an hour ago.

Just about to leave—I'll see you in a couple of hours! Xxxxx

She always tells me she's not a morning person, but the honest to God truth is she absolutely is. What she is, is the kind of person who likes a *lazy* morning. She'll wake up an hour before she has to be at work just so she can spend some time curled up under the covers reading, or jotting things down in the powder-blue notebook she takes everywhere with her.

Today must be a special occasion, though, for her to have been actually up and out of bed so early. Well—either that, or after three days being home with her twin sister and parents, clearing out her childhood bedroom and the attic to get ready for her parents to sell up and downsize, she's been going stir-crazy and can't wait to get home.

Yeah, I think, it's definitely that one. She's been putting this weekend off for as long as she can; she's been living in denial of her parents selling the house since they announced it a couple of months ago, and I can't say I blame her. My parents divorced when I was ten and after that, they both moved around a couple of times. If I had to say good-bye to the kind of home Charlotte's known her whole life, I'd be pretty upset about it too.

I can only imagine how tough this weekend has been for her; it makes sense she'd be on the road before eight o'clock.

What doesn't make sense is how much I've missed her the last couple of days. It's genuinely pathetic. I can just imagine my friends telling me, *Ethan, grow a pair, any guy would give his right arm to have the place to himself for a weekend, get the girlfriend out of the way, have a break from her!*

I *did* see a couple of mates on Friday night, but that was for a Fortnite livestream for my Twitch channel. And *see* is stretching it a little—we all joined from the comfort of our own homes. Real crazy, frat-boy kinda stuff, of course. While the cat's away, and all that.

But I've missed her.

It's not like I can't *cope* without her, like I'm some mummy's boy who never learned to do the dishes or make a bed or do the laundry or anything. It's not like that. If anything, *I'm* the one who does the bulk of the cleaning around here, always tidying up after her.

It'll be good to have her back home, that's all.

I stay in bed for a while checking my other notifications—YouTube, Twitter, WhatsApp. I clear through some emails saying I've got new patrons on Patreon, which sends a thrill of excitement through me, as it always does, and finally I haul my lazy ass up to take a shower before Charlotte gets back.

We can catch up on *The Mandalorian* this afternoon, maybe, if she doesn't want to spend some time writing. Or we could watch a movie. I wonder if she'll have a bunch of stuff from her childhood bedroom we need to find the space for—old exercise books and homework projects we'll have to shove in a box under the bed, or Beanie Babies.

Maybe she'd let me put the Beanie Babies on eBay, if they're worth anything.

I can't complain too much if she does want to keep them. It's not like I don't have my fair share of action figures and collectibles in the apartment. And the giant Charizard plushie . . .

I dread the day my parents get the same idea; I hope that by the time they do, I'll at least live somewhere with enough space to store my entire collection of Neil Gaiman books, my old PlayStation, records from my vinyl phase that I can't quite bear to get rid of.

It occurs to me now that when Charlotte thinks of us moving somewhere with more space one day, she thinks about it in the context of a guest bedroom, or a potential future nursery. Or a library. Actually, I could definitely get on board with a home library.

Breakfast made, I'm sat on the sofa watching old episodes of *Parks and Rec* and daydreaming about the studio space I might have one day that *isn't* just a dedicated few square feet of the living room, when my phone rings. It's Charlotte, which is weird, and I answer with a knot in my stomach, visions of her car broken down on the side of a motorway or—

Come on, Ethan, take a breath and answer the phone.

Sliding my thumb across the screen to answer, I manage to *not* start with, "What's wrong?" and instead say, "Hey, what's up? Did you forget your key?"

"Ethan," she says. Her voice wobbles. The catastrophizing part of my brain kicks into high gear for a second, thinking I was right, her car broke down, something is horribly wrong. She sounds upset, but it's not just that—she's agitated, angry. "Ethan, you have to get down here. He's saying I'm not allowed in the building."

"What? Who?"

"Mr. Harris," she tells me, meaning the building's live-in caretaker. "He's—Ethan, can you please come down here and talk to him? And wear a mask."

Confused as hell, I can only hold the phone near my ear even after Charlotte's hung up on me, before kicking myself into gear. I leave my plate of half-eaten bagel on the sofa and root through the set of drawers in the hallway. She thought it was ridiculous when I ordered a bunch of blue surgical masks online a couple of weeks ago, before they even started using the word *pandemic* in the news; now, I can't help but feel a little smug. Anxiety: 1, Charlotte: 0.

I wash my hands and put the mask on, then snatch up my key and leave the apartment. There's a scrap of paper on the floor someone's pushed under the door, but I'll check it later. I go down the single flight of stairs in just my socks, almost tripping over my own feet in my haste.

Mr. Harris is standing near the main doors to the building with his arms crossed, wearing white latex gloves and a mask like mine. On the other side, with her bags on the floor and her hands bunched into fists on her hips, is Charlotte. My glasses steam up from the mask so I nudge them up on top of my head, where they balance on my thick blond-brown hair, and I squint at him instead; Charlotte's head becomes a fuzzy patch of orange where her hair is a mess.

"What's going on?"

"Ethan, tell him!" she yells, voice muffled by the door. She raises a hand to pound against the glass, leaving smudges on it. "He's locked me out! He can't do this!"

The caretaker sighs. It's a long-suffering sigh, like this is a conversation he's already had a thousand times. He turns to give me a frown and I can imagine his teeth grinding behind that mask.

"Ethan, please tell your girlfriend she can't enter the building. You got the note, right?"

"What note?"

"Bloody hell, what was even the point of me . . . ?" He trails off with a sharp sigh, rubbing the back of his forearm against his brow. "The whole building's on lockdown. You remember I put a notice out when all this started that said if anybody in the building got sick, if we had a confirmed case, we had to lock down for everybody's safety? Nobody in or out."

"Yeah . . . ?"

"Confirmed case last night. Someone, *not naming any names*, caught it from her *divorce lawyer*, if you can believe it. She got a test done and it turned up positive. So we're on lockdown. Nobody's getting *in*, or *out*. Including your girlfriend."

Oh shit.

I bump my glasses back down to see Charlotte's face, still scrunched up in anger, her lips in a tight little pout. They steam up again just as she gives me a look that says, *Ethan, I swear to God, if you don't open this door right now, I'll break it down myself.*

For someone so small . . . what's that Shakespeare quote again?

Charlotte has it printed on a tote bag. It's very accurate right now.

"Come on, Mr. Harris," I say, with a nervous laugh. My hand moves up like I'm going to step toward him and clap his arm, until I remember the six-foot rule and think better of it. "It's us, you know we're good. Charlotte lives here. Where's she gonna go?"

"Where's she been?"

"At her parents, but—"

"Well, she's going to have to go back there."

"But . . . "

I wouldn't exactly say I was *friends* with our caretaker, but we're on good terms. His apartment is directly below ours, and apparently he's glad to have us there, because the previous owners "might as well have been practicing tap dancing with all the noise they made." He watches my YouTube videos, too, he told me a while ago. He said he likes having "a celebrity" in the building, and we always stop for a chat if we see him.

I don't know why I think I'm going to convince him to let Charlotte in when he looks so determined, but for a second I really believe I can. We've never made any fuss. We're good neighbors, good people, he even knows us by name.

And how can he say no?

Charlotte lives here, this is her home. Of course he has to let her inside.

"I can't let her inside," he tells me sternly. "Nobody in, nobody out, no exceptions. Well. Exceptions are by emergency only, and this doesn't class as one."

"What about food?"

"Get it delivered. I'm setting up a sanitizing station, make sure everything's clean before it gets through."

For a second, I imagine having something like that for Charlotte, and Mr. Harris setting up a giant hose to douse her in Dettol spray before she's allowed inside.

"Unless she can show me a negative test," he says reluctantly, as though he's risking his job by even allowing us that much, "she's not getting in. Quarantine's lasting a week. Sure you two can survive being apart for that long, eh?"

He shrugs, and his scowl softens just long enough for me to see he actually *is* sorry about this whole mess; I know he doesn't have too much say on the matter, that this really is up to his bosses, the mysterious, faceless, building management we've never set eyes on but who occasionally send us threatening letters via Mr. Harris to remind us there are no pets in the building, there is no renovation work to be done without clearing it with them first, that if nobody owns up to who damaged the window on the third floor they *will* be charging an equal share of the (absolutely extortionate) cost of repairs to each resident.

I always picture them in the same way as Station Management, from the *Welcome to Night Vale* podcast—some mysterious, dark, writhing, many-headed mass of condemnation. Charlotte says they're more like Mr. Rochester's mad wife in the attic from *Jane Eyre*. Either way, I don't imagine petitioning *them* right now would make a blind bit of difference.

Mr. Harris steps back, but he doesn't leave. He's got to make sure I don't try to smuggle Charlotte indoors, I guess.

I do the only thing I can, which is to turn toward her and give her a helpless shrug, pulling a face even though she can't really see it because I'm wearing a mask. I can't see her expression clearly enough because of my fogged-up glasses, but I can guess how disappointed she is.

She gestures widely enough for me to see, though, and I get the message. I tell Mr. Harris "Thanks," even though it's really thanks for nothing, and head back upstairs. Inside, I wash my hands again, take off the mask, and pull my glasses back down so I can see the world in all its high-definition glory again. My phone is already ringing on the sofa and I grab it, answering as I head out to the balcony, leaning over it to see Charlotte standing below.

She runs a hand through her short ginger hair, shaking it out, and pouts up at me, looking so desperately sad. Through the phone, she tells me, "I thought he might listen to you."

"Because I'm a guy?" I flex a nonexistent bicep and kiss it.

"Because he likes your YouTube videos, you *idiot*." She laughs, but it fades away quickly. "I'm going to have to go home. Just as well my parents haven't gotten rid of my old bed yet, huh?"

"Do you need your stuff? I could drop a bag down from the balcony. Clothes, or . . . ?"

She shakes her head. "Thanks, sweetie, but that's okay. I've got some stuff, and my laptop and things. I can borrow some of Maisie's clothes. She has terrible taste, but she *is* my identical twin. Give or take a few pounds." Charlotte grabs her love handles, cracking a grin.

"Didn't you both buy the same dress last Christmas?"

"Shush. Look, I'll . . . I'll just go back home. I'll see you next week, I guess."

"Providing this is all over by then." And someone else in the building hasn't contracted the virus, and then someone else, and we're not in this strict lockdown for the next several months, and Charlotte never gets to come back to our apartment, and . . . My chest constricts, and suddenly looking out at the empty common area in front of the apartment is like surveying some scene from an apocalyptic disaster movie. And *I am on my own.* I'm basically Will Smith in *I Am Legend*, except without the dog, and not half as cool, and—

"I'll be back next week when this silly lockdown thing is over. I promise. I'll scale the walls if I have to, okay? Don't spiral."

"I'm not spiraling."

She raises her eyebrows, squinting up at me, not buying it. Despite the fact that she's the one locked out of her home for the next several days, somehow she's the one comforting me.

"It'll be fine. It's—it's not a big deal, really, is it? In the grand scheme of things. We can FaceTime, and text, and you can have some peace and quiet to film a few videos and get some work done without me walking by in the background and messing up your edits. It's fine. It's just a week."

We talk a little while longer, until Mr. Harris opens the main door long enough to tell Charlotte to please collect her bags and go, and I wave good-bye from the balcony. Charlotte blows me a kiss on her way to her car, and I catch it.

Just a week.

It'll fly by.

Chapter Three

"Serena," Zach yells from the bathroom, "can you bring me some toilet paper?"

Four years of a loving, caring relationship, and this is where it gets you.

At least he still closes the door. Romance isn't completely dead for us. Yet.

I pause my movie and toss my phone down to grab a few new rolls of toilet paper from the jumbo pack stuffed into the top of our wardrobe, taking them to the bathroom. I open the door, passing them through to Zach one at a time.

"I thought you were going to refill it when you cleaned the bathroom last."

"I forgot," he tells me.

"How can you forget? You can see the cupboard's empty and we need more out."

"Well, I must've gotten distracted," he tells me, teeth gritted. He snatches the last roll out of my hand just as I'm yanking the door shut again.

Four years of a loving, caring relationship, I think, and it can't always be sunshine and rainbows and sparkles, or whatever. You're bound to get annoyed with each other about things, like forgetting to replace the toilet paper in the bathroom, or—

"Are we still going to the shops?" Zach asks, coming back into the living room, where I'm back with my movie. I pause it again. Maybe by bedtime, I'll have gotten through to the end, and I'll find out if Stephanie ditches her lawyer fiancé from The Big City to stay with hunky Jared from her hometown who's been helping her fix up her parents' old farm.

"We can do," I say, with a tone that makes it clear I really don't want to.

I'm in my unicorn onesie. It's a Sunday afternoon. I just want to veg out.

"I thought we were going before my shift starts."

"I can go later."

"But it's Sunday, the shops will be closed."

"Oh my God, *fine*, we'll go *now*."

"You can go tomorrow on your way home otherwise," Zach tells me.

Relationships are all about compromise. Which side of the bed you sleep on, if you need a new car or a nice holiday more, whose family you live closer to. Apparently, that kind of compromise also now includes Zach letting me do the grocery shopping by myself on my way home from the office.

Lucky me.

I don't mean to say it out loud, but I must do because he sighs and says, "Fine, then, we'll go now. *I'll* go. You finish your movie."

"It's all right, I can go with you."

"Serena," he deadpans, peering over his glasses at me for dramatic effect, something which should be annoying but which I actually still find kind of endearing, "I'm twenty-nine years old. I think I can buy you another box of tampons and get the right brand of cheese from the supermarket."

"Don't forget the halloumi," I tell him, reaching for the remote and snuggling back down, my butt becoming one with the sofa for the next hour. "Or the chicken breast for fajitas. Get diced chicken, though."

"What's the difference?"

I can't be bothered to explain that if he buys a whole chicken breast, he'll chop it up, and I don't like the idea of using the same chopping board for vegetables as he'll use for meat, even though one of us will obviously clean it beforehand, so buying precut chicken is easier for both of us, and it might stop some of the "meat is murder"/"you squeamish plant-eater" snipes we always seem to make at each other.

So instead I wave a hand in the air, not bothering to look over at him. "Just get whatever, Zach, it'll be fine."

Zach potters around our little one-bedroom apartment, getting ready to go out to the shops, collecting our list from the notepad on the fridge and checking the cupboards for anything we might have missed that he needs to pick up. I zone out, losing myself in my corny romance movie.

Just when Stephanie and hunky handyman Jared share a kiss in a rainstorm, the music swelling, the TV pauses.

"Hey!"

I sit up abruptly, glaring at Zach and reaching for the remote in his hands.

Everything about him gives me pause, though. A deep frown creases his forehead and he sighs heavily through his nose, his mouth pressed into a thin line. The TV remote hangs at his side, and his other hand is clutched tightly around a piece of paper; his shoulders are squared, stiff.

My glare disappears and I get up. Nervousness starts to creep through me, even though, rationally, I know that some scrap of paper can't be *that* bad. What's it going to be? I mean, really. A neighbor asking us to be quiet? Some junk mail?

But then, I have to wonder: Why does he look so worried about it?

"Zach?"

"We have a problem."

*

The kitchen is an absolute mess when Zach gets back upstairs. I abandon my collection of tinned tomatoes and Dolmio pasta sauce to rush into our little hallway, grabbing him by the shoulders before he even gets the chance to put his keys down, before the door has even closed behind him.

"What did he say? Zach, what did he say?"

He tries to give me a patient smile, but he can't really manage it. He puts his hands on my hips, though, which does do something to comfort me. Being trapped in the building is a pretty terrifying notion, but at least I won't have to go through it alone.

Zach shakes his head. "No luck. I'll have to call work, tell them I can't come in. I mean, I wouldn't be able to anyway, you know, the hospital's on pretty strict instructions to self-isolate if you think you've been exposed to the virus, but—"

"*Zach.*"

"Right. Yeah, so, we can't go to work. Mr. Harris said we can't even go out for groceries. He said we can get a delivery, but he wants to make sure everything gets sanitized and cleaned properly before it comes into the building."

"What, so he's going to stand outside spraying Dettol on our cereal and bread before we can have it?"

"I don't know, Rena."

"Well, did you *ask* him?"

"I was a bit busy trying to get my head around it all. We're in full lockdown until next Sunday, he said. You'll have to call the office in the morning. Shall I place a food order? Where's your iPad?"

He follows me into the kitchen, stopping to stare, wide-eyed at all the food I've emptied out of the cupboards while he was downstairs. "What are you doing?"

"Seeing if we've got enough food to get us through a week."

He laughs, coming close enough to wrap his arms around me from behind, planting a noisy kiss on the side of my face. One of my hands automatically reaches up to hold his arm, my thumb brushing back and forth. "I'll get my ration book ready for stamps, shall I?"

"Oh, shut up. We might have to live on pasta and pesto for three days straight, but I think we'll survive. We *definitely* do need more toilet paper, though. And we've got absolutely nothing for breakfast— we'll run out of bread tomorrow, and there's only enough cereal left for one bowl."

Zach's face scrunches in a curious frown and he peels away, reaching over my head for a cupboard. "I thought we bought some Cheerios on sale a few weeks ago?"

"Yeah, and I'm telling you we're almost out."

"No, no, I'm sure we bought more."

"I literally *just* looked in there, Zach. This is what happens when you come in from shift at all hours and eat a bowl of cereal before you do anything else. We run out, and we need more."

He gives up looking, conceding the argument with a small grunt.

"Better get started on that online order then," he says, clapping his hands together. He goes off in search of my iPad to get started while I tidy up the kitchen. The note the building's caretaker left under our door at some point today is on the counter, and my heart leaps into my throat at the sight of it.

With the news around the pandemic gradually ramping up and the hospital Zach works at trying to prepare for the worst, it's not as though I thought we'd just skate by totally unscathed, but . . . I guess I wasn't expecting to be put on house arrest in our apartment for an entire week, not this soon. And I hadn't even stocked up on extra toilet paper!

Still, I remind myself again, at least if I have to be put on lock-down, I don't have to go through it alone. At least I've got Zach by my side.

Chapter Four

"Stay," I tell him, leaning in for another kiss.

I cling to Danny's jacket as though I might physically be able to keep him here. As though he's not about a foot taller than me, with those big broad shoulders, and like I don't have to shop in the petite section half the time. Me, the girl who doesn't use the top shelves in the kitchen cupboards because she can't reach them, versus the guy who used to play rugby at university.

But he lingers, laughing that deep, rich laugh that makes my stomach fill with butterflies, letting his bag drop to the floor in favor of wrapping his arms around me again. He kisses me on my nose, cheeks, forehead, lips, and I sigh into him.

Is it bad how much I don't want him to leave?

Is it bad how quickly I'm falling for him?

Danny and I have only been dating a few weeks—a month, last Wednesday, actually. I'd been with a friend for her birthday on Wednesday, though, so he'd come over on Friday after work to spend the weekend. We'd had plans to go out and celebrate, except . . .

Well.

They hadn't been *firm* plans—it wasn't like we'd had tickets to anything, or reservations, so . . .

Plus, *why* would we ever need to go out for a fancy meal, when Danny was such a good cook? And *why* would I ever want to suggest getting out of bed to go somewhere, when I had my very lovely, very sexy, very wonderful boyfriend right there with me?

And, you know, I hadn't spent all that money on lingerie for nothing. It was our one-month anniversary. I had to make at least *some* effort. (Although, in hindsight, I guess I made a little too much effort, considering we never got around to leaving the apartment. And by *too much*, I mean *the perfect amount*.)

I know Danny has to go home, and he can't stay any longer because he has to do the food shop before everywhere closes for the day, but . . .

"Just a couple more minutes," I wheedle. I pout, which I know must look silly, but I can't help it. "I don't know when I'll get to see you again if all this gets worse."

"All this" meaning the apparently super contagious virus that has become not just the main, but the *only* topic on the news recently. Forget snow days taking over everything. Now, you turn on the TV, even the weatherman is saying, "It's a good day to stay inside!"

I'm really, *really*, hoping it won't turn into something more, that everything will stay at least fairly normal, but this past week, it's been impossible to escape the fact that the tone of the news has gone from *fine* to *borderline sinister*. It's kind of hard to hold out hope for everything staying normal when the tone has changed so quickly.

A sensible person right now might be worrying about their supplies of tinned food and hand sanitizer, and if they have enough tea bags to last a quarantine period.

It's not that I'm not sensible, but I am in the rosy glow of a new relationship, so honestly, my biggest concern when I've been seeing the news alerts is: If they are going to make us stay inside, who knows when I'll get to see Danny next? What if we have to go an entire *week*—or longer!—without seeing each other? I don't think I could handle it.

I know I'm falling for him. How could I not? He's so bloody *perfect*. He's everything I've ever wanted in a boyfriend. And judging by the way he looks at me sometimes, despite us not having been together for that long, I'm sure he feels the same way.

But, well, what if he doesn't? What if that's just the new-relationship, lots-of-sex-and-spontaneous-romantic-moments glow? And what if, if "all this" *does* get worse and we can't see each other for a while, he forgets about me? What if easy conversation and cute dates can't translate into drinks over Zoom and texting? We'd been spending at least a few nights a week together since we started dating. What if all that suddenly goes away?

Everything could change like *that*.

In an instant we could go from this warm, fuzzy glow and not being able to stop thinking about each other, to being total strangers who just . . . drifted apart.

The idea of what could happen, what very well *might* happen, makes my entire chest feel tight. And not in the good, "Danny, I like you so much it takes my breath away" kind of way.

Really, is it *so* terrible that I want him to stay for just a few more minutes?

He groans, drawing away from one more "one last" kiss.

"Isla, I really do have to go."

"Okay. Okay!" I say it more to psych myself up, afraid I might come off as too needy if I go in for yet another one last kiss. The relationship is still new enough that I'm worried being too full-on or too clingy will send him running for the hills.

Be aloof, I try to tell myself. *Guys like that, right? Not hard to get, just aloof. Do not, for the love of God, Isla, do not kiss him again.*

I do peck his cheek, though, unable to help myself, and take a wide step back to smile at him.

Danny picks up his bag, shouldering it, and hesitates with one hand on the door handle. "I'll call you when I get home?"

Yes, please.

Play it cool, Isla, come on.

I tuck a bit of my blond hair behind my ear, glancing away from him to give a small shrug. "Sure. I mean, if you want. That'd be nice."

"Great!" He clears his throat hastily, voice distinctly deeper when he repeats, "Great. Yeah. Well, I'll, um . . . I'll call you later."

This time, he dips forward, his arm scooping around my waist for what is *actually* one last kiss that makes me feel completely and utterly delirious, and then he says a quiet "Good-bye," and . . . he's gone.

I stand in the quiet of my empty apartment for a moment, my arms wrapped around my torso like I can hold this feeling in a little longer that way. The scent of Danny's cologne lingers, and I can still feel the impression of his lips pressed to mine, making me smile.

And then I get back to the reality of it being a Sunday afternoon: I have laundry to do, there's a whole heap of dishes to do from Danny cooking us a fancy brunch earlier with whatever he scrounged from my (apparently) poorly stocked fridge.

Now he's gone, at least, I can put things back to normal. I can get the weird (but adorable) avocado cushion my best friend Maisie got me one birthday back out of the wardrobe, I can bring my *Little Mermaid* music box out of its hiding place inside the dresser. Much as I've been telling myself for the last month that I put them away every time Danny comes over to make the place look tidier, I know it's really only because I'm worried he'll laugh at them and think they're stupid and childish and embarrassing and I'll just . . . gradually bring these things out of hiding the longer we're together.

Not that I think he's going to break up with me over an avocado cushion.

But, you know. He *might*.

I scrape my hair into a ponytail, put some leggings on so I don't feel silly for parading around my apartment in just a T-shirt and my underwear, and get to work.

I'm elbow deep in bubbles, doing the dishes, when there's a knock at the door.

Huh. Weird, I think. I wasn't expecting anybody.

My heart does a quick little flip: maybe it's Danny. Maybe he's back! He probably just realized he forgot something, is all. And, shit, I must look such a state now. I'm so glad I didn't take my makeup off as soon as he left.

(I might have even snuck into the bathroom before he even woke up this morning to put some on. Just a little bit. Primer, foundation, concealer. A little blush and mascara. And I fixed up my eyebrows. But just a *little* bit.)

Frantically, I scrub my hands dry on the tea towel, yank the hair tie out of my hair, and try to shake it out into something more presentable, before hurrying to the door.

Should I lean against the frame, trying to look sexy? Try to entice him back inside, convince him to stay a few more hours, because really, is making sure he's got something for breakfast tomorrow morning *that* important?

No, no, that's so silly. And *I* would probably look silly, trying to pull that off.

Instead, I open the door like a regular human being, startled when Danny's on the other side with an awkward smile that's really more of a grimace. For such a confident guy, he appears disturbingly nervous right now.

"Forget something?" I say. It sounds a little more sultry and flirtatious than I expect it to, but Danny doesn't even appear to notice, doesn't even decide to flirt back.

"Um . . . " He sighs, and runs a hand through his thick, dark curls. "So, apparently, I'm not allowed to leave."

"You're not allowed to leave," I repeat, squinting slightly as I scrutinize his face. Is this a joke? Is it some weird, flirty . . . I don't know, some game I'm not really getting? Is he going to break into a grin any minute, come inside, scoop me up, carry me back to bed?

But he continues to look strangely serious as he tells me, "Yes. At least, according to the guy downstairs, who . . . honestly, Isla, I'm assuming he works here, but I'm basing that off the fact he had a big bunch of keys hanging off his belt, and—"

"Bald guy? Maybe forty?"

"Yeah."

"Oh yeah. That's Mr. Harris. He's the building manager, caretaker, sends us notes when . . . "

Notes like Danny is holding out to me right now.

"It got stuck on my shoe, which he was kind enough to point out to me, during the very, *very*, extensive lecture he gave me about 'no unnecessary travel' and 'following the guidance of health experts on the news.'"

"What is that?"

Danny finally does break out into the big grin I was expecting, and he laughs, but there's still something totally off about his entire demeanor. It's no longer nervous, but it puts me on the back foot. I'm still not getting the joke.

"You know that virus you were so worried about? The one that might've meant we'd spend weeks, maybe even months, apart, having to watch movies over Netflix Party instead of going on actual dates to the cinema, like we were some long-distance couple instead of living like, thirty minutes on the bus away from each other?"

I am really, really not liking the sound of this. My stomach begins to coil into tight knots.

"Yeah . . . ?"

"Well, you don't have to worry about that. No, you do, but . . . " He laughs again, stepping inside, and putting down his bag. The hand holding a crumpled, slightly muddy note, falls to his side. "What I'm trying to say is, some lady here has it, so the whole building is on lockdown—and I'm not allowed to leave. Which means . . . "

"What?" I dive forward, snatching the note from him, smoothing it out to read. The words float around the page and it takes me a few tries to actually understand any of it. My heart is thundering. "A whole week?"

I know I said I didn't want him to leave, but . . . not like *this*.

The idea that someone in the building is so sick that nobody is allowed to leave, not even Danny, who doesn't even *live* here, is suddenly so real and terrifying that I forget how to breathe for a minute.

I want to bleach the entire apartment.

And Danny went *outside the flat*. He went into *a public space*.

How weird would it be if I grabbed the antibac stuff from under the sink and sprayed him with it? Probably the kind of weird I should leave for the six-month mark, at least.

He'll be here for an entire week. A weekend is blissful, but a week? Oh my God.

He's going to be here when I *poop*.

That's not the sort of thing that happens in the first month of a relationship, right? Is it? It's not, right?

Oh my God, am I going to have to try not to poop for an entire week? Is he going to dump me over a—a literal dump?

Don't be silly, Isla, he is fully aware you're a human being. He's not going to freak out because you need to use the bathroom.

He's definitely going to see me without makeup at some point this week. Or with my hair a mess. There's no way I can keep up my appearance constantly for the next seven days. Two or three over a weekend, sure, but a whole week? Not a chance. And what if he finds the music box or the avocado cushion, or the other little trinkets I've been stashing away? (Oh, I'm so happy Mr. Harris didn't lecture him long enough for me to actually get around to taking them out of their hiding places.) Not to mention I don't think I have enough lingerie to last me an entire week. What's he going to think when he sees me in plain old granny pants that don't match my faithfully comfy used-to-be-white-once-upon-a-time bra, without a bow or frill or bit of lace in sight?

Suddenly, I regret every moment of our relationship so far: I've put in all this effort, and now I've set his expectations way too high.

"A whole week," Danny confirms, grinning all over again, like this is the best news ever. He seems so upbeat, so enthusiastic, so damn happy to be stuck with *me*, that it makes me forget about the germs and how horrifyingly weird this entire situation is. And really, it's . . .

It's actually pretty great news, isn't it? A whole week, just me and Danny. Isn't this the sort of thing I wanted, for him not to have to leave?

If this weekend was anything to go by, the next few days will be nothing short of idyllic.

And he can cook for me! All week! How great will that be!

Plus, come on, he probably won't even notice if I wear an old, ordinary bra. Right?

This will be really good for us, come to think of it. This might really help cement what we have as something real, and serious, and if we *do* have to spend some time apart, we'll be all the stronger for this one week together. I shouldn't look a gift horse in the mouth. This isn't a problem, it's a blessing.

Right?

Danny seems to be on the same page, because he spreads his arms wide, and then lifts me up, spinning me around once before setting me back on my feet and planting a noisy, smacking kiss on my lips. "I'm all yours, baby."

Chapter Five

*H*ost a DIY wedding weekend for all the bridesmaids, Liv! It'll be so fun, we'll have a great time. You could host it at your place, Liv! Save us money, rather than renting some cottage somewhere. We can spend that cash on some bubbly and Indian takeout instead, haha!

I like to think I'm the perfect candidate for maid of honor. I'm organized, I'm prepared, I'm good at putting other people first and making sure they're having fun, and most importantly, I know how to have a good time.

And, quite frankly, I have been an *incredible* maid of honor. Kim is lucky to have me.

But damn if I'm not relieved this weekend is over.

We'd had this weekend planned for ages. It's only six months until the wedding, and four until the bachelorette party; although, right now, it's looking like that weekend up in York going from club to club in neon-pink feather boas and draping Kim in a cheap veil and *Bride to Be!* sash isn't going to happen if all this virus nonsense carries on. Or if the wedding will even go ahead, for that matter. But that's a problem for another time, I tell myself.

Kim always swore she wouldn't be a bridezilla, but those of us who know her all laughed and reassured her that we were fully prepared for her to lose her mind to wedding prep. She's the kind of person who was *born* to get married. She's so dreamy eyed, such a romantic. Nothing like me, let's face it. She and Jeremy have even already started working out when they want to start trying for babies, and how they'll manage it when babies *do* come along.

(Plus, you know, they're thinking about *trying* for babies. Intentionally coming off birth control, not just forgetting to take it. I break out in a cold sweat just thinking about that kind of commitment.)

My best friend is sweet and thoughtful and always there as a shoulder to lean on, but she also likes everything to be done *just so*. Kim didn't spend three weeks planning a six-person dinner party to celebrate my twenty-first birthday on a whim, after all. (Seriously. There were balloon arrangements and a dress code and everything. And that was her idea of "something small and intimate.")

So, yeah, Kim was *definitely* going to be a bridezilla.

It was never a matter of if, but of when.

She's had her moments, throughout the last year, since Jeremy proposed. There was the meltdown when her mum and grandma got stuck in traffic and missed the wedding fair, and another when she decided she'd found The Dress but it was double the cost of the wedding dress budget even before she considered shoes, a veil, or alterations, so she and Jeremy had a big row about whether it was worth it or if they should cut costs elsewhere and did she *really* expect them not to pay for the absurdly expensive hotel room for his grandparents the weekend of the wedding? Oh, and there was the time she *actually* screamed at the hairdresser who did a trial run, because it didn't look the way the picture on Pinterest did (although, to be fair, the highlights were a little on the orange side, rather than the warm honey tones she'd been looking for).

I held her hand and consoled her through all of it, and reassured her that she wasn't overreacting while apologizing to people behind her back on her behalf.

It was all my job, my *duty*, as maid of honor. And besides, she's probably been doing the same for me for years, whenever people think I'm being rude and don't like them, when really, I'm just that blunt and have the same resting bitch face with everyone.

Admittedly, I've quite enjoyed it all. The maid of honor stuff, that is, not the incurable resting bitch face. Kim and I had always joked about me being her maid of honor since we were little kids, and I love having a project to sink my teeth into. And Kim's wedding has been a pretty fucking big project.

I dared not complain whenever things got . . . intense.

I did, however, dare to float the idea a few days ago that we should, maybe, perhaps, sort of, somehow, *cancel* this weekend.

After all, there's a pandemic going on. You shouldn't be traveling, they're saying on the news, unless you have to. You should stay at home.

A stickler for rules, I dared to say as much to Kim. "Maybe you should all stay at home."

"Don't be ridiculous," Kim blustered over the phone, puffing and panting because she was out power walking at the time. (Part of a strict prewedding exercise regime, to counter all the cake testing.) "We've had this planned for ages. How else am I going to get all the wedding favors and the centerpieces done? Don't you *remember* we had to cut the entire budget almost to nothing after I agreed to let Jeremy plan that ludicrous weekend in Budapest for his bachelor party?"

It was hardly a budget of *nothing*, I thought at the time, looking at the boxes of dried rose petals, netted bags, and individually wrapped chocolates and sweets that had just shown up at my apartment that day, ready to be tied into little wedding favors.

"And besides, Addison's not been out anywhere, and *you've* not been out anywhere, and you both live alone, and Lucy's been living with her parents but she's not been out anywhere else and honestly, Liv, I cannot deal, this whole thing is just—it's such a *pain*. It's not like they'll be taking public transport to get to your place! And if Jeremy loses all that money on the bachelor party when *I* had to go and get a cheaper dress, I'll be absolutely *furious*. It'll be fine. If anyone gets so much as a sniffle, we'll rearrange, but right now everything is *fine*."

She said it so venomously, like she could fix this entire thing just by sheer willpower alone, that I didn't really have it in me to protest.

I did message the other bridesmaids—her future sister-in-law, Lucy, and her friend from her year abroad in America and current job, Addison—outside of the group chat, saying that I wouldn't blame them if they didn't want to come over . . .

Obviously, Kim had already got to them, though, or else they'd already expressed their doubts to her just like I had, because the messages I got back from them were a little *too* enthusiastic.

> Lucy Kingsley:
> Oh, don't worry about it! I know how important this weekend is to Kim. Really excited to meet you both properly and spend some time together! We're all being very careful right now so sure it'll be fine xxx

> Addison Goldstein:
> GIRL, don't even! I haven't hung out with people outside of work in waaaaaay too long, I need this weekend! (Plus I think Kim will actually have an aneurysm if we don't get those centerpieces sorted out, LOL!) Thanks again for putting us all up for the weekend, hon—see you both in a few days!

> Olivia Barton:
> Sure! No worries! Just thought I'd check :) Got the champers all ready and can't wait! xxx

Obviously, I couldn't tell them not to come.

Well, I could have, I suppose, but just thinking about dealing with the fallout gave me a headache. Not to mention *someone* still would have had to put the centerpieces together, and I absolutely did not want to face doing that alone.

It's not like this weekend hasn't been fun. Actually, it's been some of the best fun I've had in a long while. We decided to treat it as a sort of test-run bachelorette party: there was karaoke, a near-constant marathon of cheesy rom-coms playing in the background, plenty of greasy takeaway food, popcorn, and of course, prosecco.

We got about halfway through constructing the centerpieces and wedding favors, but Kim had been in such a good mood she didn't even seem to mind that things hadn't gone to plan, for a change. She was more like her old, fun-loving, prebridezilla self; that alone made it all worth it.

It's been a really great weekend.

But dear God, I'm glad they're leaving.

I can't wait to get my apartment back. Deflate the air mattress, tidy up all the blankets and pillows, clear up all of yesterday's takeaway containers, and maybe treat myself later tonight to the last of the open bottle of prosecco left in the fridge. And, God, have I had enough wedding talk to last me a week. Two, even.

Plus—no offense to Kim's friend Addison, but she is *loud*. And she doesn't half like the sound of her own voice, cracking jokes all the time, or telling stories. I'd call her obnoxious, but I've only known her for three days, so I guess I should give her the benefit of the doubt. Maybe it's just because she's American? Kim doesn't seem so phased, but I figure she's used to it even if she does notice it. And Lucy's way too polite and soft-spoken to say a remotely mean word about *anyone*, so I doubt she'd agree if I asked her opinion.

I mean, she's cute. *Very* cute. With those little sidelong glances when she makes a joke, and a warm laugh like honey . . .

But my *God*, is she loud.

The girls are all packed up, and I, for one, could not be happier.

Kim kneels in the corner of the lounge, rifling through the boxes to count the centerpieces for the eighth time.

"Seventeen," she mutters to herself, and then, "Liv! Olivia, where are the place cards?"

"Aren't they in that box?" Lucy asks.

"No! No!" She waves a packet of beige parchment-style cardboard rectangles. "I can only find the blank ones! Oh, please don't say we threw them out. After all that time spent on the calligraphy . . . "

If anything has taught me patience, it's being Kim's maid of honor. I step forward, opening another box and picking up a clear Ziploc bag, filled with more place cards. "Looking for these?"

"Oh, thank God! Thanks, Liv. Oh, what would I do without you?"

"I really don't know."

"Hey, Livvy, you've got some junk mail." Addison walks back into the lounge, shoving a piece of paper at my chest. I catch it as she walks away, throwing herself onto the sofa and tapping away at her phone. I'm not sure why *she* can't leave, why she's got to wait for the others. Addison came here in her own car. She's not getting a ride from Lucy, like Kim is.

"It's Liv," I tell her. I've lost count of how many times I've had to correct her this weekend. The stupid nickname grates on me so much.

I glance at the junk mail. It's a simple, printed notice with the building management's logo at the bottom. Probably someone snuck a pet in again, or, I think, with dread curdling in my stomach, maybe we were so loud with the karaoke and stuff, someone complained about the noise.

But no, I quickly discover.

It is much, much worse than all that.

"Guys?"

They all look at me expectantly, obliviously, and I swallow the lump in my throat.

"I don't think you're going anywhere."

*

"This could be worse!" Kim says, with maybe a little *too* much enthusiasm. Her usually bright, warm smile is toothy, bordering on feral. "At least we're all together! And we'll be able to finish all the wedding stuff! Think how much we'll be able to get done!"

She *does* have a point there, I concede. At least I won't have to go through the hassle of organizing yet another wedding DIY weekend, or have to do it all myself to get it finished. That's something.

"What about work?" Lucy asks, perched on the edge of one of my dining chairs, biting her thumb nail. Her gray-blue eyes are wide with panic.

"We'll call our bosses tomorrow," Addison replies, waving a hand dismissively, not even glancing over. She's still sprawled on the sofa, having not moved since she passed me the note a few minutes ago. Her mouth smacks as she chews some gum, and I can't help but turn my nose up at it. "No big deal. It'll be fine."

"What about *clothes*?" Lucy cries.

Addison doesn't have such a quick solution for that, but I do.

"Call Jeremy," I tell her. "He can pick some of your stuff up from your parents', and bring some things for Kim. *And* he can get us groceries, too, while he's at it. I've got plenty of bubbly left, but I think we might run out of cereal by Tuesday, otherwise."

"Good idea. I'll, um . . . " Lucy stands up, phone in hand, gesturing toward the kitchen, looking desperate to do something proactive. "Shall I start putting a bit of a grocery list together, then?"

"Knock yourself out," I say. I stand stiffly in the center of the room, still surrounded by the carnage of our weekend-long sleepover, mourning my plans of cleaning up and relaxing for a couple of hours later this evening.

"I know you said we should make ourselves at home, Livvy," Addison jokes, twirling her long blond hair around one finger, her full, pink lips pulling up into a wide smirk, "but I'm not sure you meant for the whole week, huh?"

"Not exactly."

Kim must catch the way I say it through my teeth, because she beams, standing up from the wedding favors she's been unboxing onto the rug in my living room to grab my hands. "Oh, come on! This is going to be so much fun, Liv! We'll get so much done. Think of it as—as—wedding planning on steroids! It'll make a great story for the bachelorette party, won't it!"

Damn it, why can I never say no to her?

Then again, she's been my best friend for almost twenty years. She bloody well should know *exactly* how to make me feel better.

I take a deep breath and grin back at her. "I'll get the prosecco, then, shall I?"

Monday

APARTMENT #15 – ISLA

Chapter Six

It's nice to wake up beside Danny.

It's eight minutes before my alarm, but instead of getting up straight away, I decide to spend that time lying in bed, hand tucked under my cheek, admiring my boyfriend.

In a noncreepy way, obviously.

He's just so, so *lovely*. Those long, thick eyelashes resting against the olive tone of his skin—Spanish, on his mother's side, he told me. The perfectly shaped cupid's bow of his full upper lip that's just so very, very kissable. There's a small cluster of spots around his forehead, his curls are in complete disarray, and his nose does a weird twitching thing like he's part bunny rabbit in whatever dream he's having. Not entirely flawless, I think, but he's all the more lovely for it.

I shiver a little and tuck myself into his side, stealing some of Danny's body heat, resting my head gently against his shoulder. I close my eyes, feeling totally and completely content.

Is this normal? I have to wonder. I know there's always that glow at the start of any relationship, that bubble you get so wrapped up in where it's all about sex and romance and making so much effort and gushing about them to your friends every chance you get, but—this feels *different*.

This feels like so much more than just a honeymoon period. I've never liked a guy this much, or felt so comfortable around someone this early on in a relationship. Not that I've got *that* many guys to compare Danny to, but the two or three that come to mind—they don't even come close.

Maybe it's a sign. Maybe it's because we're meant to be, because we're so perfect for each other.

The more I think about it, the more utterly *perfect* it is, that the building is on lockdown for the week, and Danny's got to stay here. This will be such a brilliant way to take our relationship to the next level, even if it is a little bit early. (Or, all right, a *lot* early.) It'll be a great way to test if we're really compatible.

It'll be like the *Love Island* villa!

Only without the swimming pool and weird challenges and skimpy bikinis, or the snarky comments from a narrator.

My alarm beeps, and I roll over quickly to turn it off. Beside me, Danny groans, flopping onto his front and hugging his pillow to his face.

"What time is it?" he mumbles.

"Six."

He stills, head shifting until he can narrow one eye at me. "Shut up. You don't start work this early?"

I laugh. "Of course not. Remember? I work out in the mornings, usually."

He groans again, like this is an even worse concept than having to start work early. It's not that Danny isn't the athletic type, just that he prefers his workouts to be a team sport once or twice a week.

Before now, whenever we've spent the night together, I've skipped my early-morning workouts, but I really need it today, after the stress of finding out we're on lockdown. It's less embarrassing than my habit of spending hours in the evening scrolling through Instagram, at any rate.

Danny throws one heavy, muscular arm over me as I sit up, dragging me back down onto the bed. I giggle, allowing him a few seconds of cuddling before I ease myself away. I kiss the only exposed bit of his face I can see.

"Go back to sleep for a bit. I'll be quiet."

He grumbles, but the pillow swallows all of his words. I think for a moment he might've suggested an *alternative* sort of workout, but if he did, he's obviously not serious: he nestles back into the sheets and hugs his pillow closer, maybe even already asleep again.

I smile at him once more before tiptoeing around my bedroom, popping on just a light layer of makeup (only some tinted moisturizer, a bit of mascara, a quick go-over with my eyebrow pencil) and I change into some workout clothes. Perks of being employed by a fitness company: staff discount and the occasional trip to the warehouse, where you get to nab some out-of-season freebies.

One major disadvantage of being shut up in my own apartment for a week with my hunky, brilliant boyfriend: I can't go out for a run.

Ah, well, it's only a week, I remind myself. Until then, there's no shortage of workouts on YouTube. I even have a designated playlist for my favorites, for days when the weather's too bad to go outside. I pick a Pilates one, pausing it while I do some stretches and warm up.

I hear noise from the bedroom and turn the volume down a little. Danny's joked a couple of times about how he's never been very much of a morning person, but . . . well, once you're awake, how can you *not* get out of bed? And he's got to get up for work, anyway, so I can't be disturbing him very much.

But, even so, I think I ought to let him sleep. It's the nice thing to do. He'll be up soon enough, I'm sure.

My workout wraps up within half an hour and I'm midway through making a smoothie before I realize how loud the blender is going to be; maybe loud enough to wake up Danny, who *still* hasn't gotten up yet. I sigh, leaving everything in it ready for later, and make myself a cup of green tea instead.

I take my mug out onto the balcony, collecting my journal on the way. It's a gratitude journal my best friend, Maisie, got me for Christmas. I'm a *huge* fan.

Monday
Number 1 — I'm grateful for my gratitude journal, and lovely friends who know me so well
Number 2 — I'm grateful for my boyfriend, and the extra time I'm able to spend with him
Number 3 — I'm grateful for online workouts and my yoga mat

I close the journal and take a minute to meditate on it before I take a photograph of the view from my balcony, holding up my still-steaming mug of tea into the frame. I upload it to my Instagram Story first with a sticker in a curly font reading *Monday*, and then post the same photo to my grid with the caption:

islainthestream Sometimes life misses the memo about sending you lemons and sends you a week of lockdown instead—but we'll make it through. Take some time to breathe. Drink a cup of tea. Remind yourself about all the good things you can still enjoy . . . like quiet mornings with the sunrise before work. Stay safe, my lovelies.

I stay on the balcony a little while longer, relishing the peace and quiet. This balcony, this view over the grounds of London Lane and the nearby park and streets, was the reason I bought this apartment. I couldn't afford somewhere with a garden, but this is definitely the next best thing. Actually, it's a bit of a stretch to afford it every month, but this part of my day always reminds me why it's worth it. This, I think, is my definition of *mindfulness*.

Heading back inside once I finish drinking my tea, I make breakfast, and decide to make some for Danny too. I'm not a very good cook, but I do know how to make a good poached egg. And I'm very skilled at making perfect toast. I even add some bacon to a frying pan, thinking how much Danny will love it.

It's only when I'm plating it up that I think this might backfire horribly, and I hope he doesn't expect this sort of thing all the rest of the week too.

I put our breakfast on the dining table and go to get Danny. He'll be starting work in twenty minutes, so I expect to find him dressed and ready to start his day.

He's awake, but that's about all I can say for him. He's still in bed, not even having combed his hair yet.

"I made breakfast," I tell him, not really sure how to deal with this lazy creature I've yet to become familiar with. "If you want."

"I thought I smelled something good. Worth waking me up for," he says, cracking a smile even though he's still bleary-eyed. He yawns widely, rubs his hands over his face, and finally gets out of bed.

He pauses in the doorway to kiss me, and I melt against him.

See? I tell myself. This week is going to be just perfect.

*

After breakfast, after we've both logged on to our computers for work, I decide to use a break between my meetings to sort out the food shop. I saw what people were saying on social media this morning: the *stay home* messages are starting to scare people, supermarkets suddenly seem scarier than skydiving, and food delivery slots are beginning to fill up even for people who aren't literally trapped in their own building. I'm scared if I put it off much longer we won't get a delivery at all.

Danny leans over my shoulder at the dining table, after setting down the cup of tea he's just made me, and asks, "What're you doing?"

His hand smooths over my hair and he kisses my cheek. I know he doesn't mean to be all *in my space* but it feels weird to have him hanging over my shoulder like this. We're sharing the table to work at, but I'm not too sure how long this is going to last. It's a little *too* close. Maybe we can take it in turns to work from the bedroom?

"Just ordering some groceries," I tell him. The HelloFresh website is open on my laptop, for me to place my usual order. Well, almost usual. I have to order for two of us, now, instead of just me.

"On HelloFresh?"

"Yeah, it's great. Hey, if you've never used it, we should sign up with your email! Get one of those first-order offers."

When I twist around to look at him, his cute face is all scrunched up. It's that look he got when I asked him if *Phantom Menace* was worth watching, so I could get an idea what was so interesting about *Star Wars*, if he was such a fan.

He looks judgemental as heck.

"What?" I ask him, frowning and pulling away.

"Are you seriously going to order us a delivery from HelloFresh?"

"You know I'm not much of a cook," I laugh. Smoothies and breakfast food are kind of my limit. I'd probably live off salad and instant noodles without my HelloFresh boxes. I'm terrified to admit it to Danny because he's such a natural in the kitchen, but I just don't *get* food. I don't understand which flavors are supposed to go together or what the hell it means to sauté something, and the one time I tried to use the slow cooker I impulse-purchased off Amazon, everything burnt to the inside of it.

At best, I currently have maybe three days' worth of food left in the cupboards—unless we're going to live off Ben and Jerry's and Oreos.

So, yes, I'm getting a HelloFresh delivery.

I add, "Come on, I'll even let you pick a box, huh? Since you're probably going to end up cooking all week anyway, that's probably only fair, ha ha!"

He laughs, like it's such a cute idea. "We can split the cooking, Isla."

"In that case, I'm *definitely* getting HelloFresh."

"That's batshit crazy. And it's so expensive! Come on." Danny pulls up the chair next to me, pulling my laptop toward him, closing the tab, and already tapping away in the search bar. "Let's just get, like, a regular food delivery from Tesco, or something."

I catch myself scowling at him and take a calming breath. I take a sip of my tea, even though it's a little too hot still. Somehow it's still easier to swallow than his attitude.

It's fine, I tell myself. It's going to be absolutely fine. Danny can do most of the cooking, and if he's really so bothered, it's fine. It's totally not a big deal. At all.

"Well," I tell him, "then you're definitely cooking all week."

APARTMENT #6 – ETHAN

Chapter Seven

Charlotte's alarm clock goes off and I groan, but it keeps bleeping.
"Charl," I mumble. "Charl, turn it off."

I reach over, but the bed is empty.

I sit bolt upright, blinking the sleep out of my eyes, and it takes me a second to remember.

Right. Of course. *Lockdown*. She's stuck back at her parents' place.

Oh, yeah, and no big deal, there's just a *deadly virus on the loose in this building and I am on my own and*—and I've been awake for all of thirty seconds, but already my brain has managed to place me in the plot of a dystopian YA novel.

Not that this is wholly unusual for me. Well, I mean. The virus is; the general sense of impending doom about *something*, not so much. My body is already doing breathing exercises I learned years ago, my brain talking itself back down.

I lie in bed a few minutes longer before deciding there's no way I'll be able to get back to sleep, so instead I reach over to grab my phone. I scroll through some notifications and reply to some comments on YouTube and Twitter.

After wasting an hour watching videos and combing through social media, I finally drag myself out of bed.

One day without Charlotte and my whole routine's already gone down the pan, I realize bitterly, annoyed with myself. I rarely ever stay in bed like that; I get up when she does, and I'm at least dressed and sat down with my first cup of coffee before I spend all that time on my phone.

When I started out being self-employed, I spent about two months sleeping in until midday, staying up well into the night, working in my pajamas unless I was actually filming a video. It was great for maybe a week or so. Then it just made me feel lethargic and stressed out.

Charlotte noticed. Because, of course she did. And I have to hand it to her, she really knew how to help me out without making me feel like she had to take care of me and fix my life. Gentle nudges like, "I really love it when you make me a cup of tea in the morning," or, "I think it's sweet when we go to bed at the same time so I get to fall asleep next to you."

She never made me feel like I was failing or being a complete loser.

Just one of a million things I love about her.

I wonder how she's getting on at home, with her parents and her sister, Maisie. Has her routine gone to shit today too? She's an editor for a company that produces educational resources and textbooks for A-level students, so she normally works from home a day or two a week anyway, but I wonder how it's going for her there. I wonder if she's in a meeting or if I could call her.

Despite the fact it's already late morning, I'm on autopilot, grabbing her favorite mug before I realize what I'm doing and set it back, rolling my eyes at myself. *Come on, Ethan, get it together. She's been gone three days, you can't be falling apart already.*

On the subject of getting it together, though, I really should see what kind of food I've got in, maybe place an order online.

I'm writing up a list in the Notes app on my phone when there's a knock at the door.

For a second I just stand there like a dummy, trying to puzzle out who could possibly be knocking on my door at eight o'clock in the morning.

It's gotta be Mr. Harris, I reason.

There's another knock at the door, which jolts me into action.

"Coming, I'm coming," I call out, already on my way. I throw open the door, only wondering then if I should be in a mask and gloves like our caretaker was yesterday. But it's not Mr. Harris on the other side of the door.

It's Nate, from the apartment above mine. And he looks . . . I don't know if that expression is pissed off or concerned, but it's not good, whatever it is. His jaw is clenched, his brow furrowed.

"Nate. Uh, hi. Everything all right?"

"Yeah, yeah, I'm—I'm doing good."

"You wanna come in?"

He starts to say yes, then cuts himself off with an awkward grin, and I realize my faux pas. "Best not."

"Right. Yeah, sure. Pandemic. Lockdown for the whole week. Bit weird, isn't it?"

Nate looks me dead in the eyes, and lets out a long, weary sigh. "Ethan, you have *no* idea."

We're not especially close, I guess, but I'd call him a friend. Nate moved in here a year ago. Charlotte thought we should introduce ourselves when we noticed him tromping up and down the stairs, carrying boxes and suitcases of stuff; I ended up helping him move in. We go to the pub together every so often; Charlotte even set him up on a date with one of her friends, a couple of months ago, although that was a short-lived romance.

I assume he's here because he needs to, I don't know, borrow some toilet paper or something, and he can't leave to go grocery shopping or wait for a delivery.

I do *not* expect him to open his mouth and rattle off some story about how there's a random girl in his apartment he hooked up with on Saturday night, and, "I know I shouldn't have invited her over, but . . . you didn't see the way she was texting me, you know?"

"What, like, sexts?"

"No! No, nothing like that. Just . . . she had me hook, line, and sinker, that's all. It was like she really *got* me, like we had a connection, which I know sounds totally pathetic because we matched on a dating app and we've only been talking for a few days. And she didn't even remember my *name*! But I said sure, come on over, which is fucking crazy, right?"

"Uh, sure," I say, because that's obviously what he wants to hear.

Nate paces a few steps in a circle outside my door, and drags a hand back and forth through his hair.

"So she's still here?" I ask. "Like, *in your apartment*, still here?"

"Yeah."

"I mean, kudos on setting the record for the longest one-night stand anybody's ever had."

He laughs, but it turns quickly into a groan, and Nate bends double, arms wrapping around his head before he straightens back up again. "Can I ask you a crazy big favor?"

"She's not staying here," I tell him, and then add, "*You're* not staying here."

Nate scoffs, shrugging one shoulder. "No, can I—look, she's literally only got the one outfit. You can say no, I swear, I just figured I'd take my chance asking, but you think I could borrow some of Charlotte's clothes? Imogen's taller, but she's skinnier, so I figure that must even out a little, right? And honestly, man, I don't know how I'm supposed to sit on a call doing work with her lying on the sofa in one of my shirts and her underwear with her legs out and her ASOS order won't arrive till Wednesday and—please, dude, you've gotta help me."

"The sex was *that* good, huh?" I tease.

Nate just shakes his head. "She's . . . I don't know. She's like one of those people that makes you want to pack a bag and go travel the world, forget you have any responsibilities or that real life even exists, you know?"

"Not really."

"I just need her to at least *look* normal, so I'm not suddenly inspired to quit my job and decide to go look after baby elephants in Thailand, that's all."

"Do you want to go look after elephants in Thailand?"

"I really, really don't," he tells me gravely.

I laugh. "Let me ask Charlotte, but I can't see it'll be a problem."

"Thank you. *Thank you.* Wait, where is she, anyway?"

After explaining that she's locked out for as long as *we're* locked *in*, I call Charlotte. She makes Nate send her a photo of his week-long one-night stand, and then she gives me strict instructions on which few items of clothes I'm to hand over that she thinks will fit Nate's houseguest.

"We'll send you the dry-cleaning bill," I joke. "Give us a shout if you need anything else, okay?"

He makes a show of peering past me, squinting at the shelf of action figures in the hallway, the cool minimalist Marvel movie posters. "Unless you've got a working TARDIS in there to stop me inviting her over on Saturday night . . . "

"Well, good luck."

"Thanks," he says. "I'm gonna need it."

Yeah, you and me both, buddy.

Chapter Eight

Nate is clean.

Objectively, this is a good thing. Especially during a pandemic. When I got here on Saturday night, I breathed a sigh of relief. It's never attractive when you're picking your way through sweaty, dirty socks and old take-out containers, and a layer of grime clings to everything. It really puts a dampener on the sexy mood you've been building so carefully. (Not that plain beige walls and a lack of artwork or any real *character* are very sexy, either, but definitely the better option.)

However, it's also not particularly attractive to be told to take the hair out of the plug in the shower and have the guy lurking in the doorway to make sure you do it properly. He's on his lunch break; I got up late and have only just taken a shower.

Nate sighs.

In the single day into our week of quarantine, I have lost count of the number of times he has sighed. Because I didn't use a coaster for a cup of tea. Because I put a glass on the floor, and again because I forgot about it and kicked it over, spilling water on the rug. Because I made a sandwich and got crumbs in the butter, and on the counter.

And now, apparently, because a few strands of hair missed the memo that they're supposed to stay attached to my scalp while I'm here.

It was obvious as soon as I got here that Nate is a minimalist. There was no clutter *anywhere*, not so much as a candle or coffee table book to jazz the space up a little. An orderly bookcase in the hallway and another in the living-room space, a dark TV stand that I could only assume hid a mess of wires and his *stuff*. I mean, jeez, he only had one bottle of shampoo in the shower! Where were the half-dozen "almost finished but there's still a bit left and I'll get around to using it at some point so don't throw it away yet" shampoo bottles? He did, at least, have a blanket on the sofa, a couple of snake plants, and a nice navy-blue feature wall in both the living room/dining room and his bedroom, which made it less boring.

Minimalists are a mystery to me, but I can handle it.

The intense tidiness, not so much.

"You're a neat freak," I tell him, wrapping the wad of my wet hair in some toilet paper and tossing it in the bin.

"And you're sloppy," he bites back. He turns away, muttering under his breath, "Glad I'm not stuck at your place."

I know he didn't mean for me to hear that, but I bristle, glowering at his back. So what if the walls in my place aren't a nice, boring shade of magnolia, and maybe have a couple of damp spots under the wallpaper in some rooms? Mr. High-and-Mighty who probably dusts the skirting boards and doesn't have a single expired product in the fridge.

I pull a few faces at him but decide not to say anything. I probably shouldn't pick a fight with Nate when he's being generous enough to let me stay here for the week.

Not that he's got a choice, but he *has* been very decent about the whole thing.

He also let me order some extra clothes on his credit card because mine is maxed out, and he told me he wouldn't take any money off me for the food delivery order he managed to get. Which was really sweet of him, actually.

And he went to a neighbor to borrow some clothes for me in the meantime, so I have a pair of leggings and a tank top to go with the button-down shirt I stole out of his wardrobe this morning.

I hear Nate filling the kettle in the little kitchen next to the living room so I stick my head in. The cabinets are an almost blinding white, but it's not that I can't see, it's just that there's so little to see. No over-flowing recycling bin nobody can be bothered to take out, no pile of dirty plates by the sink, no random packets of food abandoned on the counter waiting to be put away at some point. The kitchen is probably the most cluttered place in the whole apartment, if only because he has some of that magnet poetry on the fridge, and there are appliances and a mug tree and a metal dish rack out on the counter, but even that's all horrifyingly orderly.

He looks over at me, hearing me in the doorway, and I nod my head in the direction of the kettle.

"Go on, then."

He sighs—*again*—shaking his head, but gets an extra mug out to make me some tea too. I blow him a kiss and retreat to the living room. I throw myself down on the sofa, opening up Instagram to see if there's anything new in the six minutes since I last checked it.

"Remind me what you do?" he asks me, once he's back in the living room. He sets the tea down on coasters on the table in front of the sofa, and gives a pointed look at my feet. I tuck my knees up to make room for him, but immediately put my feet back in his lap.

He looks a little startled by it, almost as though he's never seen feet before.

I mean, for God's sake, we've *had sex*. Three times.

Forgive me for making myself comfortable.

"I'm a primary school teacher," I answer him. "And you work in project management at a bank, right?"

Nate looks genuinely surprised that I remember and runs a hand through his blond hair. It's not so neat now as in his pictures on the dating app, but it's fluffy and it's a cute look on him. So are those gray jogging bottoms, actually, now I think about it.

How *dare* guys look so good in something so basic.

Maybe I should try that, next time, I think. Just show up for a date in a white T-shirt, gray joggers, no makeup—see how *they* like it.

Nate clears his throat, but he's oblivious to how distracted I just got. He seems to be making every effort *not* to look at me right now, actually.

"Right. Yes. I do remember you saying, now you mention it."

He definitely doesn't remember.

"I guess you can't really work from home if you're a teacher."

"Probably not, but our headmistress has had us prepping for this since the whole *very dangerous contagious virus* thing first started cropping up in the news. She's had us all prepping lesson plans and work sheets and sending out letters to parents with instructions on how to download and use Zoom." I roll my eyes. "We all said she was overreacting and watches too many horror movies and conspiracy documentary things, but, hey. Look at me now."

I stretch out, waving my hands in a grand flourish and tossing my hair, but it doesn't seem to amuse him. Yesterday, I obviously text the WhatsApp group with some of the other teachers and the headmistress to explain my predicament to them. They've had to class it as sick leave, since *stuck in a stranger's apartment due to a super infectious disease* isn't on our clunky old HR system—yet. They got someone to cover my classes for the week, though, and nobody's mad about it. Hell, they *can't* be. This isn't like that time I lost my passport and got stuck in Brussels on a weekend away that went on a *little* longer than planned.

Nate's obviously not impressed with my blasé attitude and I decide he probably won't totally appreciate the Brussels story—at least, not right now. So instead I straighten up and add, "But you're obviously doing okay, working from home."

I look at his laptop on the coffee table, a black leather notebook and fountain pen resting beside it, and a neatly coiled pair of headphones. There's a very detailed, boring-looking spreadsheet open on the laptop screen. The kind with *pivot tables*. I shudder at the thought.

"Oh. Yeah, it's . . . I mean, we work from different locations some-times anyway. Client sites, and stuff. It's not ideal, but I'll manage."

"How's the rest of your day looking?" I ask, scooting a little closer, using my feet in his lap to hook my legs between his. "Any big, important meetings you just can't miss?"

Nate's eyes narrow slightly and he cocks his head to one side, let-ting out a nervous chuckle. He doesn't know me *that* well, but obvi-ously enough to know I'm not asking to be polite. "Why?"

I shrug. "You know, if you're not busy, maybe we could watch a movie or something?"

"Or something."

I think, for a second, he's going to say yes. His eyes are dark and one of his hands drifts distractedly to my legs, grazing from my knee and down my calf.

Since Sunday morning, Nate's tried to be—corny as it sounds— he's tried to be the perfect gentleman. We haven't so much as cuddled. I guess he's being nice, and I appreciate it, but I kind of want to tell him he doesn't have to stand on ceremony for little ol' me.

He's even given up the bed for me.

"No, no," he'd said last night, smiling but insistent. "Really. You take the bed. I'll sleep on the sofa."

"That's not fair. It's your bed. I'm the one who got stuck here."

"You're the guest."

"Not by *choice*."

Nate had scooped up a pillow and a pile of carefully folded blan-kets, his smile gone and a stern look on his face. His eyes had been doing that adorable crease-around-the-edges thing, though, like he was trying not to laugh. "You're taking the bed, Imogen, and I'm taking the sofa. It's my house, I make the rules."

And, fine, I'll admit: even if the whole chivalry thing was just an act, it was still hot.

"You could just *share* the bed with me, you know. I don't mind.

We did last night. We did a lot more than *share a bed* last night, my friend."

Nate blushed, but shook his head. "Yeah, but that was . . . different?"

I didn't see how, but I'd taken the bed anyway.

"Don't tell me," I joke now, while he's hesitating, retracting his hand from my leg, as if catching himself, and turning his head away from me to face forward. "I don't look as good in real life as I did on my profile."

He laughs. "Imogen, you remember that *you* were the one that ran out on Sunday morning, right? Without so much as a good-bye?"

"So?"

"*So,*" he says, his hands fidgeting in his lap, "I don't get it. Did I do something wrong?"

I gawp at him. "What gave you that impression? Is this your way of asking me if I faked it? Because, you know, you could just ask me. I had to borrow your boxers, and my underwear are currently on your radiator." I point at them. "I'm pretty sure you don't have to worry about offending me, at this point."

Nate runs a hand over his face, and he lets out an awkward, half-hearted chuckle. "I'm not trying to feed my ego, here. My point is . . . my point is, you were just going to disappear without a trace. I thought . . . I dunno, I thought after all that time we spent talking, you wouldn't just ghost me."

"I wasn't going to ghost—"

The deadpan look he cuts me makes me stop midsentence.

I smile sheepishly at him, and even though I *know* I don't have to explain myself, he looks so sweet, so confused, that I do anyway.

"We had a one-night stand. You told me you weren't looking for anything serious. I figured it was just, you know. Easier. I didn't want to make you feel awkward, make you feel you had to see me again or take me on a date or something, when you *said* you weren't after something else."

"But . . . " Nate frowns at me, and looks away. He drags his hand back and forth through his hair again. "Yeah, I mean, I *said* that, but . . . I liked you. I thought that counted for something."

I'm not sure how to respond to that.

Nate clears his throat when I stay quiet, obviously not sure how to follow that up. I sort of expect him to crack a joke about it, say something like, *Or at least liked you enough to have sex with you,* but as soon as I think it, I know he wouldn't. Nate's not that kind of guy. Even over text, he was straightforward. Not blunt, or rude, just upfront. Honest.

With nothing else to say, I go back to my original question. I raise my eyebrows and ask him, "So, you wanna watch that movie? Sack off work for the rest of the afternoon?"

There's *definitely* a smile playing at the corner of his mouth and I'm *really* tempted to kiss him, but then he turns suddenly serious and sits up straighter, pushing my legs off his lap.

He reaches for the TV remote, handing it over to me, and then he gathers up his laptop and notebook. "You can watch a movie. I'm gonna go work in the bedroom for a couple of hours. Big, important meetings I just can't miss, you know."

I watch him go, feeling a little out of sorts.

It's not like I've never been rejected before. I'm a big girl, I can handle it. Plus, he *is* working. But there's something about the way Nate seems to be holding me at arm's length that I'm not used to, and my heart sinks as he closes the bedroom door behind himself.

Tuesday

Chapter Nine

Nate's alarm on his phone goes off across the hallway in the living room. His phone vibrates angrily once, twice, on the table, a contrast to the tinkling chime noise that accompanies it. He turns it off, and then I hear him get up.

What kind of . . . ?

Who does that? Who just hears their alarm, and gets up, like, straight away? I mean, fine, Lucy does, but that's *Lucy*.

Oh God, speaking of Lucy, that's a problem. Her stupid wedding-planning DIY-centerpieces weekend thing for her future sister-in-law is only taking place *upstairs, in this very building*, isn't it? Of all the goddamn gin joints. When I realized, half of me wanted to run around hammering on doors until I found her so I could tell her *everything* (and maybe borrow a T-shirt or something) but . . . well, duh. I can't do that.

I can't let her know I'm with Honeypot, or that the quirky little mishap of the week is that I got stuck with him in quarantine. I mean, shit. Even I know how bad that sounds. Plus, she'd only worry, and it sounds like she's got plenty of her own problems to worry about this week with Kim the bridezilla and a quarantine of her own. No, I have to—I *want to*—handle this myself.

And, I guess, I probably shouldn't go around pounding on apartment doors and talking to strangers in the middle of a pandemic or whatever.

(Keeper of Keys, our jailer, bald and beardless Rubeus Hagrid, also might actually kill me if I do that. Which would be kind of inconvenient.)

Anyway, Nate's alarm goes off, and I hear him get up and go into the bathroom to take a shower, and I'm already wide awake anyway for some stupid reason, and my brain is going at a thousand miles an hour, so I do what any other reasonable human would.

I get up. I open the blinds for Mr. Neat-Freak Nate, and feel a little bad about how much of a bombsite his lovely, boring bedroom is right now. Considering I arrived here with basically just the clothes on my back . . . Said clothes are dumped in a pile on the floor by the wardrobe, despite there being a chair set out apparently for that exact purpose. The little hairbrush from my bag is on the dresser, along with the other miscellaneous crap I was carrying around: sunglasses, a little paperback copy of Jane Austen's *Emma*, some lip balm.

I do my very best to make the bed. When I say that, I mean I don't just yank the duvet back up, I mean I even try to tuck the top sheet back in, I smooth out the wrinkles, I fluff the pillows back up, and put the two decorative cream cushions back on the bed from where I'd tossed them into a corner last night.

The room is transformed. *Hey, look at me, Nate, living up to your stupidly high standards.*

And speaking of Nate . . .

The bathroom door is cracked open slightly, steam pouring out of it. The extractor fan whirrs low and loud. I bang an open palm on the door and push it open slightly to shout inside, "Yo, Nate-Nathan-Nate, you want some coffee?"

"Jesus!"

There's a wet scuffle, like he's slipping, and the clatter of his one, lonely shampoo bottle falling into the bathtub.

"Imogen, I'm *in the shower*," he shouts back. I can practically hear him blushing.

"I'm not *looking*," I point out, from the other side of the door. I'm not. I've got my back to him and I can't see anything except some tiles on the wall. "I'm just asking, do you want coffee?"

He stammers for a long moment before babbling, "Uh, t-th-yuh-sure, yeah. Coffee. Yes. Now please *go away*."

I pull the door to close it, and then open it back up to call in, "You want me to shut the door?"

"Yes!"

Well *ex-cuuuuse me*, mister. It wasn't like *he* had shut the door in the first place. How was I to know? There isn't a window in the bathroom; maybe he needed to leave it open to let the steam out. *Excuse me* for being considerate.

It takes me a few minutes to figure out the fancy coffee machine, although I don't have any trouble finding the little pods to go in it. To be fair to Nate, the kitchen is orderly, but it makes total sense. The flow and organization of the cupboards alone is worthy of its own Netflix special.

I open the lime-green roller blind in the kitchen. There's not as much light on this side of the apartment as in the bedroom and it's a cloudy morning, so I have to put the lights on as well. Actually, I realize as I survey the kitchen, there *is* a color scheme going on in here: green blind, green tea towel, green backsplash tiles. Even the Swiss cheese plant on the windowsill, I guess, counts into the green theme.

Imagine being *this* organized, I think. Imagine picking out backsplash tiles. And I bet he actually keeps his plants alive and they don't die however much he reads up on how to look after them and no matter what he tries.

Must be nice.

By the time I've finished pouring a second coffee for myself, Nate joins me in the kitchen. He's wearing jeans and a T-shirt but manages to look pulled together. Smart-casual, not slouch-casual. It's a second later it hits me why he looks so different in that outfit to the guys I'm used to: he's ironed it. His blond hair is damp, hanging in a mess over his forehead.

"Sorry," he tells me, dithering in the doorway, apology written all over his face. "I promise I'm not a grouch in the mornings. I didn't mean to snap at you."

Oh.

An apology.

Okay, wasn't expecting that.

"It's your house." I shrug. "You don't have to apologize to me."

Not that I'll apologize to him, though. I don't think I did anything wrong.

"Of course I do. I'm sorry," he tells me again, emphatically.

"It's okay. I did kind of barge in."

"No! No, you uh, you didn't. You just took me by surprise, that's all."

"Nate, sweetie, if I wanted to take you by surprise, I would've wheeled in a confetti cannon and serenaded you in full costume as *Phantom of the Opera.*"

(It would not be the first time. Although it would be the first time I'd done that in a bathroom.) (Look, it wasn't as weird as it sounds, I promise. Lucy wanted to go see it for her birthday but we couldn't all afford the tickets because it was just after university finished so we were all, like, putting down deposits on apartments and waiting for our first paycheck and things, so I got everyone to come as one of the characters and got Lucy an outfit to be Christine and we all had this epic sing-along to the movie version. I mean, tell me I'm not the greatest best friend ever. Even if I do owe her a shit-ton of money.)

"You're up early," Nate says then, taking the mug I offer him. "Did I wake you up?"

I shake my head. I'm still a little thrown off by his apology, and trying to think if I've already told him the story of Lucy's *Phantom* birthday. I lean against the counter, cradling my coffee in my hands. Nate takes up a similar stance across from me, leaning against the wall, both hands around his mug.

"I'm sorry, too, for the record," I blurt.

"It's okay."

"Not for the bathroom thing," I clarify, suddenly as awkward as he was a minute or two ago. "Um, for . . . I'm sorry for running out, on Sunday morning. Or trying to. It really wasn't anything against you, personally. Or about me," I add quickly, slamming a palm into my chest in defense. "It's just, you know. There's always . . . this."

I gesture between us and Nate's eyes follow my flapping hand before he repeats, "This," in a deadpan voice that makes it clear he's got no fucking clue what I'm talking about.

"You know! This! The whole awkward morning-after thing. The coffee. Breakfast, where you have to make small talk like either of you plan on seeing each other again."

Alarm bells go off in my head as soon as the words are out of my mouth. The sirens blare, the lights flash, and my brain takes us to DEFCON 1. This is where he'll get a judge-y look even though he's trying not to be judge-y and say, "Oh, so you do this a lot, huh?" and like, sure, I do it *sometimes*, but excuse me for having a healthy relationship with sex even if I can't always have a healthy relationship, period, and uh, *hello*, double standards.

I didn't even have to defend myself to him. I didn't have to apologize. I should've kept my mouth shut.

But Nate doesn't say anything like that, doesn't even *look* at me funny. He just nods. And then quietly, head bent slightly over his coffee, he tells me, "Although for the record, I would've planned on seeing you again. I told you, I liked you."

"Oof," I joke, "past tense already."

"You know what I mean, Imogen. Although jury's officially out again now I've had to live with you."

"You might be the first guy I've ever met who's judging me more on my ability to make a bed than what I was like *in* bed."

Nate took a sip of coffee at exactly the wrong moment because as soon as I say that, he chokes on it, sputtering it all over the floor before he can cover his mouth. I crack up laughing even as he coughs and switches his mug for some paper towels to clean it up.

"Not, I guess, that guys usually get a lot of time to judge me. It's usually all over within five dates, at most." I hug my drink a little closer into my body, not really sure why I'm telling him this, but apparently not able to stop. "I'm not really *girlfriend material*. Not the kind they want to take home to meet Mother. You know the last guy I dated told me I had 'Wine Aunt energy,' which I think is a compliment. I took it as one, anyway. But that's okay because he wasn't boyfriend material either. Or, I guess, he was. Just for the girl he'd already been dating for six months, who I found out about on Instagram."

"Ouch," Nate says. I'm not sure which part he's referring to—maybe all of it—but I just nod and mumble, "Yeah."

"But what about you?" I ask him, and fix him with my best coy look, batting my eyelashes and leaning forward, my lips pulling into a smirk. "Are you girlfriend material, Nate, or are you a Wine Aunt too? Mr. Just-Looking-For-Something-Casual?"

He mumbles, like he can't pick a word to start with, and I hear him gulp. He drags his hand through his hair, pushing it back from his face, and I notice him clench his jaw.

Oh shit. Great. Well done, Imogen, you overstepped. See that tiny speck in the distance? That was The Line, and you just unwittingly ran right past it.

I'm about to apologize—*again*, for a *second time* already this morning—because I've so obviously made him uncomfortable and this is so obviously a topic he doesn't like talking about, but then—

"I'm a serial monogamist. Or so my mates tell me." He gives an awkward chuckle, and scuffs a foot against the kitchen tiles. "You know those people who have basically no downtime between relationships? Like, they say they need time and space to get over someone, and then just hurtle right on into the next one even though they didn't mean to? That's me. Three girlfriends in the last six years, and I've probably been single a total of, I don't know, four months? Including this last month."

"*Ohhhh*. Oh, I get it! I was the rebound!"

Nate's face turns pale, but I laugh and wave a hand to shush him. "No, seriously, it's okay. You said you wanted something casual, and casual is like, my MO. I'm cool with being a rebound."

"That's not what . . . " Nate huffs, messing with his hair again before slumping against the counter beside me. His arm presses against mine. "Not to sound like a total dick, but I was sort of . . . I was *trying* to be one of those guys."

"What guys?"

"Like you said you date. The ones who just date girls and have fun and because they're only ever going to go on a few dates, they don't make, like, serious, exclusive commitments, and . . . Don't *laugh* at me," he says, nudging me gently when I start giggling at the idea of this awkward, sweet, serial monogamist being some kind of womanizer. "I thought it'd be good for me, which, now I'm saying it out loud, I realize sounds really stupid. And dick-ish. I just thought I'd try to change things up a little. Commit to *not* committing, for a change."

"And how's that working out for you, mate?"

"Oh, *so* awesome. This girl I just hooked up with has already moved in with me."

I laugh again, and Nate grins at me with a sidelong glance, nudging me with his elbow again. He's standing so close I can feel the warmth of his body against mine. I can smell the scent of the shower gel lingering on his skin. His lips are soft and parted in that smile and I want to kiss them. I want to taste the coffee on them. I want to kiss him and have him turn me around to sit me on the counter so we're more of a height with each other. I want to bury my face in the crook of his neck and press my lips to the skin just above his T-shirt collar while his arms wrap around me to hold me flush against him.

And I want to stay in this moment with him grinning at me like that and laughter on my lips forever.

And *that*, I realize, is most definitely a first.

Nate breaks the spell, though, clearing his throat. He steps away from me and starts fixing himself breakfast, looking at the digital clock on the oven and saying something about having to start work soon.

Right. Work. The real world. Back to reality, where we're just the universe's weirdest, most unlikely pair of temporary roommates and where Nate clears his throat to say, "Why don't you go and get dressed, Imogen? I'll put some toast in for you," like the gentleman he is.

I'm almost out of the room when I find myself pausing, turning back, and leaning through the doorway. He's concentrating on making himself some porridge, oblivious to me. I open my mouth to say something, but think better of it, and sigh a little as I leave.

All things considered, Honeypot, I think I would've liked to see you again too.

Chapter Ten

It's not so bad, I tell myself for the billionth time. Zach's worked shifts as long as we've been together, so I'm used to being disturbed all hours of the day, or him being home while I have to work.

But usually, I was, you know, *in the office* when he was at home and I had to work.

Right now, I'd take the early-morning wake-up as he got in from a night shift over . . . well, *this*.

Because he's a nurse, there's no way Zach could go in to work—the hospital he works at is still waiting on a huge shipment of tests for the virus, and his colleagues are able to cover his shifts in the meantime. There's no way he can do any of his job from home. Which means he's spent the last two days playing video games in the bedroom, while I've been trying to work from our dining table, squashed into the corner of the room by the balcony doors. Squashed, because the table is a hand-me-down, and it's too big for the room, and it's *round*, but, you know. It was a hand-me-down. So it was free. And we never got around to replacing it. Something I'm deeply regretting now, sat on an uncomfortable chair that creaks every time I move, wedged into the corner of the room to keep the sun's glare off my computer screen.

In theory, working from home should be easy enough, since I can dial into meetings and I've got my work laptop with me, but . . . I'm really, really struggling without the whole office environment, and not being able to talk to people face to face. And the whole lack-of-a-desk situation. Zach tells me it's just teething problems, that I'll get into the swing of things, but so far all I feel is stressed out about it. I swear I can barely focus long enough to send two emails in a row all day long.

Right now, at least, I have a full hour between any meetings, so decide I've earned at least a bit of a break. I go to find Zach pottering around in the kitchen, mashing bananas up.

"I thought we were throwing those out," I say, looking at the pile of brown-spotted skins on the counter. The bananas were one of our more recent arguments, last week: Zach forgot to buy them, and we both like to take them to work as a snack, so I'd made a big deal out of how I had to go out of my way after work one day to get some—only for Zach to apparently ignore me, and *also* go out of his way after work to buy a bunch.

And honestly, there are only so many bananas you can eat in a day.

It bugs me just to look at them. Because, seriously, did he not listen to anything I said? Or did he like going out of his way to ignore me?

"I'm making banana bread," he tells me, nudging his glasses back up his long, straight nose with the back of his hand. "I saw someone post about it on Instagram, thought, why not? Not like I've got much else to do."

I feel an initial flicker of resentment that yeah, he should do something productive like this and I should be so lucky, but it quickly gives way to just thinking how nice it is that he's baking something. I step over and kiss him, dust some flour off his sleeve.

"What do you want for dinner tonight?" I ask him then, stepping to the fridge. I open it, even though I know exactly what's in it. Our grocery order doesn't arrive until tomorrow, so our options are pretty limited. There's pasta and pesto, which is what we've had for dinner three nights in a row now, or we could have oven fries and veggie fingers, but I'm not sure we have enough of those for two, and Zach doesn't even *like* veggie fingers.

This is what we get for not keeping the freezer stocked full to the brim, like my parents do.

"Why don't we order pizza?" Zach suggests. "Save cooking. Hopefully have some leftovers for tomorrow. I know you love cold pizza the next day."

"I really do. Oh, go on. Why not?"

Once we moved in together, we created a pretty tight budget. It was Zach's idea; I put the spreadsheet together for us in a shared Google document. We wanted to be able to save for a deposit on a bigger place, maybe even a proper house. (Although, God, do I wish we'd splurged on a new dining table right now.) One of the first things we decided to cut out was takeaways. We don't often order in anymore, but when we do, it's not usually pizza. Chinese, or Indian, for the most part. Thai's our favorite, but Zach's also partial to a burger on Uber Eats. But I really, really do love a pizza.

"Not like we're going to use the socializing budget this week, right?" I joke.

"We'll have happy hour here on Thursday," he says, flashing a grin at me. "The house special: Quaran-tini. Shaken, not stirred."

"Oh my God."

"Served over ice . . . -*olation*."

"Oh my *God*."

I stare at Zach, who is completely deadpan now, and we both crack up at the same time.

"You're such a dork," I tell him.

"Yeah, but you love me."

I roll my eyes, bumping him with my hip as I stand back beside him. Zach's been using my iPad for his banana bread recipe. He suggests we order it now, in advance. I agree, if only for an extra excuse

Beth Reekles

to procrastinate getting back to work, and open a new tab to bring
up the Dominos website, picking one of their deals, and scheduling
the delivery for dinnertime. I add a vegetarian pizza for myself, and
then turn to Zach, who's carefully stirring the mixture.

"So pepperoni?" I ask. "Or the chicken one?"

"Nah, get me a Hawaiian, would you?"

I stare at him, sure I've misheard.

He's oblivious to my slack-jawed expression, though.

"Get some extra dip," is all he says.

I'm in such a state of shock I do as he says.

And all I can think is, *He likes pineapple on pizza?*

Since when has Zach *ever* liked pineapple on pizza?

*

I'm barely able to focus on work the rest of the day because I'm too
preoccupied by this hideous and abrupt turn of events.

The moment has been replaying on loop in my head for the last
few hours, and now I'm drinking a cup of tea on the sofa, eating a
freshly baked slice of banana bread while Zach talks to his parents
on FaceTime beside me. I'm still thinking about it when Zach goes
down to collect the scheduled pizzas.

Because seriously?

I know pineapple on pizza is a pretty polarizing subject, and honestly, I don't even care that much. So he likes a nice sweet fruit on his
savory pizza. It's weird, but hey, Zach's a little weird. He's a grown-ass
man with Iron Man action figures, and his favorite feel-good movie
is Disney's *Atlantis: The Lost Empire.* Liking pineapple on pizza is
definitely not the weirdest thing about him.

But . . .

How can I not know this about him?

How have I been with this guy for four years, and I don't know
something as basic as where he stands on pineapple on pizza?

What next? He moonlights as a serial killer? He has a secret second life with a wife and kids? He—

Oh my God.

Does he even want a wife and kids?

I mean, we never even really talked about getting married. Not *properly*. And I don't even know if he *actually* wants kids; the closest we've come to discussing it is when someone we know has announced they're expecting, and we've said, "Holy crap, I am not ready to raise a baby. Can you imagine?"

What else don't I know about Zach?

He comes back to the apartment, but I don't get to ask him about it, because I'm too confused by the fact he's not holding any pizza boxes.

"Where's the pizza?"

He pulls a face, exasperated. "Mr. Harris has a cleaning station set up. Sanitizing everything that comes into the place. He was going to disinfect the pizza boxes but that would just make them all soggy, I thought, so he said I could come get some plates to put the food on."

"Right. I-I'll come give you a hand."

I collect a couple of plates from the kitchen, following Zach downstairs to pick up our food. Mr. Harris gives us some kind of lecture on not getting "unnecessary deliveries to the building," but I barely hear it.

All I can do is stare at Zach like he's a complete stranger, and wonder what the hell else lockdown is going to reveal about him.

Chapter Eleven

When I met Danny, it was instant sparks.

We met, of course, on Bumble. (Because, where else but dating apps do you find single guys now, without having to awkwardly tell a colleague that their best friend may be single, and may be a great person, but is that bowl cut some kind of ironic throwback, or . . . ? And yes, maybe you said you were looking for someone athletic, but you didn't mean a guy who basically lives in the gym and has biceps bigger than his head in *every* sense of the words and who pouts in all his photographs.)

Danny asked me on a date within an hour of us matching. Usually, I wouldn't have met up with someone so quickly, but maybe that was *why* I'd agreed to it. All the other guys I'd met on dating apps had been after weeks of messaging, and had all fizzled out after a handful of dates. Maybe I'd just save myself a lot of time and effort, meeting Danny for dinner that same weekend.

I was a *little* turned off by the state of his house share, which, despite him and his housemates all being twenty-somethings, felt very much like a university student house—the line of empty beer bottles on a windowsill in the hallway, the mess of mop buckets and a Henry hoover and packets of toilet paper in the open space beneath the stairs, the cobweb in the corner by the doorway. But it all paled to insignificance in the glow of a perfect first date as he cooked me a three-course dinner entirely from scratch.

He even made *soup* from scratch. I'd sat on the kitchen counter sipping wine, the two of us chatting nonstop while he made spaghetti carbonara, with Danny as at ease in the kitchen as I was on a tennis court or a treadmill. I remember being so impressed, I forgot all about the state of the house share.

It was a perfect first date, and we just clicked.

Talking to some of my friends, we all waited with bated breath for things to go wrong. Such a perfect first date was so rare, *something* was bound to mess it all up.

Guys like that didn't just *exist*. Dates like that didn't just *happen*.

It'd all go south sooner or later; even my most optimistic friends said so.

But we went out for drinks and tapas. He talked in conversational Spanish to the waiter, who gave us a free jug of sangria because of it. We went bowling on the next date, and even though he was pretty atrocious and I'm competitive almost to a fault, he was such a good sport about it that I hardly stopped smiling all night. The first time we spent the night together, after our fourth date, he didn't hog the duvet or snore and even got up to make me breakfast the next morning.

"You're obsessed with him," a couple of my friends told me, after that.

They were probably right, but could you blame me?

He was *perfect*.

And every time I saw him, I got butterflies. I'd hear my phone buzz with a message and lunge for it, hoping it was him. He'd kiss me, and I'd go weak at the knees. I'd go more than two days without seeing him, and I'd be going stir-crazy.

"Do you think he's lost interest? Do you think it's because I didn't get that joke he told, about Han Solo? Do you think he's annoyed at me because I told him I couldn't make it out for drinks because I was too tired from tennis? Look! He put a red heart emoji at the end of this text when he said goodnight! Do you think that means something? It's got to mean something. It means something, right? I know he said he was having a boys' night but we've only been dating for like two weeks, we never said we were *exclusive*, what if that's code for something and he's actually out with another girl on a date? Ohmigod look at this meme Danny tagged me in, it is *so* us! Isn't that amazing that we've only been together a little while and we already have an *us*? I just love that, don't you think it's the cutest thing?"

"Isla," whichever friend I was bothering that day with stories about Danny would say, "can you please, please, chill the fuck out. You're obsessed. It's like listening to Carrie freak out over Big, only *worse*."

I might've been offended, if I wasn't so loved up with Danny.

Well, "loved up" was maybe the *teensiest* exaggeration. We'd only been dating for a month. You couldn't just start throwing around The L Word that early on.

But Danny was exactly the sort of guy I could see myself falling in love with.

I already *was* falling in love with him.

And I got the impression he felt the same way. I could just *tell*. It was in the way he kissed me, the way he'd ask when my lunch break was so he could take his at the same time and video call me. I could tell when he brought me flowers last week, and when, the last time I went to visit, the line of beer bottles on the windowsill had disappeared.

I could lie awake for hours replaying a date or phone call with him in my mind, or end up daydreaming at work. I'd think about how his parents would just love me the first time we met—I always make a great first impression on parents. He loved dogs and so did I, we both had golden retrievers growing up and had always wanted one when we were grown-up and wasn't that just so perfect. He was always so polite, and such a good cook, my mum would adore him, and he was even into car racing just like my dad and brother were; they'd get on so well. And we both wanted three kids, the first by the time we were thirty.

How could I *not* be falling in love with him?

We were perfect together.

*

Only, it doesn't feel quite so perfect right now.

It feels, I guess, real.

I'm really starting to see what the Islanders mean in the *Love Island* villa every year. This whole living together thing is *intense*. A few days is nothing, really, I know that, and yet somehow, it feels like it's been forever since Danny "moved in."

I still don't know if I'll be able to stomach it, if the building lockdown extends past this week; tough as it is, I don't know what will happen if I can't see Danny. Or even if I should move home, back to my parents? My brother's just done that, rather than risk ending up stuck at university by himself. Even Maisie moved back in with her parents this week, worried she'd end up totally isolated. Her sister Charlotte lives in the building, too, and us getting put on lockdown totally spooked Maisie—even if she told her parents she was only moving home to help them get the house ready to sell. Should I pack up, once Danny leaves, and retreat to my childhood bedroom too? Am I supposed to ask Danny if he wants to stay with me, and—do I even want him to?

Although, that said, if the lockdown here does extend for any reason, I'm *so* glad we're stuck here in my apartment, and not in Danny's house share, even if it is currently empty. His two housemates haven't been around for the last week—one had moved in with his boyfriend when this whole pandemic mess started, and the other is stuck in Sydney with some friends, still trying to get a flight back while Australia starts to shut down too.

I guess I'm also lucky we're stuck in my apartment, and not back and forth between an airport and a hostel at the other end of the world.

It's not so much Danny, I guess.

Mainly, I'd just like a little of my own *space* back.

This morning, I got up as quietly as I could, trying not to disturb Danny. I'd set my alarm late, putting my workout off until after work, but my body clock had me awake before him anyway. I went out onto the balcony with a cup of green tea and my journal and it was just so *quiet*.

It was blissful.

Right now, I wish I could go back to that moment. I couldn't stick sharing the dining table to work at, but somehow that means I've been relegated to the bedroom. I'm sat cross-legged on my bed trying to focus on a team call, but can hear Danny on the phone in the next room. He's got the meeting on loudspeaker while he paces around. I can hear every crackly voice, muffled by the bedroom door, and his heavy footsteps tromping back and forth.

(Maybe I'm overthinking it, but it seems selfish of him to claim the dining table when he's not even *using* it.)

I'm scowling, which I don't realize until I catch sight of myself in the little window on Zoom.

My boss notices, though, pausing to say, "Everything all right, Isla? C'mon, we didn't think the new design was *that* bad."

There's a polite chuckle through my headphones, and I make the effort to smile and compose my face. "Oh, no, nothing! Just, er, my boyfriend. He's on a meeting in the living room and it's a bit distracting."

There are murmurs of sympathy.

My colleague Kaylie, who's about ten years older than me, lets out a brash laugh and says, "Just be grateful you don't have kids! Honestly, I know I'm supposed to be making the effort to homeschool them right now after their school had some cases and shut down for a while, but I sat them down in front of some Disney cartoon with some cookies *just* so I could do one meeting in peace!"

As if to prove the point of how distracted we're all getting right now, my manager's cat leaps up onto her lap with a noisy hiss, winding around the headphone wire and then stomping all over the keyboard to shouts of, "No! No, no, no, Zee, come on, get—don't—stop—*Salazar Slytherhiss, you get down right now or*—"

Our boss vanishes into blackness.

The three of us sit awkwardly on the call for a moment, waiting for her to deal with the cat and come back on the call.

I'm glad for the interruption to be honest: it gives me a moment to check over the slide deck that got sent out and refocus, still doing my best to block out the noise of Danny's meeting across the hall.

Our boss pops back up.

"All right, sorry about that! Where were we? Right, Joe, you were just talking us through the revamped branding message . . . "

And Joe, our usually very introverted and shy design guy, blurts incredulously, looking deeply judgemental, "I'm sorry, but Zee the Cat is short for *Salazar Slytherhiss?* And you *never told us this?*"—and just like that, I'm oblivious to all the distractions in my apartment and in fits of giggles.

My phone buzzes a few seconds later.

A text from Danny.

Do you mind keeping it down a little bit, please?

I shoot back a middle finger emoji, but after my meeting I make myself a cup of tea and some coffee for him, and I kiss him on the cheek, and ask him to use his AirPods next time he has a meeting.

I can totally be a grown-up about this, and make this all work.

Hell, with five more days of this to go, I don't have much of a choice.

APARTMENT #6 – ETHAN

Chapter Twelve

It's automatic, when I start my day by filling the kettle with too much water for just me, and get the cream mug with the swirly gold *Hello Sunshine* motif on it she likes to use in the mornings off the mug tree and put a tea bag in it, before I remember she's not putting her makeup on in the bedroom and I don't need to make her a cup of tea.

Yesterday, it was automatic when I picked up the TV remote and opened my mouth to ask if she wanted to watch some more of *The Mandalorian*. When I wondered what we'd have for dinner or when I ordered a large pepperoni pizza and made it gluten free before remembering I didn't *have* to, because she wasn't even here to eat it. Today, when I put away the laundry and wondered if that T-shirt was one that she hangs in the wardrobe or folds in the drawers.

And it is so, so, blindly obvious to me, all the places that Charlotte is missing this week.

At least I've not let my usual routine slip today, though. That's something. It's nice to have *some* sense of normality, even if there's a lot about this whole situation that's decidedly not normal.

Despite the whole, you know, pandemic thing, I tell myself it's just a normal Tuesday. I reply to emails, review that contract for that brand deal, send an invoice for the VPN advertising I did on my last video. I schedule some tweets, script my next video, send out invites for my Patreon livestream.

A totally normal Tuesday. I wouldn't even have needed to leave the house today anyway. It absolutely does not matter that I'm on lockdown and totally alone. If anything, it should be *helpful*. I should have the most productive day—week, even—that I've ever had. Minimal distractions.

It's all going to be great.

(Maybe if I tell myself this enough I'll start to believe it.)

It's weird to be sitting at my desk and leaning back, stretching out, looking out at the balcony, and not see her out there, carefully watering the collection of plants we bought together at the garden center last year.

After a while, I realize I've been hunched over my computer a little too long: she's not here to come and stand behind me, fingers lightly massaging my neck before she leans down to hug me and murmur, "Come on, Ethan, sweetie, you need a break."

I miss the smell of her perfume.

Shit, I even miss the smell of cigarette smoke from when she's really stressed about something and thinks she can sneak one out on the balcony without me noticing. I wonder if she's sneaking cigarettes back home at her parents' place.

When I forget to rinse my mug after coffee, I even miss the angry little look on her face when she's annoyed at me about something—in this case, the way the coffee will stain the inside of the mug. I miss the way her nose scrunches up and her lips pout and she folds her arms tight across her chest and if anything, it just looks kind of adorable and sometimes I have to try not to laugh at her for it.

Fuck, I *miss* her.

I don't need anybody to tell me how pathetic I sound.

Mostly because I'm *acutely* aware of how pathetic I sound.

I'm on the verge of going full-on Bella Swan in *New Moon* without her, and I'm not even mad that I even *get* that reference. (Charlotte and I had a great weekend watching the whole five-movie saga when they were all on Netflix last year, so she could enjoy some nostalgia from her teenage years.)

Honestly, I'd give anything to be snuggled on the sofa with her right now, binge watching the *Twilight* movies.

Breaking news: I'm a total sap.

*

I met Charlotte at the cinema, two and a half years ago.

She loves the story. She calls it a "classic rom-com meet-cute." Her green eyes light up and she blushes when she tells it, a big, goofy grin on her face.

I was on my phone, texting the girl from Bumble I was supposed to be meeting there. I didn't even see Charlotte, and I walked right into her when she turned away from the counter. She dropped the large bag of popcorn she'd just bought, letting out the most adorable squeak.

I was mortified, and fully expected some big, beefy guy to suddenly pop up behind her to ask me what the fuck I thought I was doing, almost knocking his girlfriend to the floor and spilling popcorn all over her, and all over the floor. Said beefy boyfriend never appeared, though. I stammered apologies and insisted on buying her some replacement popcorn. Charlotte let me, blushing, and asked if I was there alone.

"I'm actually waiting for someone. What about you?"

"Here alone," she told me.

I sounded way too judgemental when I asked this total stranger incredulously, "You come to the movies on your own?"

"Don't you? I *love it*," she'd told me, breaking into a smile, and that was when I noticed the hazel flecks in her eyes. "I mean, it's not like you can talk much during the film anyway. And I can't resist a period drama. I—I guess your girlfriend can't either."

"Oh, she's not my girlfriend. Well. I, uh. I met her on Bumble. I've, um, I've never actually met her before. First date."

"Oh! Ooh, well, good luck."

She had her popcorn by then, and we stood there at the counter holding up the line while she smiled at me, and I tapped my phone awkwardly against my fingers, my mouth dry.

"I hope your date goes well," she told me.

"Yeah. Thanks. En—enjoy the movie."

My date never showed. I stood there holding two tickets in one hand and my phone in the other, until the usher told me, "I think you've missed the trailers, mate. If she's not here by now . . . "

At that point, I figured, I may as well see this movie, since I'd already paid for it.

Charlotte and I somehow found ourselves leaving at the same time once the movie was over. I say "somehow," like she hadn't waved at me when I walked in by myself, and like I hadn't sat three rows behind her and kind of maybe sort of waited for her to leave once the credits began to roll.

By then, my phone had a text that said *So sorry! Can't make it :(maybe some other time?*

Charlotte told me she was sorry my date had stood me up.

And I couldn't help myself. This cute girl with her chin-length wavy ginger hair and freckles, the big white cable-knit sweater she was wearing with a short plaid skirt and ankle boots, who went to the movies on her own and was still holding a mostly full large bag of popcorn, blushing when I stared at her.

I said, "I don't think I've ever done this in my life, but . . . do you, maybe, want to go get something to eat? Or—or a coffee, or something, or . . . I mean, you don't have to, and—"

She beamed at me, and I was floored.

*

I didn't even know her name when I asked her on that date, but I'm so goddamn glad I did.

I can't imagine not meeting her. Or if the Bumble date had ever shown up. Charlotte likes to say it was fate; I love it when she does.

On our fifth date, I told her I loved her.

She suggested moving in together after three months.

It was crazy, and her twin sister Maisie laughed and told us we were, quote, "Fucking idiots, falling for a whirlwind romance like this," and she, like everyone else we knew, told us not to sign a twelve-month rent agreement on an apartment, not when we'd only been dating for a couple of months.

The twelve months ran out.

We didn't renew it, just like everybody told us we wouldn't.

Instead, we bought our own place. (Thanks to some inheritance I had from my grandpa, and a small loan from both our parents that we'd probably still be paying off in ten years to help bring the mortgage down to something we could *actually* afford, but it was so worth it.)

It wasn't exactly Charlotte's dream place, and I would've liked an extra room to use as a studio space or office, but it was *ours*.

Right now, it feels too big without her. The empty space on the dresser where her perfume usually sits, the half-empty pot where some of her makeup brushes are missing. And I really hate the empty space on the other side of the bed and I hate sitting down at the dining table by myself, the place mats still left out in Charlotte's seat.

I hate her not being here.

And I *know* that's stupid; I know she'll be back in just a couple of days and she's only been staying with her parents and sister for a week and it's all because of this stupid lockdown business; it's not like she *chose* not to be here anymore or we had a fight or anything, but . . .

I wish she were here right now.

I wish she never has to go away for a week again.

I wish I could spend the rest of my life with Charlotte sneaking cigarettes on the balcony after a bad day at work and pulling that angry face at me because I forgot to water the plants or put away the laundry even though I'd been at home all day. I miss making her tea in the morning while she gets ready and having her snuggle into my arms with a sigh and reading essays on classic literature while I play a video game.

I never want to be without that.

And then I realize—

I want to marry this girl.

Chapter Thirteen

*I*t's fine. This is only day four. Or—hmm, technically, it's day five, since they arrived on Friday night. This is only day FIVE. Only . . . oh, so many more days to go. Cabin fever? Don't know her. We are all doing just great, and everything is totally fine.

All things considered, I think, this really could be a lot worse.

Of course, that could just be the alcohol talking.

Kim has a *lot* of things on her Bridal Bucket List—which is really just a very extensive Pinterest board (separate, of course, from the centerpieces board, and the one for dresses, and the one for hairstyles she likes) but this has got to be my favorite thing on it by far.

We decided, this week, we should do one thing from her Bridal Bucket List each evening.

Tonight, it's signature wedding cocktails, personalized to reflect the bride and groom and their relationship. I'm sure Kim had grander things in mind when she saved the idea, but this has been so much *fun*. We gathered every bit of alcohol in my apartment—which was actually quite a considerable collection.

"Spot the alcoholic," Addison teased, when she counted out six different types of gin. "Rough time at work, Livvy, or do you moonlight as a bartender to pick up hot dates?"

I didn't like to admit to her I did a mixology course with some people from work and ended up dating the girl who ran the class for a couple of weeks, and that we went out a few times to some gin place she was obsessed with, where I got suckered into buying a new bottle *every damn time*.

When I ignored her, Addison only laughed and winked at me. "Who are we kidding, right? Like *you* need any help picking up hot dates."

And then, I didn't reply to *that* because I was too busy blushing and hoping she didn't notice.

Anyway, after a *lot* of taste testing, we decide we've perfected the Kim/Jeremy Wedding Special. This is a cocktail that consists of:

2 x shots of pomegranate and rose gin
1 x shot of white rum
Tonic
Twist of lime

"Do you think it'll taste this good when we're sober?" Lucy asks, sipping hers. Apparently a complete lightweight, her cheeks are flushed and bright pink after only a couple of drinks, her dark hair turning frizzy. The way I hear it from Kim, Lucy is more of a quiet-night-in kind of person—and I'm guessing those nights in are accompanied by a cup of tea rather than a large glass of wine.

"Absolutely," Kim declares. "This is *the greatest* thing I have *ever* tasted."

"We're goddamn geniuses," Addison agrees. She holds up her glass, knocking it into mine as a "cheers," and slops cocktail on my lap. She's too busy laughing to apologize, and leans against me, tucking her head onto my shoulder, her body warm and soft against mine, the smell of her perfume filling my nostrils. I freeze, not sure how to respond. *She's probably just a hugger, that's all. Just ignore her—it's nothing.*

Addison is oblivious to how rigid I've become and adds, "We should make careers out of this. Quit our jobs and just start a business making cocktails."

"Oh, I wish," Kim snorts. "The literal dream."

"Lucy can be front of house. Livvy's already got the stockroom sorted," Addison says.

"It's Liv," I say, not so tipsy I can't correct her. "And Lucy's not front of house, she's a manager. I mean, it's her *literal* job."

"Even better!" Addison leaps to her feet. "Hey, how about *charades*? Let's play charades!"

We all agree, but a round of charades comes at a cost: we have to tidy up and rearrange the room again.

Personally, I couldn't be more relieved. It gives me an excuse to stand up and move away from Addison. Who, I tell myself, is probably just a cuddly drunk. That's all. Even though she wasn't really like that this weekend. But maybe she's had more to drink tonight? Sure. That's all it is.

Lucy and Kim clear up the bottles of alcohol and the glasses we discarded, half-drunk cocktails that didn't work out, while Addison clears the stack of pillows and blankets off the sofa, and I move the airbed to stand against the balcony doors, giving us back some floor space.

My lovely clean, tidy apartment, a distant memory.

We've decided to stick with the sleeping arrangements from the weekend: Addison and Kim are sharing my double bed, Lucy is on the sofa, and I've been on an air mattress in the living room. The hostess with the mostest, giving up my own bed for my guests. No big deal for a night or two. Now, I'm not sure my back will ever forgive me, a thought which is making me feel more like eighty-four than twenty-four.

My one-bedroom, one-bathroom apartment is perfect for a single person, and probably works just as great for a couple, too, but four people?

Well, it's a push.

It's an experience made all the more bearable by some alcohol, and by me being the only person having to work.

Lucy works as a restaurant manager, but her boss already closed the place because of the virus and furloughed half the staff. Addison and Kim *probably* could have worked from my apartment just fine, but Addison totally shocked me with her no-nonsense attitude and a poker face that would give Miranda Priestley a run for her money. She told their boss first thing on Monday morning, in no uncertain terms, that they were unable to work this week (even though I think they probably would've managed, if they tried, doing emails and joining meetings from their phones). She somehow negotiated them a week's paid leave from work, without even needing to use up their vacation days, quoting "extenuating circumstances."

I've had no such luck. Obviously. Of course I haven't.

First, I have to host a DIY wedding party all weekend, and now I have to spend the week trying to focus on financial forecasts and balance sheets and meetings while the girls are giggling over a movie in the next room.

Just my luck.

I'm so jealous that Kim and Addison's manager is so fair and compassionate and understanding. *Of course, it's an extraordinary situation, we understand, don't even worry about it, you can catch up next week* . . .

Not that I even tried to ask my boss, but still.

It's giving me an excuse to not have to talk about the wedding twenty-four seven, and it's a pretty decent distraction from . . . well, fine, from Addison. With her cute smile and all the sidelong looks when she's telling a joke, like there's some secret we're both in on, and . . .

And *not*, absolutely not, like it's even worth considering. I mean, she's so *annoying*. And she's so not interested, anyway. Obviously. Otherwise, she'd get my name right.

There's no work to distract me tonight, but the bucket list stuff is doing a pretty good job. Or, at least, it *was*.

For now, at least, I've got a pleasant boozy buzz going, focus on cleaning up instead of whatever "funny" story Addison's telling now, and I'm relieved when Lucy and Kim come back into the room so we can finally get into the game of charades, which Addison kicks off. The rest of us pile back on to the sofa, ready and raring to go.

"Movie!" we yell. "One word!"

Addison acts out what we can only assume is a scene from a movie, but it doesn't make sense to *any* of us. She mimes hitting somebody, and then messes with her hair. We shout out random words: "Fight! *Fight Club*! Brad Pitt! Baseball! That Madonna movie! *Hairspray*! Something about a makeover! *Sweeney Todd*!"

She gets more and more frustrated, and eventually points violently at her face.

Yesterday, the Bridal Bucket List involved oatmeal-and-honey homemade face masks. They were gloopy and smelly and messy, but, I have to hand it to the beauty blogger who'd shared them, my skin is dewy and super soft today.

Addison, however, had an allergic reaction to something, or maybe everything, in it, because after a few minutes, she'd commented on the tingly, hot sensation none of the rest of us were experiencing, and her skin was an angry, blotchy red when she took it off.

It's still not *exactly* back to normal today.

Which is why, now, I bounce in my spot on the sofa to point at her face and yell excitedly, "Ooh! I've got it! *Scarface*!"

She stops acting immediately, gawping at me, and then turns all serious like she did when she called her boss, and plants her hands on her hips. "Excuse me?"

"Is that not . . . ? Um . . . "

I look helplessly at Lucy and Kim, who are both in fits of laughter. Lucy even has tears running down her face, clutching at Kim's arm as she wheezes for breath. I'm getting zero help from either of them, apparently, and Addison's eyes burn a hole right through my skull.

Well, I think, she's *definitely* not going to be interested now. Mission accomplished, I guess?

"*Tangled*! It was fucking *Tangled*! You know, with the frying pan, and the *hair*," she adds, grabbing a fistful of her very-much-not-tangled hair. Although, admittedly, it is very long and a shiny golden blond, which is about as Rapunzel-esque as it gets.

She huffs, glaring overdramatically in my direction. "*Scarface*. Do I look like Al Pacino to you?" she asks me, although she does it in a Robert de Niro voice, like in *Taxi Driver*. "Do I *look* like *Al Pacino* to you?"

I scoff, not willing to admit exactly how funny her impression is, and go to refill my glass of Kim/Jeremy Wedding Special from the jug on the dining table. When I glance over again, Addison is look-ing at me. She smirks, and I look away to hide the fact I'm blushing.

Which is *only* because of the cocktails.

That is the *only* reason.

Wednesday

Chapter Fourteen

I haven't slept.

A pale dawn bleeds through the end-of-summer-sale garish green curtains Zach picked out that match nothing else in our bedroom, casting the whole room in a soft glow even though it's not even six o'clock yet. It's so quiet. I lie on my back, staring at the shadows on the ceiling. I hear a car going past, out on the main road, and wonder who's out this early. Someone coming home from a shift at the hospital, or someone heading out to stack shelves at the supermarket before it opens? Or is it someone trying to sneak out for a day on the coast, to escape their back garden for a few hours against all the advice to "stay home if you can"?

There are birds singing.

Normally, this would be nice. I hate those green curtains every other time, except for mornings like this, when it feels like a hazy, springtime glow no matter what time of year it is. With the birdsong and the lack of traffic, I could almost imagine we were on a camping holiday, all our worries left behind us for a few days.

Zach's breathing is deep and even beside me. He's splayed out on his stomach, one arm tucked under his chest and the other hooked over his head. He was out like a light last night, no problem. He didn't seem to notice if he thought I was quieter than usual; or if he did notice I was stuck in my head about something, he assumed I was mad about something and decided it was better not to ask if I wasn't going to bring it up.

I don't know how he can sleep so soundly at a time like this.

He mumbles in his sleep, and I can't help but turn to glower at him. How *dare* he sleep so soundly when I've barely managed to snatch two or three hours, when I'm lying here so wide awake?

I can't get it all out of my head.

I just . . . I feel like such a *fool*.

A few endless minutes later, another car has gone by and Zach sighs in his sleep.

I can't stay here. Not like this.

Slowly, not wanting to wake Zach up to deal with this properly just yet, I slip out from under the covers. I forgo putting on my slippers so I can pad barefoot out of the room, grabbing my dressing gown on the way, and wrapping myself up in it. The bedroom door creaks on my way out and I pause, but Zach doesn't stir. Creeping into the kitchen, I want to make myself a cup of tea.

I regret the idea immediately.

The leftover pizza is wrapped in foil on the side, along with the extra dip Zach wanted to order but never got around to using. It's all there, on the kitchen counter, taunting me.

I glare at them while I wait for the kettle to boil, and my lip curls as I carry my tea out past the leftovers again.

In the hallway, I catch a glimpse of myself in the large mirror over our just-a-bit-wobbly IKEA sideboard. Even the person in the mirror looks like a total stranger for a moment.

I mean, she looks like me, of course she does: dark skin, shoulder-length curly hair, body made even softer and rounder than usual by the big fluffy dressing gown. The girl in the mirror looks like me, but she's not, because the Serena looking back at me is one who *looks* like her entire world was just turned upside down. My eyes are bloodshot and there are purplish bags under them, my cheeks burn hot, and my jaw is clenched tightly. As soon as I notice it in my reflection, I try to relax.

It takes an enormous amount of effort.

Walking away from my reflection, I try to shake it off, but I can't. Even with the pizza leftovers out of sight, I've got Zach's voice in my head, crystal clear, telling me so enthusiastically, so easily, that he wanted pineapple on his pizza.

My head was spinning too much to confront him last night.

It's still spinning.

It's been spinning all night long.

I go out onto the balcony, curl up on the bench that Zach's dad made for us as a housewarming gift, and drink my tea in the quiet morning.

This will help, I tell myself. It's bound to. This is what people do, isn't it? At least, I know it's what Isla from Number Fifteen does. She posts about it on her Instagram all the time. Her little fifteen-minute morning meditations. Her journaling at dawn out on the balcony, watching the sunrise. It *does* always look so nice, but hell, who can sit with just . . . *nothing*, for that long? Not even thinking? In fact, consciously *trying* not to think? Nope, couldn't do it.

I catch myself: I've already failed at trying to sit here and just *be*, because I'm thinking too much.

But *Jesus*. How can I *not* think about it?

The boy ordered *pineapple*, on his *pizza*.

In the four years I've known Zach, he's never done something like that. I've never seen him eat a slice of Hawaiian. I've never so much as heard him express an interest in it, never offered any sort of contribution to the everlasting controversial debate, that most persistent of internet discourses: Does pineapple belong on pizza?

"Hey."

I startle, so caught up in my own tumultuous thoughts that I didn't hear him get up, or come out onto the balcony. My tea's half-drunk but now cold; the sun is starting to burn the clouds away. I put my mug down and notice Zach frown, confused, as he looks between me and it.

In all the time we've been together, I've never known him to order Hawaiian pizza, and he's probably never known me to not finish a cup of tea.

He takes a long look at me before sitting down.

His hair sticks up at odd angles and his glasses have finger smudges on them.

I shift into the corner of the bench as he sits.

"You weren't there when I woke up. How long have you been out here?"

"Depends what time it is."

"Almost eight."

God, how have I lost that much of the morning to this whole shit-storm?

"What's up?" He reaches over to take my hand but I pull away. "Serena, babe, what's the matter?"

And even though I've been thinking about this for like, twelve hours now, I'm no clearer on what I want to say. I know I need to explain, but it's so much more difficult than that, and I can't tell him what *started* all this, can I? I'd sound totally ridiculous. Or worse, he'd *laugh* at me, and I don't think I can stomach that right now, especially since if he makes a joke of it all we won't ever actually deal with it.

So what comes out of my mouth instead is, "How long are we going to stay here, Zach?"

"What?"

"Like, here. This apartment. This was supposed to be the start, right? What's next?"

"Uh . . ."

"Like is it a four-year thing? Ten? Twelve? We've only got one bed-room. Or, like, are we supposed to wait until I get pregnant and we start having kids to even *think* about moving? Are we supposed to wait until then to even ask ourselves if we want kids?"

"Whoa, kids? Is this—where did—Serena, are you—is this you trying to tell me you're pregnant, or something?"

I scoff, rolling my eyes. "*No.* I'm just *saying.* But like, we will, one day, right? Or at least, I'm *assuming* we will, and now I'm thinking—well, I realize that I'm *assuming* that, you know? Based on *nothing,* except . . . that you've never said otherwise. But we've never actually talked about if we even both want kids. Do you *want* kids, Zach?"

He stammers and looks alarmed when I twist my face up to look him in the eye.

I know I've sprung this on him, but—well, come on. The boy's got to have an opinion, surely?

"I dunno. Like . . . I guess? If you do."

I am officially lost for words.

I gawp at him, so Zach fills the silence by babbling on. "I'm not saying I *don't,* or anything, you know, I guess I just never really thought about it much. I just always assumed . . . you know, it'd happen, if it was gonna happen. For us, I mean."

"What, you didn't think we'd, like, discuss me stopping my birth control, or something? Or *moving somewhere* with enough space to raise a kid? Or two, or three? Or however many we 'happen' to have? You didn't think that there'd be, like, *any* amount of planning in us having kids? Or that you should maybe form an opinion on whether you want them or not?"

Zach laughs nervously, rubbing the back of his neck. He takes off his glasses, cleaning them on his pajama T-shirt and clearing his throat.

I let him stall, because I really need to know what he's got to say for himself.

"Come on, Rena. We've only been going out for four years—"

"We bought an apartment together!"

"And we're only in our twenties."

"*I'm* only twenty-eight," I point out. "*You* turn thirty in June! But that's the point! Your little sister's twenty-two and *she's* already thinking about kids—and she doesn't even have a boyfriend yet! And what about your brother and his husband? Why do you *think* they bought a house in the suburbs the way they did, why do you *think* they took a loan off your parents to get a bigger deposit so they could afford the mortgage on that place? It's *three bedrooms*, Zach. Do you think Matty and Alex need *three bedrooms*, or that they're planning for kids?"

"I thought you only *wanted* one bedroom."

"Yeah, for now! Because that's what we could afford, *for now*. That's why we made a budget!"

"Exactly," he says. "We have the budget. Because we said we wanted to save for somewhere bigger."

"*I* said that, Zach. And you said, we should make a budget. But we never talked about if it's what you wanted too. Or what the plan was, how much we want to save, where we want to move to. I just— it's the fact you haven't even . . . you haven't even thought about this, it's—I can't . . . "

I trail off, so angry I don't know how to tell him. I'm also aware that my voice is climbing higher and higher, and *louder*, too, and I should probably take this inside before the neighbors file a noise complaint.

I storm back inside, and hear Zach stumbling to follow me.

"Is this your way of telling me you want to start trying for kids?"

I spin back around, hands jabbing at the air or back on myself as I talk.

"No! I just—you know, I can't wait till I'm forty to start thinking about it, you know? I don't *have* that luxury." I break off with a sigh and tug my hands through my hair. "We should be *talking* about those things, and we're not and . . . "

Zach sighs, rubbing his hand over his mouth, and I hear him mutter, "It's too early for this bullshit."

"What?" I hiss.

He blushes when he realizes I heard him, but then his gaze hardens, his jaw sets and he nods as if steeling himself before saying, "This is ridiculous, Serena, you get that, right? If you wanted to talk about kids, or if you want to get married, or if you want to move to a bigger house, or whatever, then why didn't you just *say* that? Why didn't you just ask me?"

"Well apparently if I had, you wouldn't have had a fucking opinion anyway!"

"*Excuse me* for not having planned out every minute of the rest of our lives!"

"We've been together for *four years*, Zach! You're telling me you never stopped to think how you might propose one day? Or even *if* you would? If you *wanted* to?"

"Do you *want* me to?"

"That's not the point!"

Zach scoffs, but the sound quickly turns into a disbelieving chuckle. He paces away from me and then back again, getting up close until he's only inches away. "Then what *is* the point, Serena? Why don't you fucking spell it out for me, since I'm obviously not getting it?"

I shove him back. "Don't look at me like that. Like I'm being a total bitch."

"You are! You're being a bitch! It's not *like* you. What the hell is going on this morning?"

"I'm *trying* to talk to you about it but—"

"Oh, is that what you're doing? Because it sounds more like you're attacking me for not having been part of a conversation you think we should've had, without ever telling me! You do realize how *extremely* absurd this whole thing is right now, right?"

"Screw you, Zach."

"Do you *want* to sit down and talk about how many kids you want, or when you want us to get married? Have you already picked out colors for a nursery?"

"Oh, fuck you!" I'm screaming now, and I don't even care if it wakes up the whole freaking apartment building. I grab Zach by his T-shirt to shove him out of the living room and into the entryway. "If it's so fucking absurd why don't you just do what you do best and ignore it, and go away for a pint with the boys till you decide it's all blown over?"

"Come on, that's not fair."

I don't know if he means that it's not fair because he wouldn't do that, or because he'd love to do exactly that, but he can't, because the building is on lockdown. I don't care to know the answer; I have a horrible feeling it's the second one.

"*You're* the one not being fair," I tell him, my voice hitching. "*You're* the one calling me a bitch just because I want to talk about something real for a change!"

"That's not what I meant and you know it."

"Then what *did* you mean? Huh?"

"Fuck this," Zach grumbles, shaking his head. "Maybe I *should* go."

"Yeah, you do that. Good luck. Where are you going to go, huh?"

He stands there looking at me, lips pressed tightly together and jaw working furiously as he churns over words he decides not to say. A single line cuts through his forehead and I think for a second about how I've never seen his eyes look such a bright blue. He looks ready to cry and my heart splinters.

Please don't cry, Zach, because if you cry, I will too, and then we won't get anywhere.

He doesn't cry. I watch as his posture shifts and his whole body turns rigid. His hands don't even shake. He is completely and utterly still, and then he lifts his chin. I hear the sharp, loud breath he draws in through his nose, and lets out again.

Lockdown on London Lane

What right does he have, to be so angry with me? To call *me* a
bitch?

How can he just not have an opinion on these things? How can he
just expect to *go with the flow*, over such major life decisions?

It makes me feel like he doesn't even care about the life he has with
me. It makes me feel like . . .

Like he's settling.

Like he's just with me to pass the time.

It makes me feel like *I'm* settling.

"I have to get ready for work," I say, and I shut myself in the bathroom. I actually *do* need to take a shower, but instead, I sink to the
floor with my back against the door, hugging my knees to me and
burying my face in the fluffy sleeves of my dressing gown, stifling the
sob that tears itself out of my throat.

I hold myself tighter, my body hunching as small as I can make it
go, like I might somehow be able to keep my breaking heart together
like this.

Chapter Fifteen

Sure, it's fine, go ahead and watch TV, it's absolutely not bothering me. I'm in the next room! I can totally work just fine from my bedroom! It is A-okay. Don't you guys worry about me, just have fun. It's really not a problem.

It is absolutely a problem. It is absolutely not fine.

But, I guess, it has to be fine, because I have no choice in the matter. And it's not *their* fault, I know that.

I'm doing my utmost to keep being a good hostess. I'd want them to do the same for me.

That doesn't stop me feeling totally exhausted, though. And it is much harder than I thought it would be to focus—especially with one of them knocking on the bedroom door every so often to say, "Sorry, Liv, how does the oven timer work? Livvy, sorry, just quickly—how do you get the extractor fan in the bathroom to turn on? Just bringing you a cup of tea, Olivia, love . . . and, while I'm here, where did you say the laundry detergent is, only I can't find it in the cupboard under the sink?"

Even without that, though, the state of disarray my apartment is in is enough to keep me at least mildly stressed out. Jeremy brought Kim an extra bag of clothes when he brought the shopping the other day, and he brought Lucy some of her clothes from their parents'. Addison's been borrowing some of mine since we're roughly the same size. Unfortunately, though, all this means is that everywhere you step in the apartment, there seems to be a rogue pair of socks, someone's bra, a bunched-up T-shirt none of us are sure is clean or dirty so we toss it on the laundry pile just in case. I know the girls are making an effort to keep it tidy, but it's more difficult than any of us thought.

Even the sight of the drying rack cluttered with damp laundry in the corner of the bedroom stresses me out.

I'm starting to realize that Kim isn't the only one of us who likes things to be *just so*.

Right now, I have an hour between meetings and nothing *that* urgent to do, so I decide to leave my laptop charging for a bit and take a very long tea break with the girls, who are bingeing their way through old episodes of *Come Dine With Me*, which Addison has never watched before and is totally entranced by.

"All right?" Kim asks me, as I leave "my office." "Are we being too loud?"

"No! No, of course not. Just thought I'd take a break for a bit. Anyone want a cuppa?"

There are murmurs of assent from everybody, and Lucy joins me in the kitchen to help out. She asks me how work has been so far today, sounding like she genuinely cares.

I like Lucy. She's sweet. She's the youngest of our group, and tells great stories, although the subject of most of them is her wild friend Imogen. We've never really interacted much before, past being mutuals on Instagram.

"You have such a lovely place here," she tells me, sounding wistful. "I'm living at home so I can save the money I'd be spending on rent to put toward a deposit, but God, this makes me really want to move out and have my own place. Is it really sad that I can't wait to buy my own kitchenware?"

"Absolutely not." I laugh. "Kim was always saying the same, whenever she came to visit, before she and Jeremy bought a place together."

Initially, Kim had come to look at this apartment when she and Jeremy were considering buying somewhere in the city. I'd trailed along, since Jeremy couldn't make it that day and Kim wanted a second opinion.

It didn't "feel right" for them, she said, within about twenty seconds of setting foot over the threshold. But I thought it was pretty perfect.

I tell Lucy as much now, and she smiles. "Yeah, this doesn't strike me as very Kim and Jeremy. It doesn't have 'growing space.'"

"I don't know. Four of us packed in here okay. I think they'd be able to find space for a crib, if they have a baby."

"*When,*" she corrects me. "And don't forget the dog."

"The border collie Jeremy's got his heart set on having one day. How could I?"

Lucy shakes her head, a fond smile on her face as she hands me the milk. "We always used to tease him about having such a clear idea of what he wanted from life, but he's really found it with Kim. I still remember him coming home from their first date and telling us she was the one."

"Kim did the same thing. I told her she'd better not tell him that if she wanted a second date and not scare him off."

"Match made in heaven," Lucy says softly, and smiles to herself, genuinely happy for them.

It's not that I'm *not* happy for them, or like I don't love Kim to pieces, or like I'm not a fan of Jeremy, but sometimes . . .

Sometimes, it's just a bit much. You know? All that lovey-dovey, hopeless romantic stuff being shoved in your face, all the damn time. Even when they fight, they've made up within an hour, having talked everything out and tried to compromise and find a solution. They're just so damn *perfect* together that it gets . . . it's a little exhausting.

Especially for those of us whose relationships always fail after only a few dates.

But I am happy for them. Really. I am.

Lucy glances at me expectantly, so I smile back, hoping it doesn't look as forced as it feels. Fortunately, I've finished the tea by this point, so busy myself handing mugs over to her to carry back into the living room. We find Addison and Kim in the middle of a discussion, the episode of *Come Dine With Me* paused, apparently too important to risk missing even a minute of it.

Addison looks up as I put down her mug. She snaps her fingers at me, like she's beckoning a waiter. I half expect her to call me *garçon*.

Instead, she says, "Livvy, have *you* got your plus one for the wedding yet?"

Something like dread prickles across my body and my stomach flip-flops. I'm sure my palms are sweating already. For a horrible second, I think she can read minds, and knew what I was thinking about in the kitchen a few seconds ago.

"No," I admit. My whole mouth feels like it's full of sawdust, like a bad hangover.

"See?" She turns to Kim with a triumphant look. "I don't know why you're so worried. I'll find someone to bring. Look, babe, I know you want to confirm with the caterers how many people want the vegetarian risotto, or the beef casserole, but don't stress it."

"Have you got someone in mind?" Lucy asks.

"Huh? Oh. No. But I can find someone. That's what Tinder's for, right?"

She laughs—loud and brash and grating. I stare at her in horror.

"I'm sorry," I have to interrupt, "but you'd go on a dating app and just ask someone to be your date to a *wedding*? Just—totally out of the blue?"

She turns those big blue eyes on me and blinks once, the very picture of innocence.

"Sure. Why not?"

"You don't think that's a bit . . . serious? A bit fast?"

Addison scrunches up her face. "I'm inviting them to drink free champagne, eat a free meal, and go dancing. I'm not *proposing*. What's the big deal?"

Kim pulls a face at me, and then looks away to sip her tea. It's judgemental—but directed at *me*, not at Addison, and I know instantly what she's trying to say to me. That I take commitment too seriously and take *myself* too seriously.

"Let me guess," Addison drawls, misreading the look between us, "you got this lecture about needing to confirm your plus one months before the wedding too?"

"I never *asked* for one," I mutter, directing the comment more at Kim, who only gives me a deadpan look in return.

Lucy pipes up, "I don't have one either."

Addison must not have heard her, though, because she laughs again and says, "Well, that settles it. If Livvy doesn't have a plus one by the time it comes around, and I don't, either, we'll be each other's hot date to the wedding."

My cheeks begin to heat up so I busy myself picking up my tea, because it gives me an excuse to turn away from them all for a couple of seconds. But I scoff and say, "There. See, Kim? Problem solved. Now are we watching the rest of this episode or not? I want to see who wins before I have to go back to work."

Lucy presses play on the episode, and Kim fills me in quickly on the scores so far, and who we're all rooting for—her way of making peace.

I know she and Jeremy wanted to offer all the bridesmaids and groomsmen a plus one, to make it fair, and because for those of us who are single, we might not be single by the time the wedding rolls around, and then we'd just be bitter. I know that; but I've been telling Kim since the start I don't want a plus one.

I don't want a plus one, because my parents are going to the wedding, too, and I still haven't figured out how to tell them the reason I haven't brought "a nice boy" home to meet them is because I'm not interested in bringing *any* kind of boy home. They're just so *traditional*, I'm not sure how they'd take it. And now it feels like I've kept it from them for so long I don't know how to explain I've been hiding all this from them for years.

It's safe to say I don't feel like explaining all of that to Addison, though, and frankly, it's none of her business.

Her hot date to the wedding.

Ha.

She should be so lucky.

Chapter Sixteen

"So this is . . ."

"Weird?"

"Just a bit. And . . . "

"Awkward?"

"Absolutely."

We share a nervous laugh, Danny looking relieved that I'm on the same page as him, and not totally *loving* every second of being shut up in my apartment with him. He's not quite as enthusiastic as he was on Sunday when he came back to the apartment after hearing he couldn't leave; and as much as I've been telling myself how great this will be for our relationship, I'm definitely feeling the strain too.

Actually, he's . . .

He's kind of getting on my nerves.

Like, a *lot*.

(Seriously, would it kill him to make the bed after he gets up in the mornings, instead of leaving the sheets in a rumpled pile? And, like, if I can brush my teeth and put on some makeup before he sees me in the mornings, the least he can do is not bite his nails when we're watching something on TV in the evening.)

I must be getting on his nerves, too, though, and that's exactly why we're sat at my dining table, using our lunch break to map out our schedules for the week and a chore rota. I didn't realize I had such a routine until Danny was here interrupting it.

I didn't realize he was such a pain in the butt either.

(God, seriously? Who takes. Every. Single. Meeting. with their phone on speaker while they pace around? Who gets up with six minutes to spare before they have to log on for their first morning meeting, with barely enough time to use the bathroom and put on a T-shirt? And how, God, *how* does he manage to use what seems like every pan I own when he cooks dinner?)

It was Danny's idea to coordinate our schedules a little more. I think he could see I was getting annoyed with him. I also think it's because he doesn't like my 6:00 a.m. alarm. In fact, I know he doesn't because yesterday, at his request, I turned it off and we slept in; and today, he grumped and grumbled and pulled me back into bed for a cuddle I was not in the mood for.

"Well, like I said the other day, you're cooking dinner," I tell him now, picking up the pencil and scribbling his name down in the timetable we're making. "Since you're so good at it. I'll do the dishes."

"What, *every night?*"

"You cook for yourself every night already."

"Sometimes I split it with the guys," he says, meaning his housemates. "But that's not the point."

I laugh, but it comes out sounding dry and a bit meaner than I intended. "And here I was thinking you'd planned out what we were eating all week when you did the food order. Didn't we have, like, a whole discussion about making enough pasta one night so we'd both have leftovers for lunch?"

"Well, *yeah*, but, I mean, *obviously*, I planned it, but that doesn't mean I should cook every single night. It's not fair."

Danny's thick, dark eyebrows start to pull together in a scowl. In fairness to him, I probably *am* being sort of bratty about it. (It's just the luxury of having a boyfriend who's such a good cook, and it's not like he doesn't *enjoy* it. He actually counts it as one of his interests.)

But he's got a point, so I say, "Okay. I'll cook tonight."

"We could do it together," he suggests then, smiling and reaching for my hand. He does that thing where he traces light little circles on my palm; he's done it for as long as we've been dating, and I soften a little. It's probably something he's done with every girl he's dated before me, but I can never bring myself to care. There's something about the way he does it, about Danny himself, that makes me feel like it's special, just for me.

Still, it's not quite enough to distract me from the debate of who's going to cook dinner this week.

Doing it together is a nice compromise, and I appreciate it, but . . .

"Trust me, you don't want my help in the kitchen."

I remember on our first date when he cooked us dinner, watching him chop onions so quickly, almost carelessly, that I'd thought he'd cut himself. It would've taken me ten minutes to do what he'd done in seconds. He'd been so at ease in the kitchen. Like he *belonged* there.

If I help him out with cooking, I just know he's going to get frustrated with me. I'll only slow him down and get in the way.

Danny sighs, but doesn't argue.

"Okay. *Okay*, you wore me down," he says, chuckling, still tracing little circles on my palm. "I'll cook, you can clean up after. But—what about this: If I'm going to cook and you're *not* going to help out, why don't you just do your workout then?"

I stare at him, all too aware of the indignant look on my face I can't seem to get rid of.

"Well, because I do it in the morning before work?"

"It's just the rest of the week. Couldn't you switch it up?"

I think I've already "switched it up" plenty, with not being able to go for a run, or to the tennis court down the street a couple of evenings a week—*and* by skipping it yesterday and this morning. Danny's only suggesting it because he doesn't want me to keep waking him up so early and disturbing his (obscenely long) lie-in in the mornings, now he doesn't have to commute to the office.

Sensing I'm not on board, Danny goes on with a gentle, upbeat tone. "Hear me out. I'm just thinking, I don't start work until eight o'clock. And you don't work regular hours anyway. So why would you get up at six in the morning, which wakes *me* up, too, when you could do your workout at the end of the day, when I'm cooking dinner?"

I *hate* how much sense that makes.

I also hate how this is making me realize how stubborn I am; I never thought of myself as stubborn before. I'm not sure I like this part of myself.

But, hey, he compromised on agreeing to stick to my usual plan of doing a little housework each day, rather than doing it all in one go once a week, *and* he's going to do most of the cooking, so . . .

And, you know, I really don't want to get into a fight over it.

I refuse to be the reason our relationship crumbles: because I wouldn't change my exercise routine.

"Okay," I mumble, scribbling out the lines that say *6:00 a.m.– 7:00 a.m.: Isla Workout*. "And for the record, I work *flexible* hours. It's not like I work after lunch and late into the evening every day, or something."

It looks like I'm also going to be working reduced hours soon, too, with the company already making plans to have everyone work from home if this whole "situation" gets worse. (I've been trying to ignore the news alerts because they're just making me feel so despondent; Danny is obsessed with watching them, though I can't for the life of me understand why.)

Management are talking about furloughing people, or reducing hours to avoid that, and preparing to close the offices and have everyone work from home full time. Lots of people—like my colleague Kaylie, and our boss—are already at home. Kaylie's having to isolate with her kids because there were cases at their school, and our boss has some chronic illness I don't really understand because I always feel too awkward to ask her to explain it to me, so she's been advised to stay home too. It should probably be comforting that other people are in the same boat as me, but it just fills me with dread.

Anyway, work's big positive spin is that, as a sports and fitness company, they expect to be busy if people have to adjust to at-home exercise on a long-term basis. Our yoga mats *have* been selling like hot cakes in the last week or so, but I still think that's mostly due to them getting a nice little review in *Cosmopolitan* recently. But, still, it's scary, and things have been a little slow lately as we wait to be told what's going to happen with our jobs.

Danny, on the other hand, seems to be busier than ever in his job at the local council. Which was *his* argument for me doing all the housework-style chores this week. I'd protested against that on principle, but you know, he had a point: my six hours a day versus his nine or ten didn't really hold up in that debate.

We hash out a couple more things for our new schedule—like the fact that Danny likes to listen to audiobooks before bed, and I like to keep the window open at night, that he hates the idea of watching TV while eating dinner.

It's all the kind of stuff we don't notice, spending just a night or two with each other. It's all the kind of stuff that is thrown into sharp relief now that we can't avoid each other.

And we *have* only been dating for a month or so. That's barely any time at all. Surely we have to cut ourselves some slack for that?

Danny belches, and gets up to make another coffee.

I'm not sure it's a good sign that there's a part of me that's counting the days until he can leave, and we can spend a little time apart again. Maybe, I realize, my stomach giving a sickening lurch, our honeymoon period is officially over.

Maybe if we can't even hack it this week, while we still *have* a honeymoon period, it's never going to work out with us.

No. No, I can't think like that—I *won't*. It's a much too defeatist attitude, and it'll get me—us, our relationship—nowhere. I push the thought away, hopefully for good.

We're all finished with the rota for the week, and I take it with me, following Danny to the kitchen. I tack it to the fridge with an *I Heart Rome* magnet I got from my holiday there with Maisie last year.

The doorbell buzzer sounds.

"That'll be the grocery delivery," I say quietly.

"I've got a meeting in five minutes."

"It's all right. I'll sort it."

I grab my keys, slip on some sneakers and head downstairs to collect our delivery. Well, Danny's, mostly.

Oh, no, I'm not being fair to him, I'm really not.

"Hey!" a voice barks at me, snapping me out of my thoughts as I reach the bottom of the staircase. "Six feet!"

I jump, realizing I've almost bumped into another girl, and that the caretaker, Mr. Harris, is glowering at me. Despite the lower half of his face being covered by a surgical mask, he still manages to look furious, and deeply stressed out.

I feel like I'm in trouble with the headmaster at school. Mr. Harris has always scared me a bit, though I've never been able to put my finger on why, exactly. Now, I gulp and raise a finger timidly toward the door.

"I just—um—we have a food delivery, and—"

"Yeah, yeah, you and everyone else. I've got a *process*. Nothing's—"

"Nothing's getting in or out of this building," adds the girl in front of me, reciting right along with him, "without it being adequately sanitized first."

"That's right," Mr. Harris says, with an approving nod at her. I notice the table he's set up near the door then: a box of disposable latex gloves, an open bin, a jumbo pack of Dettol wipes, some store-brand antibacterial spray, a large pump bottle of hand sanitizer. I wonder if he started preparing for this as soon as the words *highly contagious virus* were mentioned on the news. (Smart guy; I'm wishing I'd done the same.) He goes outside to talk to my delivery driver; it looks like he's halfway through cleaning someone else's groceries.

The tall, curvy girl in front of me turns around with a halfhearted smile and a shrug, which is when I recognize her. It's Serena, from next door. Her thick, dark hair is concealed under a towel turban, and she's in a guy's hoodie. She's wearing a pair of fluffy pink socks and slippers. It makes me feel dressed up, in my cotton dress and cardigan. For once, I feel more insecure wearing makeup than if I weren't.

"Better settle in," she tells me, leaning back against the wall and crossing her arms. "You're going to be here a while. He's *thorough*."

"Just as well I don't have any meetings this afternoon."

She laughs. "Tell me about it."

"Have you got the week off, for lockdown?" I ask, with a glance at the towel wrapped around her head.

"Oh! No. God, no. I wish! I'm just finding it hard to focus, so taking a shower seemed like a great way to procrastinate."

"Better than waiting for the shopping," I offer. I could tell her I completely understand, and tell her how difficult it is trying to work from home with Danny doing the same, and I'm sure she'd empathize—but something stops me.

If she notices I'm holding something back, though, she lets it slide.

"I actually *should* be doing some work right now. Zach—you know, my boyfriend—he was supposed to be down here doing this because he obviously can't get to the hospital for his shifts, but then his boss called, so . . . " She gestures at the hair and the hoodie, and then her slippers. "Bloody pain in the ass."

"His boss?"

"No, Zach."

She's obviously trying to sound like she's joking, but her voice is tight when she says his name, and something flickers across her face.

I have to bite my tongue. It's not as though we're close neighbors—we follow each other on Instagram, pick up each other's mail if we're away for more than a few days—but I *have* noticed the way the two of them snipe at each other, if I see them around. And, sometimes, if I'm out on the balcony, I hear them arguing with each other.

Danny and I *definitely* heard them yelling at each other this morning. Danny had joked, "They're really going at it, aren't they? Bloody hell. Well, that fight's either going on all day, or they're going to have *really* loud make-up sex later."

It sounded like a pretty horrible fight, about kids and marriage and things like that. I think one—or maybe both of them—cried, but if she's not going to bring it up . . . well, we're definitely not close enough that I can outright *ask* her what happened.

I know that if I'd had a blazing row with Danny, I wouldn't want her asking me about it.

"How're you finding it?" she asks me, slightly more upbeat. I'm not sure if she's just being friendly or if she's finding the silence too awkward—or worse, if she *knows* I overheard their argument—but either way, I don't mind it. It's nice to talk to someone that's not Danny. "Your new boyfriend's here, right? I saw on your Insta Story. That must be nice for you guys."

"Oh! Yeah. Yes, he's . . . well, he's a bit short on clothes," I find myself admitting. "He was only supposed to be here for the weekend, and it's not like, um—not . . . "

"Not like you were planning on wearing clothes much?"

I blush, but Serena only laughs.

"Puppy love. God, I miss that. Just seeing them and wanting to rip their clothes off."

I'm not sure what stops me from correcting her about the "puppy love," or saying it's not actually all that rosy with us at the minute, but

I know I've painted a great picture on Instagram the last few days and I'd feel stupid for contradicting that, so just smile instead. "Yeah! It's been pretty great. I think it'll be really good for us and our relationship. Really help us get to know each other better."

Serena smiles, looking a little sorry for me. We're not close, but I get the impression she suspects I'm stretching the truth a little.

"Well, your guy looks pretty built, but if you want I can lend you some of Zach's T-shirts and joggers. God knows he's got enough of them, he won't mind. If you want. If it's helpful, I mean."

"No! That'd—gosh, thanks. That'd be really lovely. Thank you."

We smile softly at each other and lapse back into silence. It might be the longest conversation we've ever had, and it makes me think that I really *should* make more of an effort with my neighbors.

And then Mr. Harris comes back inside and grumbles loudly, "Bloody hell, no wonder everyone's up in arms because they can't buy pasta. You must've bought all the penne in the country here, Number Fifteen. Leave some for the rest of us, eh?"

I scoff. "Try telling that to my boyfriend."

Chapter Seventeen

Nate's phone pings and I glance up from my own over to the small dining table he's currently working at. I'm so bored, I even found the exact make and model of that dining table on the IKEA website. And the chairs too. And his TV stand.

I am *bored*.

He waves his phone at me. "That's your ASOS order. Apparently it's just been delivered."

"Oh! Amazing."

I never knew I'd be so happy to get a multipack of basic black briefs.

Until now I've been alternating between my underwear (and then handwashing them in the sink, rather than waiting for him to have an entire load of laundry) and a pair of Nate's boxer shorts. Because, I'm sorry, but I *slept with him*, so borrowing a clean pair of his underwear is the least of my problems, and it feels genuinely icky—not to mention downright rude—to go commando in the leggings I've borrowed from his neighbor.

"I'll go down and grab it," I tell him, rather unnecessarily. Like he hasn't done enough this week without interrupting his workday to go downstairs and collect *my* clothes delivery, which *he paid for.* (I mean, I paid him back, out of the money Lucy sent me, but you know. He used *his* credit card.)

I do steal the hoodie he was wearing the morning, which is draped over the back of his chair. I wiggle it away from him, pulling it on over the Ramones shirt I'm wearing once again.

It's such a nice shirt.

"First my shirt, now my favorite hoodie," he laments, all melo-dramatic, slumping back in his chair. He must be in a good mood, because he cracks a wide smile at me, head turning to look at me.

Not that he's been in a *bad* mood, or anything, but I feel like he's so on guard with me most of the time and honestly, I'm not really sure how I'm supposed to handle that, or even if I'm, like, *supposed* to. It's a Nate thing, I keep trying to tell myself, not a me thing.

Still. It's nice to see he's taken a break from the distant attitude, if only for a minute or two.

"Sorry. Finders, keepers."

"I thought you said you owed me for the clothes order?"

"Hmm." I narrow my eyes at him and pull on the hoodie.

"I want *both* of those back at the end of this week, you know."

"But I look *so* good in them."

I stick my hands in the hoodie's pockets and strike a pose. Nate waves a hand at me, as if to say, "Go on, leave already," and I pull a face at him.

"Hey. You better show a little more enthusiasm when I bring that clothes order back. The whole experience of buying clothes isn't truly over until you've tried everything on and paraded about in a full fashion show."

"What, seriously?"

"Don't tell me you've never had a girlfriend do that. Or like, a female housemate at university. Or your mum, even. Like, *everyone* does it."

Nate looks at me like I've lost my mind.

"Like with music and everything?" he asks, looking mildly horrified.

I burst into laughter, moving over to cup his face in my hands. "Oh, my poor, sweet Nathan. Stick to your spreadsheets, okay?" I pat one of his cheeks gently, playfully, laughing again at the look of utter bewilderment on his face.

His key hangs on a hook near the door, so I take it and put on my shoes (which are inside the apartment now, and clean—if only because I was *that* bored yesterday I sat on the balcony scrubbing them with damp paper towels) and I head downstairs to collect my order.

When I picked up the food delivery the other day, I had to wait half an hour for the not-a-serial-killer, actually-a-caretaker guy to disinfect it all. I figure I'm in for the same experience with my clothes.

In the corridor, there's a heady, pungent stench of cleaning products. Bleach, and disinfectant, and something lemony. It kind of reminds me of a hospital, only worse.

I need a mask, just to be able to breathe through it. I pull the Ramones shirt up over my nose instead, chin tucked down against my chest.

When I arrive at the front door, I find the caretaker looking even *more* like a serial killer this time, in a yellow onesie made of thin plastic. It's even got a hood, which is pulled up over his head.

I snap a quick, sneaky photo. Nate definitely needs to see this. And I'll totally share it with Lucy, once I'm out the other side and I can admit to her I got quarantined with a one-night stand she told me, in no uncertain terms, not to go and see.

"What's up, Walter White?" I ask him, announcing my arrival.

He turns around, looking less than impressed, and he obviously recognizes me by the way his frown deepens. "Ramones," he greets me, and then points a gloved finger accusingly at the plastic bag full of clothes. "I'm guessing this is yours."

"Yup. Took your advice. Ordered some clothes to see me through the week. And I see you did the same. I'm *loving* this look, mister. It's very pandemic chic."

His face twitches, but since his mouth is covered by a white papery mask, I'm not sure if he smiles or if it's more a look of deep disdain he's got going on under there.

He dunks a sponge into a bucket of soapy water, and starts scrubbing viciously at my delivery. So viciously, in fact, that by the time he takes several large steps back and lets me pick it up, he's rubbed the ink clean off the postage label.

I salute him and start back upstairs.

Except as I'm getting to the first floor, one more staircase to go, voices drift down through the stairwell.

And I *definitely* recognize one of them.

Actually, come to think of it, I recognize both of them.

Shit. Shit, shit, shit.

They sound close enough that if I carry on going upstairs to Nate's apartment, I'm going to run into them. Which I guess is a slight issue because, like, there's an extremely contagious virus on the loose in this building, and whatever, but mainly, it's a problem because Lucy cannot know I'm here.

And Lucy is on her way downstairs right now.

And Lucy is going to give me *such* a lecture, and this might actually be the thing that makes her finally lose her shit with me because even I can admit it's pretty goddamn reckless, and I've already got to deal with Nate sighing at me all week.

Oh fuck.

" . . . like it's *my* fault she'll never find anyone she likes enough to invite. What was I supposed to do? Give my best friend a wedding invitation and *not* give her the option of a plus one? I just wanted her to have the *choice*, that's all."

"I'm sure she knows that," Lucy says, ever the mediator.

Her future sister-in-law, Kim, possibly the most uptight and boring person I've ever met, barely acknowledges her. "The wedding's not for six months yet, anyway! She's got plenty of time to find someone! And it's not like she even *has* to bring anyone, or like anybody will care either way, but she acts like I've done something really . . . really, *malicious*, you know? Like I'm trying to show her up, or put her on the spot, and that's absolutely not what . . . "

I tune her out and make the snap decision to bolt back downstairs. I almost barrel right into the doors, where Lucy's big brother, Jeremy, is now waiting. A couple of bags of shopping rest by his feet. He's on his phone, though, too busy to notice me, thank God.

The caretaker notices me, though.

"Ramones, what are you—"

"You didn't see me here," I tell him, and I dive under the stairs, out of sight, just as I hear Lucy and Kim starting down from the first floor.

Just in time. I could give James Bond a run for his money, I reckon.

I hunch as far under the staircase as I can get, cramped and trying not to eavesdrop as the girls greet the caretaker, explain who Jeremy is, and wait while knock-off Walter White disinfects their stuff. He does leave the door open for them, though, letting them talk to Jeremy for a little while.

Jeremy says something to Kim about how, maybe, they'll have to think about postponing the wedding. Save some money, just . . . take *precautions*. Maybe they can even negotiate not losing their deposits, under the circumstances.

"What?" she whimpers, sounding on the verge of tears.

"I just want to toss it in the ring," he says, with that same everlasting patience as Lucy has. "Put it on the table. Something to consider. This is just looking really serious right now, Kim, that's all. I don't want us to have to cancel the wedding, either, believe me, but if we *did* have to postpone it, it'd save us some money, that's all I'm thinking. And if that *is* what we need to do, I'd rather give all the guests as much notice as we can. Some of them are going to need hotels and taxis and . . . "

My phone buzzes, and I get it out of Nate's hoodie pocket as quietly as I can. I turn off the vibrate so it doesn't give me away, then check the notification.

It's a text from Lucy.

Wedding drama on the horizon. We're just picking up some food Jere brought us and he said something about postponing the wedding, which was maybe a bit my idea, a little, to save them money and hassle in six months if all this carries on, and now I think Kim might cry. This is like some horrible reality show. Send Ant and Dec in now, please. I'm a bridesmaid, get me out of here.

Uh-oh
Tell me everything

As if I don't already know *exactly* what's going on.

But, ever the dutiful best friend, I let Lucy vent over text while she stands by and waits for their shopping to be disinfected, reassure her that it's not her fault if they decide to postpone the wedding, all while Kim and Jeremy have a tense conversation about doing just that. I feel only a *little* bit shitty that I'm lying to her.

Well. I guess it doesn't count as lying, so much as embellishing the truth.

And is it even embellishing the truth if I just . . . neglect to tell her something?

They're there for what feels like *forever*. Once Jeremy is gone and the girls have collected their safely sanitized shopping, and I can't hear their footsteps anymore, I crawl out from under the stairs. My neck is stiff and my legs have pins and needles, both so numb I stagger and fall over when I try to stand up.

The caretaker sighs at me. "I don't even want to ask."

I dust myself off and hug my ASOS package to my chest.

"Thanks for not giving me away, Walt."

"That's not my . . . " He sighs again, and I have to wonder what is it with everybody sighing at me this week? "Yeah, yeah, just wash your damn hands when you get back inside. And stop lurking in my hallways."

Chapter Eighteen

"I need some of your clothes."

"What?"

Zach looks at me, first with confusion, pulling off his gaming headset, and then an expression of terror crosses his face.

After four years, I know him well enough that I know what he's thinking. I try not to look too annoyed with him. (Being annoyed with him seems to be my default state, since our fight this morning. Or—oh, or maybe it's my default with him normally, now I think about it.)

"I'm not about to set fire to them and throw them off the balcony in some sort of symbolic cleanse, Zach." I roll my eyes, even managing a thin smile back at him when he laughs. "Isla next door, she's stuck with her boyfriend and he doesn't have any clothes."

"Oh no. How terrible for them."

I smirk, opening up the wardrobe to rifle through. "I said I'd lend him some of your clothes."

"Oh. Uh, sure. That was nice of you. But—isn't he, like, you know. A beefcake?"

I do laugh at that, because Zach's not wrong. From what I've seen on Isla's Instagram account, her boyfriend (Danny, I think?) is built like a brick shithouse. He's got broad shoulders, big arms. Typical rugby player build, and he's also really tall.

Although, Isla *is* a tiny slip of a thing, so maybe he just looks huge by comparison. But Zach's tall too. And he's *fairly* broad shouldered, even if he's skinny. Looking at him now, I'm suddenly reminded of the first time I ever saw him.

*

Three months out of a serious relationship, I was ready to get back out there. I'd dated the guy through university and been so loved up. We made it work for two years after getting jobs and going "out into the real world"—by which I mean, we both tried way, way too hard to make it work, even though we lived in different cities and were so obviously going different ways in our lives. Anyway, three months after we finally called it quits, I was *so ready* to get back out there.

I'd show him, I thought. I'd move on and meet some amazing, really cool guy, who was everything I was looking for, and I'd forget all about him and the relationship we had in the glow of a new romance.

Except, God, was dating this hard for everybody?

Seriously. I gave up on Tinder. The one guy I dated from Hinge was so . . . intense, I ended up just deleting the app. A dozen Bumble dates and I was met with either the blandest personalities in existence or guys who were nice, sure, but there was zero chemistry once we met in real life. (To be fair, one of the guys with no personality *was* crazy hot, and he was really good in bed, but I quickly decided a healthy sex life wouldn't make up for the fact he only wanted to talk about the stock market.)

Six months out of a serious relationship, I was ready to give up on dating and romance altogether.

That shit was *hard*.

Like, to the point where I had so many first dates and so very few second dates, I was starting to wonder if I was ever going to meet a guy I liked ever again.

When one of my best friends at work, Vicki, begged me to go on a double date with her, I groaned. Loudly, melodramatically, meaning every bit of it. I laid my head down on my desk for a long moment before sitting up to say, "Vicki, I swear to God, that's the worst idea I've ever heard."

"Okay, but hear me out!"

"I'm done dating, I told you."

"Please, you always say that, and you never mean it." She gestured to toss her hair, forgetting she'd just chopped it all off for charity, her hand swooping through empty air instead. "Seriously, hear me out. You know that guy I've been talking to, Henry?"

"Is this the one with the fish in his first profile picture?"

She pulled a face at me. "He works in an aquarium. It's not the same as some dude holding up a sea bass from some fishing trip with his friends. Anyway, he asked me to go on a date on Friday and—"

"Oof, Friday. You know what, Vicks, I have plans then! Doing *literally anything else*. Although, actually, I am genuinely planning to order myself a pizza and watch some YouTube videos and do a face mask. It was going to be a whole thing."

"*This* is a whole thing!" she cried, throwing out her arms, with such earnestness in her voice that it turned heads in the office. She sighed, sounding so sad and hopeful all at once, and turned big, brown, puppy-dog eyes on me. "I don't want to go meet some strange guy at a bar alone. So he suggested I bring a friend."

"Vicki, listen to me. I love you. And you know I think you have great boobs and I'm very jealous of them. But I'm not going to have a threesome with you."

She snorted before her seriousness returned. "He's bringing a friend too. We'll have our date, and you guys will . . . be on a blind date. Or you'll just hang out and get drunk and laugh at how awkward me and Henry are being on our first date, and you'll never see him again. Come on. Please? For me?"

"Fine. But only—*only*—for you."

When we got to the bar, we recognized Henry from his pictures on the app. He smiled and waved. And the guy next to him . . .

God, the guy next to him was so not my type. Skinny, almost gangly, his brown hair a little messy and a little long (what, did he think he was in a boy band, or something?) and wearing these thick-rimmed glasses and a Thor T-shirt underneath his flannel shirt, and I knew immediately, he was not my type.

It wasn't going to be a blind date. It was going to be us getting drunk and being polite to each other while we mocked our friends on *their* first date.

The one thing Zach had going for him was the way he'd rolled up his shirt sleeves.

What can I say? I'm a sucker for guys' forearms.

He had a great smile too. He stammered a little when he introduced himself. When we left Henry and Vicki to it, taking a table a short distance away, I joked that we should get shots to see the two of us through the night, and he got us a round of tequila slammers, which he did *not* down like a champ, and I had to pat him on the back, he coughed so hard.

There was zero pressure. I mocked his T-shirt, so he mocked my charm bracelet. We shared a bowl of cheesy fries and talked about our jobs and our lives and how we knew Vicki and Henry, and at one point we were both just buzzed enough that when I said, "I love this song," Zach pulled me up to dance, right there in a crowded bar, twirling me on the sticky floor like it was a damn ballroom.

He was so very far from my type, and he told me that was okay because I wasn't his, either, but I'd never laughed or flirted so much in my whole goddamn life.

Vicki's date with Henry was okay. She gave it a six out of ten. Decent, but not great, and not good enough that she'd want to see him a second time.

My date with Zach? Oh, easily a ten out of ten. It was the best first date I'd ever had in my life.

*

Zach helps me pull together a few items of clothing to lend to Isla's boyfriend. We do it quietly, but there's a rhythm and coordination to it, bred from four years of familiarity. We know each other so well.

And yet, we know each other so little.

I think about that first date. I think about all the beautiful, wonderful, spectacular moments we've shared since. The cute days out, the nights snuggled up together losing track of entire hours as we kissed, the rush of looking for an apartment together, the comfort of spending Christmas with his family and New Year's with mine, all those times he's made me smile and we've laughed until our sides hurt and one of us (me, it's always me) would have to rush to the bathroom before they (me) peed themselves.

I love him so much.

It's so easy to love Zach.

That's why it hurts so much, to feel like the guy next to me right now is a complete stranger.

We haven't talked about it since this morning. We've settled into this clipped back and forth of, "I'm making tea, do you want one? Can you close the door? Do you know where my laptop charger is?"

For a few minutes, though, we manage to forget all about that. I finish packing his clothes into a tote bag when there's a weird rummaging at the door. We both go to look out of the peephole, and find Mr. Harris there, all masked- and gloved-up, a scowl on his face I'm pretty sure he was born with, spraying antibacterial spray on our door and scrubbing it down. Zach stifles a laugh into his hand and I nudge him, shushing him, before he makes me laugh too.

When Mr. Harris moves to scrub down the bannister on the stairs to the floor above, Zach whispers, "I don't think those clothes are getting to Isla without a strict quarantine period first. Or a good soak in some bleach."

"What am I supposed to do?"

"I'll cover you."

We wait until we hear Mr. Harris move upstairs. Zach opens the door, peering around it, and then waves me out. I hurry down the hall, knocking on Isla's door as quietly, *quietly*, as possible, hopping on my toes for her to answer and collect the bag. I shush her before she can say "hello" or "thank you," pointing upward, where Mr. Harris can be heard muttering to himself and aggressively cleaning people's front doors.

"Oh!" she whispers, and nods, taking the bag from the floor. She gives me a thumbs-up before disappearing back inside.

Zach's humming the *Mission Impossible* theme under his breath, his back against the door and hands poised in front of him, fingers folded in a gun shape as he squints dramatically at the staircase. He waves me over and when he follows me inside, he dives to the floor, doing a forward roll and then getting his finger gun back out like he's surveying the area, which sends me into peals of laughter.

I catch myself, remembering we're supposed to be fighting, and clear my throat, muttering something about having to get back to work. He coughs, straightens his hoodie and glasses, and shuffles back into the bedroom.

God, he's such a dork.

I don't know how to feel about the idea of him *not* being *my dork* anymore. So I decide it's better to not think about it at all.

Thursday

Chapter Nineteen

I t's automatic, when I tap my pen erratically against the table, a page full of useless scribbles staring up at me, the anxiety creeping up from the pit of my stomach, squeezing around my heart and crawling into my lungs.

Okay.

Okay.

Okay.

I can do this. I can do this, I have nothing to be so worked up about. It's not like anybody even *knows* about this, if it does go wrong, or I don't think I can go through with it for some reason.

This is not a big deal, I tell myself. I am just taking a break from work for a little while.

God, how can I post so much utter crap throughout the day on social media that people engage with, but I can barely string a sentence together right now?

I can totally do this.

I've had days to think about all the things I love about her and all the things I miss so much now she's not around; I've had days to mope around like a soppy, pathetic, romantic bastard. I can *do this*.

It should not be this difficult.

Dear Charlotte—I . . .

Dear Charlotte. You're not perfect, but you're perfect for me, and . . .

Dear Charlotte, this week has been hell, and I don't . . .

Okay, it's impossible, and I absolutely cannot do this, and I have very, *very* good reason to be breaking out in a cold sweat.

I scribble out the latest stupid line I just tried to write out, sighing and burying my head in my hands. Eight pages in, and I can't come up with a single entire sentence that doesn't sound completely cringeworthy or even comes close to telling her how I feel about her.

You'd think, after two and a half years, I'd know what to say to her. This is useless.

I'm never going to figure it out.

She deserves better than this paltry attempt. I should be singing "Can't Take My Eyes Off You" with a marching band as I dance down the bleachers in front of a crowd of all her friends. I should be kissing her in the rain after writing her a whole bunch of letters. I should be climbing up a fire escape with a bouquet of roses after pulling up in a white limousine. I should march through a field in the pouring rain to tell her I love her, after bailing her sister out of a shotgun wedding to a soldier and in spite of my prejudice and her pride.

God, *all* the romantic movies we've watched together and I can't even come up with a single damn line to express how much I love her, never mind some outlandish, unforgettable display of showboating.

Who am I kidding?

The good news, I guess, is that Charlotte knows I'm not that guy. I'm awkward and shy and introverted and I look like the nerd I am.

Something tells me a dorky, gangly guy with wire-rimmed glasses and puffy, mousy hair singing tunelessly along to "Can't Take My Eyes Off You" won't have *quite* the same effect as when Heath Ledger did it, and that if I walked through the rain to meet her in a gazebo, I'd look less Mr. Darcy and more drowned rat.

"Come on, Ethan, get it together," I mutter, dragging my head up out of my hands and shaking myself. I stand up, pacing around the room, and it's official: the cabin fever is bad enough that I'm now talking to myself.

Seriously, you'd think, considering I'm an introvert who likes to spend most of his time indoors playing video games and recording vlogs, that a few days of staying in my apartment wouldn't be any kind of hardship. It should be a totally average week.

And *yet.*

Motivation feels harder to come by than usual and I find myself getting distracted by literally anything. I've never wanted to just go out for a *walk* so much in my whole life.

I'd love to look at something that's not the wall of floating bookshelves piled with Charlotte's fiction paperbacks, or the IKEA unit in the corner with photographs we've framed, or my limited-edition Stormtrooper helmet.

I close my eyes and wonder, if I pretended hard enough, if I might be able to imagine that the shag rug under my feet is grass.

(Yep, I've officially lost it.)

All right, all right, focus. You got this. Charlotte's not expecting Ryan Gosling. She'd expect it to be you. It doesn't need to be a show-stopper performance, just you. Honest. Real. Authentic. Yeah, she loves authentic stuff. What else does she love?

She loves classic books. I could do that thing where I cut a hole out of the pages in a book I know she likes, to hide a ring in there. But she'd probably be madder at me for wasting a good book, *and* I don't even have a ring yet.

An hour-long Google search later, I discover that I know nothing at all about rings, and even if I did, I don't know what she'd like more: a classic diamond, one with emeralds to match her eyes? A princess cut, whatever that is? Am I supposed to get silver, or white gold, and what's even the difference, and is she going to be offended if I pick the wrong one?

Sure, I could just pick one and go ahead and order a ring. I could find her jewelry box and try to measure one of her rings and use that as a guide to figure out which size to buy, sure, but none of the websites I look at can guarantee when they'll deliver, and if it doesn't show up until after she gets back and Charlotte sees the delivery box she'll only ask what it is and I am *the worst* at keeping secrets, so it'd ruin the whole thing.

Okay, so no ring for the grand proposal.

Which is maybe a good thing, because I bet she'd have a great time picking out the perfect ring for herself, and she'll probably do a better job of it than I would. I bookmark a couple of rings I think she'd like, trying not to look for too long at the price on any of them in case it gives me a literal heart attack, and step away from my computer to go back to pacing around the room.

I give up on that soon enough, and go to make myself a coffee. Maybe that'll help.

My phone rings while I'm in the kitchen, and I prop it against the toaster once I swipe to answer.

Charlotte's face fills the screen, and my heart lurches.

Such a sap, Maddox.

"Hey, sweetie!" she says, beaming. "Whatcha doing?"

"Just makin' coffee." I grin back at her, lifting the French press to the camera before I pour it. "How about you?"

"Just sittin' in the garden."

She flips the camera, showing off a lush green garden, the grass recently mown but already sprinkled with daisies. The red-brown fence at the back of it matches the planks of wood that make up the deck, where she's sitting on a sun lounger. I can see her pale legs stretched out in front of her on it, as she swings the camera around the garden.

She flips it back on herself and I notice she's wearing the blue earrings I bought her on holiday in Tenerife last year.

"I'm starting to think we should've just said *screw it* and quit our jobs and moved out to the country and bought some little cottage in the middle of nowhere just to have a garden. I *miss* having a garden." She sighs.

I laugh. "It's your job we stayed near the city for, remember?"

"All right, Mr. Self-Employed. We can't *all* make a living selling ad space on our vlogs about video games."

"I talk about Reddit threads too."

"Yeah, and Pokémon, I know. You think I'm not fully aware of that giant stuffed Charmander in our living room?"

"It's a *Charizard*," I correct her, like she doesn't already know, and Charlotte giggles. "What're you reading?"

"I found my old copy of *Lady Chatterley's Lover* from when I was, like, seventeen." She waves a slightly faded–looking book with a nondescript green cover at the camera. "It's not as good as I remember, but it's okay. What are you doing?"

"You mean in the last hour since I text you?"

Charlotte laughs again, lips curving up in a bright smile and God, I wish she was here. I can't believe it's been almost a *week* since I kissed her. She waits for me to answer, apparently oblivious to the fact I'm distracted thinking about the next time I'll get to kiss her.

"Uh . . ."

Shit. Shit, I can't tell her what I've *actually* been doing this morning, since we last messaged. *Oh, nothing much, Charlotte, just planning the perfect thing to say to you to ask you to marry me, because I realized I want to spend the rest of my life with you.*

Never mind a ring showing up in the post; I think saying *that* would ruin the surprise, just a little.

"Not much. I've got a vlog to film for Saturday. Some stuff to plan for my Twitch stream tomorrow night."

"Eight o'clock," she declares. "I've got my reminders all set to tune in."

I laugh, rolling my eyes at her and picking up the phone in one hand, my coffee in the other, taking her back into the living room. "Why? You hate my livestreams."

"I don't hate them."

"All right," I concede, "but they're not your kind of thing."

I was still working when I met Charlotte. I was a paralegal.

I hated it.

I hated the hours, I hated the office, I hated the work. I'd only taken the job because I didn't know what else to do with my life, and it seemed as good as any, and what the hell else did I plan to do with my law degree?

She thought my "little hobby" of a YouTube channel I'd been running for a few years at that point was really cute. A few dates in, she told me she'd watched some of my videos but didn't really get it. "Do people really like watching someone else play a video game?" she'd asked, genuinely baffled by the concept.

We'd only been dating a few months when the channel started to take off. It was exhausting to keep it up alongside my job; but I loved it too much to stop. Charlotte didn't get it, sure, but she was supportive. She was the one who encouraged me to ask to cut my hours to part time and invest more in my channel.

I quit my job completely about a year after that.

She never understood it, and she didn't really enjoy watching it, but she always said she liked how enthusiastic I was about it, and she was never scornful of it.

"I don't have to like video games to want to just watch you for a couple of hours. It's like hanging out with you."

"You're cute."

Her nose wrinkles and her shoulders shrug a little. "I know."

She doesn't know the half of it.

She starts updating me on a situation apparently happening upstairs: Maisie's friend, a girl called Isla who lives in our building, has overhead some really crazy arguments from one of her neighbors. Apparently this neighbor has been having screaming matches with her boyfriend the last couple of days (which now she mentions it, might explain some of the noise I've been hearing from upstairs this week), and it's escalated to yelling about how they feel about kids and marriage and stuff. Charlotte sighs, telling me she hopes it works out for them, but she imagines what a big, scary conversation that must be. My stomach twists the whole time she talks, and I have to work hard not to give too much away. I'm sweating through my T-shirt.

She notices *something* is up, because her mouth twists and her forehead puckers in a frown. "I'm boring you, aren't I? Sorry. I know you don't really care about some stranger's drama."

"No!" I say, maybe a little too quickly. "No, that's not it, I just—just feel bad for them, is all. I promise, I want to hear all about it."

Charlotte and I never really *talked* about getting married, or kids, or our futures, or anything like that, but I guess we never really needed to. We were serious and committed to each other so early on. I guess she's always expected me to propose at some point, but it's not something we discussed so much.

We've been to a couple of friends' weddings over the last year or so. Once one got engaged, it seemed everyone was doing it. We've had five weddings in the last year. Charlotte would say something at each one, like how she didn't want lilies at her wedding, or she thought it was tacky to have such a big group of bridesmaids and groomsmen, or that she could never get married abroad because she'd *never* expect *her* friends to pay that kind of money just to see her tie the knot.

It wasn't like I didn't have my share of opinions. When her friend from university had a kid and we went to visit, we both laughed over the name (they'd called their kid Leia, after the *Star Wars* character) and I'd joked to her that if we had a son, I'd definitely name him something appropriately dorky too.

Everything had always been such a throwaway comment, though, or part of a joke.

Hearing her tell me this gossip I don't *actually* care about, though, I wonder if we should've talked about it more, before I go ahead and propose to her.

As if she can read my mind, Charlotte turns suddenly serious and says to me, "Ethan?"

"Yeah?"

"Can I ask you something?"

My stomach lurches and my heart is somewhere in my throat, but I nod and say in the most breezy voice I can manage, "Sure, anything."

And she asks me, "How do you feel about pineapple on pizza?"

Chapter Twenty

*N*ope, sorry, Danny, I tried and I can't do it.

Even with the door shut, the noise from the kitchen is so distracting it's making it impossible to focus. It doesn't help that my head's not really in it because this late in the afternoon isn't when I'd usually be working out, so as much as I grit my teeth and try to push on, I only end up frustrated and fed up.

Like, seriously? I'm here with my whole routine in disarray, even wearing mascara and some BB cream to exercise so I don't look totally hideous for Danny, while he's barely stepped away from his computer for more than two minutes at a time today to speak to me, and now he's making a total racket while cooking dinner—and probably making an absolute mess of the kitchen I only just cleaned this morning.

There's a loud metal clatter, like the sound of a saucepan falling, which is the last straw.

Huffing, breathless, I pause the HIIT workout video I'm following on YouTube, almost tripping over my yoga mat and the wine-red rug I pushed out of the way in my haste, and storm across the hallway.

I catch a glimpse of myself in the ornate vintage mirror hanging behind the sofa: dripping in sweat, hair scraped back into a ponytail but starting to form a frizzy halo around my head from the exercise. But I can't even care about the state I'm in. I'm too riled up. No, I'm not just *riled up*, I'm plain old *pissed off*.

I throw open the kitchen door and I'm hit by a wall of steam.

"Could you *please* turn that down?"

"What?" Danny has to shout for me to hear him over the roar of the fan over the oven and the Spanish podcast he's listening to.

"I said, could you turn that down?"

"What?"

I'm grinding my teeth and resenting the interruption to my work-out; I run a hand over my flushed face and don't notice him reaching to turn off the fan on the stove and hitting pause on the podcast until it's too late and I'm yelling into a now-silent kitchen:

"CAN YOU PLEASE GIVE ME SOME GODDAMN QUIET?"

Danny blinks at me, taken aback.

I'm breathing hard, but now it's nothing to do with the workout.

"And will you open a fucking window? It's like a sauna in here."

Danny turns down the temperature on the hob, giving the bolognese he's making one last stir before turning to me. Behind him, the counter is piled with pots and bowls and knives from some earlier part of his cooking process. Somewhere in the depths of my kitchen, he's found an apron. Pink gingham. I vaguely recognize it as one that my mum bought, when she helped me kit out my new apart-ment. Even though Serena dropped off a small pile of Zach's clothes an hour ago, Danny's not wearing a shirt under the apron; I'd have teased him about it, maybe made a couple of flirty comments, but I think we both know that wouldn't go down well.

"Your kitchen windows are locked," he tells me slowly, "and I didn't want to interrupt your workout."

"Bit late for that," I mutter, scowling, but stride across the kitchen to yank open a drawer by the sink and get the key out, unlocking the windows and throwing them wide open. The fresh air feels glorious, especially when I'm overheating from my workout and the kitchen is so steamy. I take a second to try to calm down and enjoy it, to stop feeling so angry. It's not particularly effective.

Making an effort to sound at least a *bit* calmer, I tell him, "I couldn't even *hear* the workout video over all the noise you're making in here. And honestly! How can you possibly have used this many pots and chopping boards for one dish? I didn't even know I owned this many knives!"

"I'll clean it all up after."

"That's—that's not the point! What about the fact that you've been working *all day*, and you worked all yesterday evening. It's like you could barely look up from your laptop long enough to acknowledge me *all day*, and I don't want to be that couple who don't talk to each other, and—"

"Not talk? Isla, I was in meetings, like, all day! It's not like I was trying to ignore you."

Danny shuffles closer, reaching for me, but I draw away to pace the length of the kitchen again, anger boiling in the pit of my stomach. He says, "You've got all black under your eyes. I think it's mascara."

"Well at least I'm wearing mascara!"

He looks at me like I've well and truly lost the plot now, his handsome face crinkling in confusion. "What?"

Oh crap, that didn't really land with the impact I wanted it to have. Now he looks like he wants to laugh, which really doesn't help my mood when I'm so pissed off.

"I—you know what I mean!" I burst out, glowering at him, desperately trying to clean up the smudges of mascara from under my eyes. "I've been making so much effort all week and it feels like it's all you can do to brush your hair!"

Frowning, obviously self-conscious, he rubs the thick layer of stubble on his cheek. "Well, yeah. It's not like I've got my razor or nice shirts or my other pair of good jeans. In case you hadn't noticed, I'm *stuck here*, with only an overnight bag, and some clothes you borrowed from next door that don't even fit me right. *Sorry* if I'm not looking my best this week."

I'm speechless for a second, because I didn't even think about it that way.

But oh, I'm so mad with him, and that's still not the point I was trying to make, or I don't think it was, and besides, there's a bunch of other reasons I'm in such a bad mood right now.

And I open my mouth to retort again, my face scrunched up, finger raised as I step forward to jab at the air, and the second I move my leg—

Phhhhbt!

—I let out the loudest fart of my entire life.

In that second, right there in my little, six-by-eight kitchen still full of steam, standing across from my boyfriend of only a month, I want to die. I want the ground to open up and swallow me whole.

Oh God, and it's not that it was even so loud, it's the noxious smell like rotten eggs that follows, enough to make me gag.

Danny stares at me in total shock.

I can imagine exactly what he's seeing now. Some sweaty, red-faced girl half his size, cheeks smeared in mascara, looking angry enough to throw him out of a window for what seems to him like no good reason, letting out the world's loudest, most rancid fart.

It is a far cry from the image I've been striving to cultivate: keeping my legs shaved, using the nice fancy moisturizer, doing a foot mask so even my feet seem perfect and soft, running to the bathroom first thing in the mornings to cover up any new spots, not singing in the shower so I don't sound like some banshee, avoiding eating anything too smelly on our dates so I won't smell or taste gross when he kisses me . . .

And to think I was worried about him finding the wine stain on the underside of the sofa cushion, or my *Little Mermaid* music box.

Everything I've done in the last month—the last week—has been for *nothing*.

I've destroyed it all in a single moment.

So I do the only rational thing I can. I flee the kitchen and shut myself in the bathroom.

Danny isn't far behind, running after me and calling my name, knocking on the door even as I press my hands to it, like little ol' me can barricade it if he *does* try to open it.

"Isla," he pleads, knocking. "Come on, open up. Please? Isla?"

Oh God, I can't even *avoid* him, can I? We're stuck in here together and I can't pretend that didn't happen (both the fart and me blowing up at him like that). I can't hide in this bathroom for the next four days until he's allowed to leave again.

I'm going to have to . . . ugh, *deal with it.*

I give myself a few seconds, eyes shut, trying to compose myself. I'm not losing my mind. I'm just freaked out because this is an extraordinary situation that we're in, and it's a lot of pressure. I'm *not* losing my mind. I just have to explain myself, even if the idea sends a shudder through me.

It's okay, Isla, you can do this. You're a total badass, and you've got this.

He knocks again, and I steel myself before wrenching the door back open.

"Look, I gave it a shot, Danny, but this isn't working out."

He looks at me like I've slapped him, turning ashen. He gasps, as though all the air has just been kicked right out of his lungs.

"What?" he asks me, breathless.

"I'm a morning person. I'm an early bird! I *like* starting my day with a workout. I like getting up early and taking fifteen minutes to meditate when the sun's coming up, and having a cup of tea or a smoothie out on my balcony before I start my day! Not rolling out of bed barely in time to pee before my first meeting of the day! And I *hate* cooking. I mean really, really, don't like it.

"And you know what else? It's a total slap in the face to feel like you're not making an effort and like you've given up already, but . . . I can't keep this up! I keep trying to—to be the perfect girlfriend for you, to make so much effort, but I *can't keep it up.* I can't do this forever. Sometimes I like it when my legs are all fuzzy and I don't have to spend a small fortune getting my nails done and eyebrows threaded. And you know what? Sometimes—yeah, sometimes I fart too! But this is who I am, Danny, and I'm sorry, but you're just going to have to deal with that. Okay?"

Danny stares at me with those big, dark eyes, and his lovely long eyelashes, mouth hanging open, before bursting into laughter so suddenly that I jump back.

"Uh . . . "

Catching his breath, he steps toward me, putting his hands on my arms, drawing me into him.

"Isla, honestly. 'This isn't working out.' I thought you were talking about *us* for a minute, not—not your workout schedule! Jesus Christ. You scared the *life* out of me for a second there."

All the pent-up anger I've been holding on to for the last few minutes (and, all right, all the tension that I've let build up over the last few days) suddenly rushes out of me, and I'm laughing, too, brushing his hands away when he strokes some wispy hairs back from my face, pulling me toward him for a kiss.

"Don't," I say, still giggling. "Danny, I'm all gross and sweaty."

"I don't mind," he murmurs, kissing all over my face and making me laugh again before his hands are around my waist and he draws me close, his lips on mine, and I can feel myself positively *melting* into him.

I'd never had that feeling when I kissed a guy, before Danny. There was always too much tongue or bad breath or that one guy who didn't so much as kiss as just suck on my upper lip. (Which, honestly, I'd tried to work past, because he was really hot and I'd met him through tennis and on paper we were a *great* match, but . . .)

Danny, though, takes my breath away.

I don't even care anymore that all his stupid noise while he cooked and his stupid podcast blasting through the Alexa speakers was grating on me, or that he said he can't watch a movie with me this evening because he has to do some more work after dinner, or even that he's seeing me so gross and sweaty, midworkout, when he's barely even seen me *without makeup* on, before this week.

I don't *care*, because he's kissing me, and the way his tongue drags over my lower lip and the way his body is pressed against mine feels so goddamn *wonderful*.

"You know, you ruined my workout," I mumble against his lips, when we finally part for air. My hands press against the bare skin of his back, warm and smooth. "You should definitely have to make that up to me."

Danny laughs. "Aren't I already cooking dinner for you?"

"Hmm . . ."

He scoops me up so suddenly that I squeal. He pulls me against him, hands on my butt, and hoists me up, wrapping my legs around his waist. He grins at me, one eyebrow quirking upward when he says, "You know, I can think of an alternative way you could burn some calories."

I laugh, trying to wriggle down. "Get off. If I'm not going to finish my HIIT class, I need to take a shower."

"Oh yeah?"

I know exactly what he's thinking and my arms tighten around his neck, even though he's already let me go and set me back on my feet. I stick my chin out. "Yeah."

Danny's nose nuzzles against mine, his breath ghosting over my mouth. "How about I join you?"

"You'd better," I tell him, already kissing him again as I walk backward, dragging him into the bathroom with me.

Maybe having my boyfriend around during lockdown isn't *so* bad after all.

Chapter Twenty-one

L et's just set the record straight right now:
I'm not a bitch.

I'm not, typically, an impulsive person. I like to think things through, understand where they're going and how I'll get there. *Plan* is maybe a little strong, but I like to at least have an *idea* of a plan. I like to consider *consequences*.

It's safer that way.

It doesn't mean you don't make mistakes; it just means you were prepared for them and aren't caught totally off guard if (or when) shit does hit the fan.

I also don't consider myself hotheaded. It's not like I don't get angry, I'm just pretty good at keeping a lid on my temper and managing the situation. I can be snappy, sure, but I don't just *lose it*.

I am also not prone to flights of spontaneity.

End of.

I didn't use to understand how people *couldn't* think things through, or just lived in the moment like that.

It used to drive me slightly nuts when I was first dating Zach, but it gradually became one of the things I loved most about him. The way he'd show up on my doorstep after work and announce he'd made us a picnic and come on, we were going to the park for the evening; when he booked us a weekend in Edinburgh for my birthday without telling me until we got to the airport, having packed a bag for me and picked me up from work. (He forgot to pack me any bras or mascara, but I forgave him pretty quickly for that.)

He's easygoing, happy-go-lucky, and always seems to believe things will just work themselves out.

It's not like I'm a pessimist or anything, but I always feel like I have to *work* to make something happen. Zach's the kind of guy who shows up at the shopping center at peak time instead of leaving early to beat the rush, yet just happens across a prime parking spot right near the doors. He actually won a grand on a scratch card last year.

It took me a little while, sure, but I came to see this as a good thing.

They always say opposites attract, and we did.

For the last four years, *we did*.

And then . . .

Oh, *then*.

I grit my teeth just thinking about it all, and feel my blood start to boil. It's been so hard *not* to be angry at Zach, at our relationship, at lockdown, at *everything* this week. And fuck, I cannot believe we're stuck here and I can't just put some distance between us and not have to see his face all day long.

We've done our best to tiptoe around each other since our fight yesterday morning. For the most part, he's stayed in the bedroom playing video games, and I've stayed in the living room working. Aside from that one brief moment of normality when we sorted out some clothes to lend Isla's boyfriend and he was goofing around, our interactions have been civil at best.

We tried to talk about it again last night, but it just turned into another screaming row. He slept on the sofa. I didn't try to be quiet when I got up for work this morning. He slammed the bedroom door when he shut himself in there.

Right now, however, we're both in the kitchen, and I hate that he can't *actually* leave, the way he said he should yesterday.

"Will you move, please?" I grind out.

Zach's standing in front of the fridge, with that forlorn look on his face again.

God, I hate that face. I wish he'd quit it already.

Zach isn't a very tall guy, but he's lean and lanky, so it gives the impression that he's taller than he is. I bought him that shirt: the red and charcoal flannel that's half-tucked into his skinny jeans. His blue eyes crinkle behind his thick-rimmed glasses, but he steps back from the fridge so I can open it up and get the milk out.

I might be mad at him, but I am *determined* not to be petty.

He can call me *bitch* all he likes, but he can't call me petty.

Not when I'm making him a cup of tea as I make myself one.

I am the least petty of ex-girlfriends. (Ex? Ish?)

Close enough, at this point, to be honest. I haven't dared ask to find out if we *are* broken up, and Zach seems to be avoiding bringing up our argument again, too, especially after our attempt to clear the air last night.

I want to ignore him. I really, really do. I want to act like he's not here and like this whole melancholy thing isn't bothering me and like that long, heavy sigh means nothing to me, but . . .

Well, you can't just erase the last four years that easily.

"What's the matter now?" I ask him.

"What about my dad and stepmum's party?" he asks me, turning to look at me with a pout. A single, deep line creases his forehead. My eyes slide from him to the embellished gold-on-cream invitation, with its cornflower blue floral border, that's been pinned to our fridge for months.

I feel a pang of sadness in my gut.

Their anniversary. A big party, with all their friends and family, at some cute rural hotel, to celebrate their ten years of wonderful marriage. I must've looked at that invitation a hundred times in the last few days, in the past few *months*, even, but I'm so used to seeing it there I barely notice it anymore.

This is the first time it truly hits me: it's not just Zach I'm breaking up with, it's his whole family too. His wonderful, sweet mother, who always tells me how lovely and slim I look (even though I've put on more than fourteen pounds since I first got together with Zach, and wasn't all that *slim* to begin with) and makes us such lovely home-cooked meals whenever we visit. His madcap dad with his shed full of tinkery inventions and his stepmum, who works for Mac Cosmetics and always lets me use her staff discount, and tells me how she wishes she had my bone structure or my curly hair. His younger sister, with her . . . well, apart from being the most mature twenty-two-year-old I've ever met, his younger sister's pretty ordinary, but she's *so easy* to get along with.

And then, of course, there's his older brother Matty and his husband Alex, who treated me like I was one of the family from day one, their instant friendly banter a welcome relief from the polite parental inquisitions. They're the nicest, sweetest people I know. Alex has even come to concerts with me and my dad a couple of times, like *he's* part of *our* family. And Matty is easily one of the funniest, friendliest guys I've ever met. (Something Zach has *always* been jealous of, a reaction which I've always found quite cute.)

It makes my chest feel tight, the idea of cutting them all out of my life. Of throwing Zach out of the apartment, and all of them along with him.

But his family isn't enough to make up for everything that's happened these last few days.

"What *about* the anniversary party?" I snap at him instead, scowling. "Do you really think I care about that right now? Zach, it's like— it's like you're not *listening* to me. God. Of all the things we . . . That party is the last thing on my mind."

"I'm just saying," he mumbles.

"Yeah? Yeah, well maybe there were a lot of things you should have been *just saying* for the last four years."

"Rena—"

"Save it," I bark at him, the nickname he's so fond of grating on me. I finish the tea, all but hurling the spoon toward the sink when I'm done, ignoring his wince at the noisy clatter of metal on metal, and storm back into my squished corner of the living room/dining room to go back to work. I seriously doubt I'll be able to focus on work anyway. The only thing I've been able to think about this week is Zach, Zach, Zach.

Not even a phone call earlier today from one of the women on my team laying into me for using last year's data in a report by mistake is enough to distract me.

(And it really should be, because she berates me for a solid thirty-eight minutes over my slipup, which made her look like an idiot in a meeting with senior managers where she had to present the report. I don't even have the energy to point out that she had two days to look at my work and let me know, and probably shouldn't have just winged it.)

Zach potters around quietly, doing some housework. He moves quickly, silently, efficiently, dusting and polishing, sweeping the floor. He seems to be making every effort not to disrupt me, which I know I should appreciate, but really, it just makes my blood boil.

I don't think I'm an irrational person. Far from it. But I *know* I'm being irrational for resenting how much effort he's putting in to not making this worse, and I can't do anything about it.

*

"It's because he doesn't get it," I moan down the phone to my friend Vicki, looking desperately to the heavens.

While Zach takes a shower, I've shut myself out on the balcony to talk to my best friend. We don't work together anymore, but that never stopped us being friends. And God, I've been *dying* to talk to her, not just swap messages over WhatsApp about it all.

"I kind of don't blame him," she tells me, somewhat reluctantly. What a traitor. "I mean, listen, sweetie, I *get it*, I do, but . . . You've met Zach. He's not exactly . . . " She searches for a word, and apparently doesn't come up with one inoffensive enough. Instead she says, "I mean, the boy could not be more laid back if he tried. He probably didn't see this coming in a million years."

I groan, exasperated, and lean over the balcony railing. The evening is cold and the air is thick and gray with drizzle. I'm mostly protected by the balcony above ours, but the rain that falls softly on my bare arms feels refreshing.

There's a couple walking their dog out on the main road, and I'm horribly jealous of them, for so many reasons. Not least because Zach is horrified at the idea that I want a cat, and that really should've been an indication of bigger problems from the start.

"It's infuriating," I try to explain, turning my back to them. "Either I'm a total bitch going off on one, or he's just moping around the apartment like a kicked puppy and being so fucking *nice* like I'll just change my mind and everything will magically be solved."

"I think it's sort of sweet, that he wants to try to work things out," Vicki tells me. "I mean, how many girls would kill for a guy that wants to work through problems like this, and tries to talk things through?"

"And calls them a bitch?"

"You can be a bit of a bitch, you know. You can be kind of a Karen, sometimes too."

"You're one to talk," I snap back at her, although honestly, I can't come up with a single example of Vicki losing her shit over something trivial.

"Oh, I'm sorry, would you like to file a complaint with my manager?"

I snort, despite myself, and she erupts in peals of laughter.

"All I'm saying is, maybe you should hear him out. Maybe this is all just cabin fever, you know? The lockdown talking. It's a weird, scary, stressful situation, so it's hardly surprising you guys had a fight over something."

My scowl returns. "This isn't lockdown talking, Vicks. This is way bigger than that."

"Okay."

"As for hearing him out—why should I? He hasn't heard me out. He just thinks I'm blowing things out of proportion, or that it's not worth getting so worked up over."

Vicki gives a sympathetic hum. I called her for some support, some solidarity, but also so she could talk some sense into me. She's good at calling me on my shit, so I knew that if Vicki thought I was overreacting and being ridiculous, there was a solid chance I *was* overreacting and being ridiculous—but so far, she hasn't. She's just tried to offer "perspective" in case it'll help me "approach the discussion from a new angle."

(Spoiler alert: it won't.)

She obviously knows that it's not doing any good, though, because she clears her throat and moves on quickly, her voice all upbeat.

"What if we just smuggled you out, off the balcony?" she suggests, and I can hear the grin in her voice. "Hire a crane. Or we could create a whole pulley system. I'll come over with my bicycle and we can just, like, lift you out of there or something. Oh! You could tie all your sheets together and climb down, like a makeshift Rapunzel. We'll call a taxi to be your getaway driver."

The crushing weight of the ruins of my relationship disappears for a moment, and I forget about everything while we come up with crazier and crazier ways to break me out of the apartment block, and I'm in fits of laughter that leave me wheezing for breath and teary eyed.

And for a second, everything feels like it'll be okay.

Chapter Twenty-two

Bored bored bored bored bored bored bored bored bored bored bored bored bored bored bored bored bored bor—

"What are you doing?" Nate asks, rudely interrupting my brain's incessant chant.

I look at him like it's not totally obvious. I am lying upside down on the sofa, my feet up on the wall, my head just brushing the ground, my fingers drumming on my stomach in time with the rhythm of my *bored bored bored bored bored* chant.

"I'm drying my nail polish," I tell him.

It's not a complete lie. I found a bottle of bright blue nail polish rattling round in my handbag so decided to paint my fingers and my toes. And then in an attempt to stop myself touching something and smudging them before they dried, I sat like this. Although that was, like, ten minutes ago, so they should be good now.

He squints at the blue fingernails I waggle at him and scrutinizes my position carefully.

"And does this . . . help?"

"It can't not help," I point out, and then swing my legs down and twist until I'm lying across the sofa, arms now flung above my head. Nate starts pottering around with his iPad and the TV, setting up for the Zoom "pub quiz" one of his friends has organized.

I wonder if I should've offered to leave him in peace for it. Apparently, it's a regular thing, because Nate's old gang from school all live so far apart, they do a virtual quiz night once a month, which is honestly about the cutest thing I've ever heard. Like, they all "block out their calendars" (genuine quote from Nate) and make sure they never miss it, and take it in turns to host, and have theme nights.

And it sounds awesome so *of course* I was like, "Oh my God, YES. Nate, this is amazing. I cannot tell you how badly I need to spend an evening, like, not watching something on the TV. That is all I have done all week. And I've done the two jigsaws you own, which says a lot, because I do not like doing jigsaws at all. I *need* this."

Now, as he sings quietly to himself as he sets up the Chromecast on the TV, I wonder if I'm intruding.

Well, okay, I *know* I'm intruding, but it's not like I can leave the building, is it? I guess I could've not invited myself along, though. Shut myself in the bedroom instead for an hour or two scrolling TikTok or whatever. I probably should've offered to do that, at least.

But, hey. Letting me join in is the least Nate can let me do, when I've cooked us dinner every night this week. Mostly to keep myself from getting too bored, but still.

"Get us some drinks, will you, Immy?"

I startle a little at him using my nickname, but Nate carries on like it's no big deal.

It's just a nickname. It's *my* nickname, it's what everyone else calls me. It *shouldn't* be a big deal.

So why does it feel like it's, I don't know, A Moment?

Oh God, no, I cannot be having A Moment all by myself. I won't allow it. I don't have *Moments*. They're for serious people with serious relationships. Like Nate. And Nate, very obviously, is not part of this Moment.

So, it *can't be a big deal*. I won't let it be.

"Oh my *God*," I sigh, languishing on the sofa. "Just call me Cinderella!"

Nate only laughs, though, and I roll off onto the floor then clamber to my feet. Almost as soon as I leave the room, I hear a conversation start; I guess Nate's not the only one joining the call a couple of minutes early.

I wonder what he's said about me to them. I assume he's said *something*, to explain why I'm joining their quiz night.

I wonder what kind of picture he's painted of me. I know Nate's a good guy and he wouldn't exactly be bitching about me behind my back, but I also know I haven't exactly been a model houseguest, like I bet Lucy is being somewhere upstairs. My stomach twists with something a little like guilt, even though that's stupid because I've got nothing to feel guilty about, and I tune out the conversation determinedly.

I root through his alcohol collection in one of the cupboards for a minute before deciding to mix us some cocktails, finding a big plastic jug so I can make a batch. I accidentally put three cartons of cranberry juice in the food shop instead of one, but now it's a perfect mixer to make a Woo Woo. Total crowd pleaser.

Besides, Nate's wines look *fancy*. Like, I don't mean compared to my usual *whatever's cheap at the liquor store round the corner*, I mean, they look *fancy*. Like he really considers his choices. He probably even knows how to pair them with different foods.

Maybe it's how he impresses girls when he brings them over for a date night and cooks them dinner.

Either way, I'm too scared to open any of them in case I accidentally use some special, crazy-expensive bottle he was saving for whatever, so Woo Woos it is. I even dig a lime out of the fridge and cut it up to add a wedge to each of our glasses. Super classy.

Nate is sat on the floor at the long, low, oak coffee table. I guess it's so the camera is at a better height where his iPad is propped up on the TV stand, a few feet in front of him. He's got paper and pens ready for us, lined up neatly on the table. And coasters, which I make sure to use to put our drinks on.

"There she iiiiiissss," crows someone from the TV, as I grab a cushion off the sofa to sit on next to Nate on the floor.

On the screen in front of us are four windows, each looking into a different room. There's a ginger guy sat on a bed, an Indian guy whose fake background is the *Love Island* confessional room (hilarious, I love him already), one dude with golden tan skin and shoulder-length sandy hair sat cross-legged on a sofa, notebook on his lap, and finally Peggy Mitchell.

Like, I'm not even kidding. The guy's got a blond wig that looks exactly like the beloved *EastEnders* landlady's hair, is wearing pink lipstick and a leopard-print coat, and his background is set as the Queen Vic from the show.

I must be gawping because the ginger guy laughs. "Nate, didn't you warn her about Peggy?"

Nate looks at me, looking a bit awkward and embarrassed, and mumbles, "Duncan missed our last quiz. And since it's his turn to host, he has to do a forfeit to make up for it. Don't ask."

"Get out of ma Zoom!" Peggy/Duncan says, in a scarily accurate impression that has all of us cracking up. Then, in what I assume is his normal northern accent, he says, "So you're the bird who's been driving Nate round the bend all week."

I absolutely hate it when guys say *bird* like that.

"Tweet, tweet, bitches."

Nate flushes, but his friends only laugh. The Indian guy wags a finger at the screen and says, "I like her," and the dude with long hair says, "I absolutely see what you mean, Nate."

Duncan introduces the other guys, starting to rattle off names (Sam, Kaz, and Wills, in the order they are around the screen) but Nate laughs and says, "Don't bother, mate. Immy's not too great with names."

He grins at me, though.

I shove him lightly. "Shut up and drink your Woo Woo, Nikolaj."

There's a little more chatter and banter before Peggy/Duncan claps his hands and announces, "All right, folks, put down those drinks and grab those pens. We're gonna kick things off today with Round One: Things That Went Viral This Week."

*

Admittedly, I do feel a little bit like an imposter.

Nate and his buddies are all pretty different characters, it's clear, but there's a way they all gel together that makes it obvious how strong their friendship is. They lay into each other, but it's never malicious, and they riff off each other like it's second nature. Which, I guess, given that Kaz mentions at one point they've been friends for over ten years, it sort of is.

There are all these references and inside jokes I don't get; I absolutely tank on Round Three: Where Are They Now, guessing what job people from their class at school have now, but I make some really wild guesses (Percy Pinstock? Oh, yeah, he's definitely a peacock trainer. Jess Smith? Please, you just *know* she's that lady Buckingham Palace hired to break in the Queen's shoes for her) that I feel like I'm part of it all, and everyone has a great laugh.

It's nice, though. It's low stakes and good (mostly clean) fun, and nobody—not even Nate—seems to mind that some total stranger is a part of their ritual pub quiz night.

Nate's more conservative with his cocktails than I am, but I don't tease him about it in front of his friends. He does have work tomorrow, I guess, and I did make them kind of strong.

Even so, by the time we're marking the final round, we're both giggly and a little sweaty and slurring our words.

The last round was on *Lord of the Rings* quotes. I don't win it, but I do come out with a really solid score. And, thanks to my stellar performance in Round One (thank you to all those hours I've spent scrolling social media this week) and in the music round, when Peggy/Duncan reads out our totals . . .

I've won.

I leap to my feet, narrowly avoiding upending the coffee table with our last drinks and almost elbowing Nate right in the face, to do a victory dance. I stand still and throw my arms out wide to belt a few lines of "The Winner Takes It All" by ABBA, and then, finally raise my glass to the camera.

"To absolutely whooping your sorry butts," I declare in my most serious voice.

Everyone drinks, but Sam says, "Nate, I'm sorry, man, but you can never invite her again. This is humiliating."

Peggy/Duncan is a few sheets to the wind and shouts, "Get out of ma Zoom!" again. Someone offscreen barks for him to shut up, which only makes him snort with laughter and shush himself loudly.

Everyone chats for a few more minutes before deciding to call it a night. I salute the boys and tell them it's been an honor, and they all tell me enthusiastic good-byes, tell me how great it was to meet me. I think they're probably just being nice, but I'm flattered nonetheless.

Nate gets up to turn off the TV and his iPad, and I wriggle across the floor until I can lean against the sofa. The movement makes my head spin. Or is it the room spinning? I think it's both. It's probably both.

"I like your friends."

"Yeah, they're not bad."

"Sorry if I spoiled your night, or anything."

"Because you won?"

"Oh, I'm definitely not sorry I won," I assure him, cracking a smile. It seems to take all my energy and focus to drag my cheek muscles up into a smile; the tiredness hits me like a train, right out of nowhere.

"Just, like, you know. Sorry if I took over your one night a month hanging out with your mates. I know I can be a lot. Especially when I drink. I get, you know. Excitable. Loud. Really chatty."

Nate doesn't disagree that I'm a lot, but he does say, "I don't think you need a drink for that, Immy. But you didn't take over. I had a good time, anyway. Did you?"

"Sure I did."

Nate clears up, finishing his drink and taking our glasses out to the kitchen. He cleans up the lime wedges I've left on the chopping board and puts his iPad in the charger, uses the bathroom, then collects his pillow and blanket from the airing cupboard for another night on the sofa. All of this takes him a while because he stumbles around a bit, drunker than he intended to be.

By the time he comes back, my limbs are heavy, and I'm almost asleep. Nowhere, I repeat, *nowhere*, has ever been so comfortable as this spot on the hardwood floor with my head lolling back toward the sofa I'm propped up against.

"Come on," Nate says. "You look ready for bed."

It's okay, I want to say, *I'll sleep here.* He can take the bed tonight if he wants.

"I can't feel my teeth," I tell him instead, running my tongue over them to check they're still there.

"Can you ever feel your teeth?" he asks, genuinely curious, moving his own mouth around like he's testing it out.

This is an excellent question.

"Come on," he says again, and bends down to hoist me to my feet. We're both unbalanced, but Nate less so than me. He hooks an arm around my waist to take me to the bedroom.

Here's the thing: when I drink, I get . . . *more*. I'm more loud, more talkative, more excitable, more hilarious, more *everything*. And I'm already a pretty outgoing person. And when I hit my wall, I get sleepy. Often, I take catnaps on a night out—either at predrinks, or on a crappy sofa by a bathroom in a club, or on a bench—and then I'm ready to go again. I have hit that wall right now.

But even so, I'm capable of walking the few feet from the living room to the bedroom by myself.

Not that I *tell* Nate that, of course. He smells nice, and I like the feel of his arm around me and his body next to mine. And it's nice to feel taken care of. Like when someone brushes your hair for you.

He's already turned the bedcovers down (although, I notice with deep despair, he has not left a little chocolate on the pillow for me) and he sits me down on the mattress. I flop backward, crawling clumsily under the covers, and Nate helps draw them up over me.

I snuggle down, and I was wrong: screw the floor by the sofa, nowhere has ever been so comfortable as *this*. I peer through the dark at Nate.

"Goodnight."

And he must be drunker than either of us realized, because he bends down to kiss my cheek. "Goodnight."

I'm asleep before he even leaves the room.

Chapter Twenty-three

*C*aptain's—er—Maid of Honor's log, day . . . What day is it? Day *seven. (God, is it only day seven? I swear it's been, like, four months already.) Anyway. The centerpieces are finally finished. I even bunked off work a little early to help out with them. Lucy cooked dinner tonight—veggie burgers she found in the back of my freezer, from the time I was dating the vegan, and spicy sweet potato wedges. Also, I am going to lose my mind if this goes on much longer.*

We're all starting to succumb to the cabin fever a little, by now. I'm finding it borderline impossible to work; I have to start out on the balcony, until lazybones Addison and night-owl Kim both wake up and I can evict them from my bedroom and work from there instead—although I'm continually interrupted throughout the day.

And as for them—well, there's only so many days in a row you can watch rom-coms on Netflix, according to Kim. They even got bored of *Come Dine With Me* after enough episodes.

I'd give *anything* to be sat around watching my thirtieth episode of *Come Dine With Me* instead of working, I think. But even Addison seems antsy; I've caught her checking work emails on her phone when she thought nobody was looking.

The grass is always greener, I guess.

With the last of the dishes from dinner washed and put away, I gather the few remaining bottles of prosecco from the stash I bought for last weekend, finding spaces for them in the fridge to chill them for later tonight. I keep one bottle back and pop it open to drink now.

Hell, we *deserve* this.

Two days hanging out together doing wedding stuff was fine, but seven? Seven is a *lot*.

I think even Kim may be starting to get sick of it by now.

Luckily, tonight's Bridal Bucket List item is the wedding playlist, which Kim needed to sort out anyway for the reception party in the evening. Mostly, I think, it'll involve a bunch of cheesy noughties pop songs—and what goes better with a #ThrowbackThursday playlist on Spotify, than a few glasses of prosecco?

Nothing, that's what.

It's a great idea.

For the first glass or two, at least. It's the greatest idea ever, for those first rounds of drinks. It's more party than pandemic. It's bright and brilliant and the kind of night you feel could and should go on forever.

Everything goes downhill so fast, none of us could ever have seen it coming.

We're on to the third and final bottle. Addison suggests that the Arctic Monkeys song I've just played should make the wedding playlist, which gets Kim talking about the dorky dance Jeremy and his three groomsmen are planning to a similar song.

She complains about it vehemently, but she still bounces up from the floor and drags Lucy to her feet, getting her to join in recreating the dance since they've both seen the guys practicing, giggling over the whole thing.

It *is* dorky. I can just imagine how seriously Jeremy is treating the whole thing, too, which somehow makes it even more hilarious to picture. Addison is hooting with laughter, joking that they'd better take classes if they don't want their first dance to be a total joke.

Everyone is laughing. Everything is great.

None of us notice Kim's attitude flip, it happens so fast.

At first I assume she's just in hysterics. Almost as one, we all suddenly realize she isn't laughing anymore, but *crying*. She stops dancing abruptly and collapses in a flood of tears, lamenting the wedding playlist and the DJ and then saying, "But what if the band cancels on us? Because of all this?"

"You can get another band," Lucy says, crouching next to her and rubbing her back.

"What about the DJ?"

"We're all the DJs you need," Addison declares. This is followed by what I can only describe as her *throwing shapes*. It's awful. It's also hilarious.

Lucy cuts her a look—and me a look, when I snort with laughter at Addison's moves—but she tells Kim, "Exactly! But I'm sure the DJ won't cancel."

The DJ is the least of their worries, I think. The DJ, the caterers, the venue . . . The dress shop could close, if all this carries on, and then how will Kim get to her fittings? And that assumes she even *needs* a dress—if this gets so bad they start to cancel public gatherings . . .

And I blurt, "That's even if it all still goes ahead at all."

Kim wails. Loudly, heart wrenchingly.

I know I shouldn't have said it as soon as the words are out of my mouth, but it's too late by then; the prosecco has loosened my tongue. Lucy stares at me with her eyes wide, and Addison clutches both hands to her hair, which is damp and tied back in two French braids, her face flushed from the drink, and utterly mortified.

Uh-oh.

Time to be Maid of Honor Extraordinaire, not just Kim's friend.

"Well, I'm just saying," I add hastily, trying to backpedal, my tongue heavy and tripping over the words. "With everything going on, I wouldn't be surprised if the whole thing got postponed. Nothing to do with Jeremy, obviously. You guys have seen the news, everything they're saying about how this might go. It could be next *year* before you get to walk down the aisle."

Kim stares at me, stricken, the tears drying on her pale face. "Next year?" she rasps, hands clasped to her throat.

Behind her, Addison makes slashing gestures across her throat, her eyes bugging at me. It's a very clear message and I can just imagine her saying, *Quit while you're ahead, Livvy. Just. Stop. Talking.*

But Kim looks so distraught that I have to fix it, and explain that I didn't mean anything bad by it, and it's nothing *personal*, obviously, it's just that if this week is anything to go by, it's all totally out of our control and might even get *worse* for a while before it gets better, and even though Lucy and Addison look like they want to rugby-tackle me to the ground and stuff a pillow over my face, I can't seem to stop talking.

"Well, yeah, you know," I say. "I guess it wouldn't be the *end* of the world. They're already talking on the news about canceling flights, sports . . . Hey, at least Jeremy will probably get all the money back for the bachelor party in Budapest! That's something, right? Although we probably will need to redo all the gift bags." I look around the carefully packed boxes from the weekend, containing all the immaculate little chiffon bags of dried rose petals and chocolates, the little packets of Love Hearts sweets, each one tied together with a lavender-colored silk ribbon. We'd gotten the sweets and chocolate on sale from a manufacturer Lucy knows, and the best before dates on them will be up by Christmas. If the wedding gets pushed to next year, we'll have to replace them.

I don't mind the idea of eating all the sweets by myself so much, to be fair. That wouldn't be the worst part of this whole thing.

Kim is still looking at me, completely aghast, so I explain all of that to her too. (Minus the part where I plan to eat all the sweets.) Addison groans, burying her face in her hands and pacing to the other end of the room before turning, her arms crossed, chewing on her lip as she watches me dig myself into a deeper and deeper hole. By contrast, Lucy is still and silent, almost like if she doesn't draw attention to herself, she won't get caught up in any of it.

But I don't see what the problem is, not really.

I'm just being honest. I'm just being practical.

It's my duty, as maid of honor. Isn't it? To make sure Kim keeps her head screwed on right. To plan for all eventualities. Although, honestly, I was sort of assuming those potential catastrophes would be, like, the wedding car blowing a tire, not a highly contagious virus driving everyone to stay at home.

That *definitely* hadn't made it onto any of the Pinterest planning boards, shockingly enough.

"Oh, sure!" Kim cries suddenly, shooting to her feet and almost knocking Lucy over. She storms toward the nearest box of wedding favors, snatching a handful out and tearing at them. The chiffon packets were dirt cheap, and they tear easily. Love Heart sweets and petals and tiny purple foil-wrapped chocolates spill onto the floor at her feet. She throws the scraps in her hand down after them, grabbing more out of the box.

Lucy lets out a quiet squeak of protest; the noise I make is distinctly more pissed off, but I don't try to stop her.

If she wants to destroy all the wedding favors, bloody well let her. If she wants to throw a tantrum and throw away all our hard work, *fine*. See if I care. I've put up with her bridezilla shit for months, and this, it appears, is my limit.

Because honestly, how dare she? What goddamn right does she have to get so upset over something *none of us* can control, and ruin what's been such a fun night? Like her and her wedding is the only thing that's suffering? What about me, and my lovely tidy apartment, and my calm, organized life, completely upheaved by having to host my best friend and two relative strangers for over a *week*? You don't see *me* ripping things up and crying and making a scene.

But sure. Sure. Let's all indulge Kim. Let's all coddle Kim. Let's all let Kim have her fucking moment.

If she notices my silent seething, she decides to ignore it.

(Who am I kidding? Of course she doesn't notice. She's so wholly self-absorbed right now, there's not a chance in hell of her noticing how *I'm* feeling.)

"Sure!" Kim barrels on. The tears are flowing again now. "Let's just eat all the wedding favors! Hmm? Why not? The wedding's obviously ruined now anyway! If it even ever goes ahead! All that planning, all the work, all the *waiting*, and now—now we were—it was so close, it was . . ." She hiccoughs, gasping for breath. "His grandparents won't be able to fly over from Spain! The honeymoon! The Amalfi Coast! *Everything* is going to be ruined! Who cares about stupid fucking little wedding favors?"

More chocolates hit the ground, clattering noisily. Kim abandons the wedding favors, marching toward the pile of carefully cut and arranged fake flowers and twigs we've all just been working on for the centerpieces, the ones we trimmed to precise sizes and paired up so carefully, tying with lavender ribbons, per Kim's Pinterest DIY wedding board. She kicks the pile and Lucy gasps, hands flying to cover her mouth, looking unsure whether she should let Kim get this out of her system or stop her.

"Kim, sweetie," Addison tries gently, sternly, stepping forward.

"Who needs centerpieces!" she screams. "When at this rate, there won't even be a wedding to need them!"

She deliberately stomps over the pile, snatching up the prosecco bottle and draining the last little bit we'd left in there, tipping it right into her mouth. Kim is so livid that her face is blotchy and red in spite of her fake tan. She looks like Addison, after the face mask disaster on Monday night.

Instead of defusing the situation like I have a thousand times before, I find myself yelling right back at her.

I am so, so done with her shit.

"Do you mind *not* trashing my apartment?"

"Do you mind *not* ruining my wedding?" she shoots back.

"Why do you always have to be such a bitch? Not everything's about you!"

"Just because *you* can't hang on to a relationship for more than a month, doesn't mean you have to try to spoil things for me! You've always been jealous of me and Jere, just admit it! I don't know *why* I ever thought I could—"

"Oh, what, so now I'm sabotaging your wedding? Excuse *me*, but some of us are pretty happy being single and not letting our entire lives revolve around somebody else."

"He's my *soul mate*. You're just bitter because you know even if you *did* find someone who could put up with you for longer than a couple of weeks, it wouldn't matter, because you *still* haven't come out to your parents!"

"*Knew iiiiiit*," Addison sings quietly from the back of the room.

"Oh my God," Lucy gasps, grimacing as she looks between us.

It knocks the wind straight out of my lungs. My glare disappears and I stop grinding my teeth to gawp at her, my jaw somewhere on the floor.

She did *not*.

Except . . . she *did*.

It's not like I care if Addison finds out I'm gay; I'm pretty sure Lucy already knows. It's not like it's a *huge* secret; just when it comes to my family.

I don't care that she said it in front of the girls.

I care that she said it *at all*.

It's a low fucking blow, and—and who does she think she's kidding, anyway, talking about *soul mates*? She only dated *one* guy before Jeremy, and that was when we were fifteen! This whole stupid argument is *nothing* to do with me or my failed relationships or me not coming out yet to my family—and the fact that she even *went* there has my blood boiling.

She's acting like such a brat, but that . . . Oh, that was downright malicious.

I can hear a ringing in my ears, and my hands ball into fists. I can taste bile in the back of my throat and choke it back down, along with a million and one things I'd like to scream at her right now.

She thinks I'm the one being spiteful?

She hasn't even *seen* spiteful.

"You know what?" I snap at her. "I don't know why I've put up with any of this. We're supposed to be best friends, but my best friend turned into some narcissistic bitch the second she got engaged. The rest of the world stopped existing, if it wasn't to do with your fucking wedding. So you know what? I hope the wedding *does* get canceled."

"You'd *love* that, wouldn't you? You've wanted this to fail since the beginning! Do you think I don't hear you, always gossiping to my parents, or Jeremy, when you think I can't hear? Saying I'm a bridezilla?"

"Uh, hello? Have you taken a look in the fucking mirror lately, *Bridezilla?*"

That's when she hurls the prosecco bottle at the wall, screaming wordlessly, and it shatters into a thousand pieces.

Friday

Chapter Twenty-four

*M*aid of Honor's log, day eight. *The lounge is littered with the remains of broken wedding favors. The bride is clutching a mascara-streaked pillow, face dismal even when she's fast asleep. Addison is snoring from the bedroom—I blame that for being the reason I'm awake so early. Recycling bin in the kitchen is overflowing with prosecco bottles. Stepped on some of the broken glass last night and sort of hoping it does turn out bad enough that I need to go and get stitches just so I can leave this godforsaken apartment and—*

I shake myself.

Definitely, definitely losing it.

I lift up my foot, taking a peek, just to reassure myself. It wasn't even a big cut, and it's not even bled through the plaster I put on last night. No stitches required.

Bitterly, I think that Mother Hen Lucy probably would've clucked that she was also a trained first aider and able to do that for me to save me a hospital visit, but I quickly remind myself that's not fair either. She was *very* sweet last night, the first one to hop up and go looking under my kitchen sink for a dustpan and brush to clean it all up, and then gently advising me to clean the cut on my foot with an antiseptic wipe and some cream before I put a plaster on.

I definitely shouldn't be getting annoyed at Lucy right now.

Besides me, she might be the only rational person in this damn apartment. (I'm not sure *rational* is a word I'd use to describe Addison at any point in time, to be honest.)

God, I *wish* I'd never agreed to all this.

I look now at the clutter of empty buy-one-get-one-half-price prosecco bottles in my recycling bin and sigh. My head is throbbing just looking at them, although I'm sure the booze isn't the real reason for my headache this morning.

I wince, remembering the sound of the bottle smashing against the wall, Kim wailing.

No, sod her. I hope she wakes up feeling even worse than me. She bloody well deserves to. None of this was my fault, I was just being honest, and she was completely out of line.

I don't have the energy to be angry again. I don't have the time to mull over it too much longer, either, not when I have to start work soon. And, honestly, I'd much rather throw myself into trying to concentrate on work than dwell on last night's argument.

It's not like Kim and I have never argued before, but it's never gotten so personal, or so nasty. And neither of us will even really get the space to sit with it, when we're still stuck inside for a couple more days.

Not being able to run away from the fight is probably a good thing, but it doesn't feel like it right now. It just feels like it enforces an expectation that we have to forgive and forget, and move on, and have everything be just fine again.

I want us to talk things out and swap apologies and move on, of course I do, but I don't want it to happen just for the sake of keeping the peace, rather than because we *want* to sort this out, because we care about our friendship. But, I should've known it was only a matter of time before Kim's bridezilla attitude turned on me. I'd just figured it would be on the bachelorette party, and that she'd be mad over someone not showing up and that would somehow be my fault, or because I didn't book her a stripper. (Even though she's maintained every damn time it comes up that she *does not want a stripper at the bachelorette party*, "No matter what Addison says.")

While I had a feeling it would happen at some point, I just didn't think it would go down like *this*.

What a complete shitshow.

Maybe . . . maybe if I ignore it for long enough, just go about my day, I can put off having to deal with it for just a little while.

Quietly, I fix myself some cereal, not daring to use the toaster in case the *pop* of it wakes any of the others.

I can't believe I ever thought hosting this cute little weekend for the bridal party was a good idea. Just two days! No big deal! They'd be gone soon enough. I can't believe I ever thought it was going *well*, that I was having *fun* with it.

Oh God, I *wish* they were gone.

Chomping down on a spoonful of cornflakes, I scowl out of the window, and then turn when I hear someone walking into the kitchen behind me. It's Addison, in her slouchy pajama shirt and teeny-tiny pink shorts, hair piled up in a lopsided bun on top of her head. She yawns loudly, her neck popping as she rolls it.

I really *hate* when she does that.

It was a weird party trick the first time she did it, on Saturday morning. She's done it a dozen or more times since then, though, and the novelty quickly wore off.

I grimace. But instead of, *Can you maybe not do that?*, I figure it's probably best I don't incite another argument and say, "Morning. Didn't hear you get up."

"Oh, sure," she says, too loudly, in her thick southern-American drawl, "I'm an early bird after I've had a few drinks! It's, like, the main reason I can go out drinking on a work night, ha ha!"

She wasn't an early bird on the weekend, or after the signature wedding cocktails, I want to say. She's slept in late consistently all week. But I don't have the energy to argue with her about it; and besides, it's probably just another one of her try-hard, weird jokes.

I offer up a weak smile, trying not to freak out as I watch her rummage around my kitchen to find the bagels, which she promptly puts in the toaster. Could she make any more noise? She'll wake the whole damn building up at this rate.

She starts to make coffee, and after setting a mug out for herself, she gestures at me with another. "You want one?"

"Yeah, go on then. Please," I add, as an afterthought.

Coffee made, I take the mug off her when she hands it over. Her bright purple manicure is chipped, her fingers brushing against mine, and once she's passed over my drink she runs her hand through her hair, effortlessly pulling out the hair tie and shaking out her long blond waves. I have to admire how soft and smooth her hair looks right now.

As annoying as she is, I suddenly find myself picturing what it would be like to run my hands through her hair, hold her close, how soft her lips would be.

She pops her neck again, effectively yanking me out of the daydream and back to this reality, where I definitely don't plan to act on whatever *this* is, because even if she's attractive, she's *absolutely* not my type. She's just so . . . *everything*. So *much*.

Too much for me, anyway.

She stands munching on her cream cheese–smothered bagel while I sip my coffee, both of us leaning against the kitchen counter in our pajamas.

"I know all this wedding stuff has been stressing her out, but I *really* didn't expect her to lose it like that last night," Addison mumbles, this time quiet enough that there's no chance of her voice carrying out to the bedroom, where Kim's still fast asleep (we hope). She catches my eye, her face twisting in sympathy. "I mean, it's not like you were being *that* unreasonable. She *has* been a bridezilla. And it *might* all get canceled. Even Jere said so."

"Wait, he did?"

"Sure he did. When they went to get the groceries from him on Wednesday."

Addison shrugs like this is no big thing.

Jeremy has been our knight in shining disposable face mask and latex gloves this week, doing supermarket runs for us and bringing us several bags of food—once on Sunday afternoon, when he also brought clothes for Kim and Lucy, and again on Wednesday.

Our savior—or so I'd thought. I'm willing to bet that whatever he said to Kim contributed to last night's meltdown.

"Nobody told *me* he said anything about calling off the wedding," I say now, barely daring to whisper it out loud.

"Oh, I mean, *calling it off* is a little strong. She was a little weird when she and Lucy got back, so when she was in the bathroom I made Lucy tell me what happened. Apparently, he just said maybe with all of this going on, they might have to end up postponing it. Which is exactly what you said last night. Lucy said not to mention it to you, or let Kim know she'd said anything. She said she didn't want to bring the mood down."

"Kim managed that all by herself," I mutter.

Addison leans toward me, looking serious for once. The usual quick smile and gleam in her blue eyes has vanished, her face earnest, and she reaches over to squeeze my arm. The contact sends an electric shock through me. "For the record, I think it's totally fair, what you were saying. You were just being realistic. She was *way* outta line."

"Would've been nice to have a little of that support last night," I snap, jerking my arm back, forgetting to keep my voice down this time. I check myself, whispering, "Instead of just cuddling her and telling her you were sure it wouldn't come to that."

"What did you want me to do, tell her you were right and that the whole thing *would* get canceled and yes, actually, she has been a complete bitch for the last few months? She hurled a bottle at the wall, for Christ's sake, Livvy."

"It's just Liv," I say, scowling. It's a reflex now, after an entire week.

Addison seems faintly amused by my insistence over her *not* using that name for me, but tosses her hair and carries on, "If the two or three of us had ganged up on her she'd have probably thrown herself off the damn balcony. And you know as well as I do, if you're not with Kim on something, you're against her. There's no being Switzerland with her. *Sor-reee* for trying to make things a little better and defuse the tension."

I huff, but know she's got a point.

After all, isn't that exactly what I've been doing with Kim for the last year? Except this time, Addison was me, and I was the Evil Bringer of Wedding Tragedies she had to apologize to while Kim lost her shit.

"Plus," Addison goes on, looking downright angry now, "she had *no right* to say any of that stuff about you."

My cheeks flush. I sort of assumed (hoped) she wasn't going to bring it up. "Oh. Well, I mean . . . "

"Talk about a low blow," she says, and then cracks half a smile and winks at me to say, "Like, bringing your commitment issues into it? Wow."

Some of the pressure in my chest seems to ease, and I find myself smiling back.

"Seriously, though," she says, touching my arm again, "if you—"

Oh God, she's going to say, "If you want to talk about it," and I really do not. It's too early in the morning for a serious heart-to-heart with a cute girl.

"You're right," I say instead, interrupting her, "she really lost it last night. If it does all get canceled, it might be a blessing in disguise. I don't know how much more of this I can take. You know, part of me is sorry I ever got involved in this whole damn thing in the first place."

And then there's a gasp, and both our heads snap to the doorway, Addison jumping away from me, and Kim stands there, her hair a tangled, greasy mess and her face still streaked with yesterday's mascara. My heart plummets to somewhere in the pit of my stomach and Addison whispers, "Shit," under her breath.

Kim's face contorts and I think she's going to start bawling again, but instead, her eyes flash and she spits out words like poison.

"If *that's* what you think, Olivia, maybe I made a mistake in making you my maid of honor. Maybe I made a mistake in making you my *best friend.*"

Chapter Twenty-five

It's drizzling outside. Rain pitter-patters against the balcony and the double glass doors, and pale-gray clouds linger across the sky; they seem to muffle the noise of traffic and people, like cotton wool.

Nate is nursing a hangover, the poor lamb. I had to make him some bacon and eggs this morning to help get him back on his feet. He looked at me with narrow, bloodshot eyes and asked how I could be so perky after drinking even more than he did, and how much schnapps *did* I put in those drinks, exactly—no, you know what, don't tell him.

Poor lamb.

Meanwhile, I've got only the barest of headaches, and I am so deeply, horribly bored, that I have spent my day trying to catch up on a little work. I persuaded Nate to let me have free reign over his iPad this morning and have been using it to catch up on some emails, even joining a staff meeting where the headmistress talked us through a detailed plan for preparations for moving to remote lessons.

I hope this all blows over. I really, really do.

Especially because I don't trust myself to work from home.

I'll be leading classes over Zoom wearing a blouse and my pajama trousers. I'll be sending emails from bed. At least I won't need to struggle through a commute if I'm hungover, I guess. (Not that there's going to be anywhere to go, but when has that ever stopped me?)

Nate has been incredibly disciplined with his work this whole week. I've been woken up by him sneaking into the bedroom for clean clothes in the morning after he's taken a shower; he's been nice enough to make me a cup of coffee in the mornings when he makes himself one for breakfast. Usually, by the time I've got bored of scrolling social media and am hungry enough for breakfast, he's already thinking about lunch.

I have no idea how he does it.

I know I will never be able to do that when—*if*—it's my turn to work from home.

Right now, I'm starting to run out of the motivation that had me doing some work. It might be time to call it a day and abandon my lesson plan. Even Nate has clocked off early because it's Friday, his work things packed neatly into a backpack he leaves under the coat hooks in the hallway.

He's sat at the other end of the sofa, and he's staring at me.

I can *feel* his eyes boring into me; I'm just not sure if it's a "let's go to bed" look or a more scathing one. Judging by the cautious approach of "let's pretend we didn't sleep together and we're just friends" that he's taken this week, I can't imagine it's the former.

Neither of us has mentioned him kissing my cheek goodnight. I don't know if he even remembers it. I do, but I obviously also don't think anything of it. It was just a peck on the cheek. It was no big deal.

It was *nice*, though.

Still, it was nothing, and he was drunk anyway, and I'm pretty sure that's not what's on his mind right now anyway.

"You're staring at me," I say to Nate, not even looking up.

I glance up just as he turns his attention back to his phone, but his cheeks flush a faint shade of pink. He glances back, eyes lingering on the iPad, my lesson plan open on the screen.

"Sorry. It's just . . . you really don't strike me as the teacher-y type, you know?"

I know, because it's what Lucy tells me on a frequent basis, and it's nothing I haven't heard before from my family. My little brothers still think I'm scamming everybody, and that my real job is something bonkers and scandalous that I could never tell my family about.

But because he's blushing, and he's way too easy to tease, I cock my head and frown curiously at him and say, "No? What do you mean, Nate-Nathan-Nate?"

Nate almost seems to steel himself for a minute, stalling by reaching for his mug of tea, taking a long, long sip. He sets it back down and then says to me, not quite able to look at me, "I don't know, you just seem a little . . . *chaotic*, I guess."

Oh.

Oh wow.

WOW.

Free-spirited, absolutely. Fun and fancy-free, you know it. A zest for life, 100 percent. Immature, even, I've heard that plenty.

But straight-up *chaotic*?

Ouch.

"You know," he goes on, not noticing that I'm sat here like a slack-jawed idiot, "just your whole attitude. The whole persona you've got going, the party girl thing, like you don't care about anything. It's just . . . not what you'd expect from someone who teaches little kids, I guess."

He's right, my whole persona is major party girl vibes. Wine Aunt, like that one guy told me on a date. But the way Nate says it . . .

It's not with that sort of long-suffering "we love you anyway" sigh I'm used to getting from my parents, or my housemates, or Lucy and her family. It's not reverent and jealous, like a few of my friends who feel like they settled down too quickly.

It's not particularly *judgemental* either. If anything, it's very matter of fact, the way Nate says it.

And it doesn't sound like such a good thing.

I'm thrown back to Lucy answering the phone last Sunday and immediately assuming I was in trouble and needed to borrow money. It's a funny, sweet little in-joke.

But it's also totally, almost painfully true.

And I get the feeling if I were to joke about it out loud—not just to Nate, but to—well, anyone—it would sound kind of sad.

Well, what does he know?

Who does he think he's calling *chaotic?*

Anybody would seem chaotic to him. With his meticulously structured day and his carefully ironed T-shirts and his hair-free shower drain and crumb-free butter and yeah, no shit, Nate, of course I seem a little wild, compared to you. We can't all be a stick in the mud. He's not even a stick in the mud, I think, he's—he's Weetabix. He's plain, nasty, Weetabix, and I am porridge with fresh fruit and syrup and all the trimmings, and he's just *jealous.*

I'm jealous.

I chew on my response for a little too long; Nate cringes, his shoulders hunching and he twists toward me, cradling his tea in his hands.

"I just meant—"

"I know what you meant," I say, my voice sounding unusually cold and curt. I would *love* to stand up, toss my hair, tell him where he can stick his stupid opinions and what a fantastic fucking human being I am, that what he thinks of as *chaos* is just pure enthusiasm and I'm *so sorry* his life is so mundane, and storm on out of here with my head held high, ready to tell my friends about what a prick Honeypot Guy is.

Except, I can't.

(And he's not *that* much of a prick.)

Nate begins to stammer out an apology, and I think of all the brilliant stories I have that could prove him wrong. The all-night bender the night before the school nativity last Christmas, and showing up to school in the same outfit, wrapped in tinsel and with glitter on my face, and everyone thinking I was just in a particularly festive mood. The massive party I threw for my friend Jaz when she officially qualified as a doctor, which she claimed made all the years of studying and training worth it. The Beanie Baby I tracked down for my mum for her sixtieth birthday, because she loves collectables like that, and I had to go all the way to Edinburgh to collect it, and it cost me one hundred pounds plus a signed McFly CD, and my tire blew out halfway home and I didn't have roadside assistance so got my dad to come and pick me up and help fix it, in the middle of the night.

My life is a myriad of adventures.

It's goddamn *delightful*.

My bank balance, not so much. The constant leak in the kitchen sink and the permanent weird musty smell lingering in our lounge, not so much. But what do those things matter?

But *anyway*, I tell myself, I don't need to prove myself to Nate. Nate-Nathan-Nate, the one-night stand I'd talked to for a week or so before coming here, who doesn't even have a single chocolate bar in his kitchen cupboards, he's so boring.

"It's fine," I tell him, to shut him up.

Nate falls quiet quickly, but is clearly uncomfortable. And I can't say I blame him. I'm scowling and clenching my jaw so hard I can practically see the storm clouds clustering around me.

I give my teeth one last grind and pry my jaw apart, doing my best to smile at him instead.

"Do you want to watch *Tiger King*?"

Chapter Twenty-six

My final meeting of the day is a drag, and one that is too easy to tune out when I'm not in the room with everybody. Distracted, I do the only rational thing I can think of to try to resolve this whole situation.

I make a list.

There are a lot of reasons it's not going to work out between me and Zach. So many reasons.

Here are a few of them:

1) He's easygoing to the point of simply *not giving a damn* about things, which honestly, at this point, is just infuriating. I don't want someone agreeing to get married to me because "whatever, I don't care," just to appease me. I want someone who *wants* to marry me. Is that really so much, so *impossible*, to ask? And is it really so absurd of me to be bothered by how *not* bothered he is about it, how much he *doesn't* have an opinion past: "Well, it's just a lot of money, isn't it? Look at what some of our friends have spent. But, like, yeah, I'm sure they always have a nice day and everything."

2) And on that note—it's *impossible* to have an argument with him sometimes. Which is nice, sure, I guess, because the most I get is a snarky retort. But isn't that part of what got us into

this mess? Because we can't *talk* about the important things? Sure, I get that whose turn it is to take the bins out might not be life or death, but I have a thousand and one examples of things like that, and Zach's usual eye roll and the fact he gives in if I'm belligerent enough (or, I get sick of bickering and I'm the one who gives in) means the disagreement ends there, but it's never really *solved*.

3) We fight. A lot. It's never a big fight, and we've always dis-agreed on stuff, but I'm pretty sure we snipe at each other way more now than we used to. Is that normal? Is that what I should want from a relationship? Is that what he wants?

4) He's *perpetually* annoyed by me being a vegetarian, and my occasional foray into veganism. He'll joke that am I allowed to wear that woolly sweater, don't I know how much I'm missing out on at his family's barbeques, am I *really* going to be so pedantic about using a different pan to fry vegetables than the one he just cooked some meat in? I think it started off as some weird little in-joke that was never serious, and I always know he's *not really* serious and isn't doing it to upset me, but I don't know where it came from or *why* it's such a thing for him. I know I make plenty of comments back at him about all the sweet little piggies he's so callously murdering just for a bacon sandwich when he's hun-gover, after all. But still, it pisses me off.

5) He always mixes up the names of the characters in *Game of Thrones*. Like, it's not that hard. It's not like Daenerys Stormborn of the House Targaryen, Queen of the Andals and the First Men, Khaleesi of the Great Grass Sea, Breaker of Chains, doesn't have enough titles. Surely he could remember *one of them*. And not still be saying, "Oh, look, isn't that the girl with

the eyebrows?" whenever she pops up on TV. It's *not that hard*. (I don't care if the show's over now, it's infuriating. I know he could do it if he wanted to.)

6) He's shorter than me when I wear my good heels.

7) He always says I iron his shirts wrong, when it's my turn to iron the laundry. (And yet, he still lets me do them, rather than just telling me, "Don't bother, I'll do them myself later," which he should if it's such a problem. And I *still* don't understand what I'm doing that's so wrong, even after two and a half years of living together.)

8) He organizes his books alphabetically by title, instead of by genre or by author, and I cannot deal with it. It hurts something deep inside my soul.

9) He said he hasn't even thought about when he wants kids, or even *if* he wants them, which brings me back around to my first point of him being easygoing to a fault. I mean, was he seriously thinking that if we had kids, I wouldn't want to talk about that with him first? And was he *really* going to just not make a decision on that for himself, and go along with whatever I wanted? Do I even want kids with someone who *doesn't care* that much?

I don't mean for the list to turn into *A Series of Unfortunate Events: Zach and Serena Edition*, but that's how it turns out.

I thought it would help, but I don't feel any better for it.

I still feel just as confused, just as crappy, just as resentful and heartbroken as I did when he ordered that Hawaiian pizza on Tuesday night. I sigh and close the cover on my iPad, and try to pay attention to the rest of my meeting before I can finally log off for the week. Maybe, I think, maybe I just need a fresh perspective like Vicki was trying to tell me last night, and she *is* always right about stuff.

Yes, that's it. I'll take a shower, try to clear my head, and then I'll try to make a *different* list—one of all the reasons it should and can work out between us, and why I love him so much.

*

"What the hell is this?"

I look up to see Zach standing in the doorway of the bedroom, my iPad clutched in his hand and his knuckles white, his jaw clenched. His eyebrows are drawn tight and his eyes look dark, furious.

I've seen Zach annoyed plenty of times, but in the four years I've known him, I have never known him to be anything more than angry. He's been angry when he argued with me this week; his cheeks got flushed, turning blotchy, his eyes watered because if there's one thing he really hates, it's a *proper* fight.

But this is different.

Now, his face is ashen, paler even than his knuckles. I can hear his breath rattling, which is when I realize I'm holding my own.

I've seen Zach annoyed plenty of times. I've seen him angry, on occasion. But I have *never* seen him this furious.

It's so disconcerting, I don't even have it in me to snap at him for barging in when I was getting dressed after a shower. I ignore him long enough to pull on some leggings and a clean T-shirt, and swallow the lump in my throat before I face him again.

I have the most horrible, sinking feeling in the pit of my stomach, seeing him holding my iPad.

"What are you doing with that?" I ask him.

It's mine, I want to say, even though that never mattered before.

"Your dad FaceTimed."

"You didn't *tell him*, did you?" I demand, because I really can't face having to tell my parents about all of this when Zach can barely accept it himself—when I'm not even entirely sure what there is to tell. (But my dad was *so slow* to get on board with me dating Zach at first, because he thought we were so different and didn't get Zach's sense of humor at all, so I get the feeling I'll have to deal with an "I told you so" once he does find out about whatever this is.)

"Course I didn't," Zach bites back, visibly offended. "But you were in the shower, so I answered to chat to him and say we're doing fine and we didn't need him to bring us more shopping because we sorted ourselves out with that already."

I breathe a small sigh of relief, but then Zach says—

"And then—then I saw this. You made a fucking list? Are you serious? Who do you think you are, Ross in that one episode of *Friends*? If you're going to make a list, maybe you shouldn't leave it open on your iPad."

"Maybe you shouldn't be snooping, *Rachel*," I retort, but it's weak, and my heart isn't in it. My heart is hammering so hard in my chest I think it might make me physically sick, and all I can think is how right he is. It's not his fault I left the Notes app open, with that list, that stupid goddamn list, and that I left my iPad just out on the dining table and it's not even got a passcode on it, and . . .

I would hate to read a list like that too.

It's not even softened by a *good* list. It's just straight-up *bad*.

"If me making jokes about you being a vegetarian pisses you off so much, why didn't you just *tell me*, instead of going along with it? I thought it was like . . . our thing. Joking about each other's food."

"Why would that *ever* be a thing?"

"You don't remember our second date?" Zach says, the ire in his face dimming only slightly, giving way to nostalgia. "You ordered that vegan, gluten-free white truffle risotto and I had that massive double-stacked burger with bacon and onion rings and, like, three types of cheese, and they put your risotto down and it just smelled *so bad* I swear you literally turned green. And you kept saying, 'No, no, it's fine! It's really yummy!' and forced it down and I could see you trying not to puke it back up and you were eyeing my burger like you'd much preferred to have ordered that and—"

"Wait. *That's* why you always crack jokes about how jealous you bet I am of your food?"

"How can you *not* know this?"

"Because . . . !"

Because it's just *our thing*, like he said, and it's gone on for so long now, it's just what we do.

I don't think I ever even connected it to that date. I'd pretty much forgotten all about that, actually—and I'm surprised Zach remembers it so clearly.

He sighs, and then lifts the iPad again, his whole demeanor shifting in an instant.

All right, this is definitely worse than the fury. His sadness is palpable, and this time I know it really is all my fault. He's not even a little bit to blame for this one. He sinks onto the edge of the bed, setting my iPad down gently next to him, and his glasses, too, and hunches forward over his knees, covering his face with his hands for a long, long moment before sighing and dragging his face back up to peer at me.

"Where did we go so wrong, Serena?"

Where did we go so wrong?

Oh, I wish I knew. These last few days, I've asked myself that a lot. Where did we go so wrong, because how long ago could I have known all this stuff, or how long have I gone without asking it and when was the *right* time to have asked it? When did this whole thing become work? When did being snippy with each other become so normal I forgot we were ever any other way?

Where did we go so wrong?

Zach rubs his knuckles to his eyes before putting his glasses back on. I feel like I'm on the back foot, but I don't even know *why*, and

I dither for a second, wringing my sweaty hands before deciding there's only one thing to do right now.

I move beside him, pick up the iPad, and sit down on the bed next to him.

I rest the iPad in my lap and lean sideways until my head rests on his shoulder. I can smell Zach's aftershave on his shirt, and close my eyes for a second, drinking it in. I love the smell of his aftershave. I've always loved it.

I love how easy it's always been to just *be* with him. I used to dread a time when Friday nights in with a boyfriend would be catching up on *Gogglebox* and eating pasta bake on the sofa, instead of making plans to go out somewhere and *do* something, but it had never felt mundane with Zach. It was part of the reason I was so happy to say *yes* when he suggested we look for a place to move in together, after not even being together for a year. It was part of the reason I got a new job nearer him, so eager to start our life together. Because if even the boring bits were that good, just think how incredible the good parts could be.

Zach's head tips to rest against mine.

"What happened the other morning, Serena?" he asks me softly.

"You called me a bitch and said you should leave," I say. It comes out quiet and wobbly, which I really wasn't expecting, and then I find myself sniffling. I gulp, not sure when this lump appeared in my throat.

"Rena . . . "

I sniffle again, scrubbing the heel of my hand across my face before he can realize I'm crying. God, I know we have to at least *talk* about this, even if it's all over, and maybe now he's finally going to listen.

So I say, "You ordered pineapple pizza. That's what happened, Zach."

It hangs in the air between us for a while, the silence stretching out, pressing down around us.

Until, eventually, Zach laughs.

He pulls away from me so that he can look at me better. I refuse to raise my face to his, but out of the corner of my eye I can see the incredulous look on his face, the nervousness in his eyes when he laughs again.

"What?"

I tell him again, my voice a little more steady this time, "You ordered pineapple pizza."

"Um . . . yes?"

I sigh, and meet his gaze this time to give him a deadpan look.

"I'm sorry," he says, still laughing, though I know he's trying so very hard not to, "did it offend you? I wasn't aware you had such strong and intense opinions on the topic."

"It's not that." I'm not yelling this time, just . . . hopeless. Helpless. I take a deep breath to steady myself, and explain, "It's that we've been together for *four years*, Zach. We own an apartment together, for Christ's sake! And I don't even know what kind of pizza toppings you like, or where you stand on something like *pineapple* on pizza. And it just made me wonder, what else don't we know about each other?"

"Wait. *Wait*."

Zach stands up, pushing me back from him when my hand automatically reaches for his arm, and he stands across the room from me, his hands pressed over his mouth. He frowns at the floor for the longest moment before looking at me, one thick, dark eyebrow quirked up.

"*That's* why you started that whole thing about kids and houses and getting married? That's why you went off on one?"

"I went off on one because you called me a bitch, and you didn't even have an opinion on any of those things," I tell him, my teeth already grinding again.

Zach scoffs, but it's not the angry, exasperated sort of noise I heard the other morning. If anything, he just sounds tired. "All right, I shouldn't have called you a bitch. I am genuinely sorry about that. But you *were* . . ." He catches himself and whatever he was about to say, swallowing it back down and offering instead, "acting very out of character. I mean, jeez, I wake up and you're sulking out there on the balcony, and suddenly start yelling at me about how we should have a three-bedroom house out in the suburbs like Matty and Alex, and about how your body clock is ticking—"

"All right, I *definitely* never said that."

Zach cringes. "Well, you know. Words to that effect."

I grunt, but give it to him.

"It's not that I don't have an opinion on whether I want to marry you, or have kids, or whatever. I just figured it wasn't time, yet."

"But what if you *didn't* want kids? Or what if you did, and I really didn't? You don't think that would be worth us breaking up over? How long would we have been together before we realized all that?"

Zach's face crumples, and I see him *finally* get it.

"Oh."

"Yeah, *oh.*"

I get up now, too, standing in front of him.

"I'm not saying this should've been first-date conversation, or that we should've been on our third or even thirtieth date talking about where we'd live that was close enough to family but had *great* schools for the however many kids we'd decided we wanted to have, or that we should've been settling on if we wanted to get married one day or both just wanted to spend the money on a few nice holidays before we moved in together but . . . *Four years*, Zach. It just made me realize that maybe, at some point during all that time, we should have talked about some of these things."

"And you realized all of this . . . because I ordered a pineapple pizza."

Zach looks at me with such gravity, such a serious pout, no hint of amusement anywhere on his face or in his voice now.

And we both erupt into laughter.

Zach bends forward to clutch a stitch in his side, hooting loudly, and I collapse onto the floor, hunched over my knees and wheezing.

"Over *pineapple* on *pizza*," he repeats, and sets us both off laughing again.

He's right.

It is properly and completely bonkers.

And what else can we do right now, having already spent days yelling ourselves hoarse over it, except laugh?

When we've both caught our breath, Zach folds himself onto the floor opposite me, and holds his arms out in a gesture that feels so second nature now that I don't even hesitate. I've skirted around him the last three days, banishing him out to the sofa to sleep, glaring at him if we so much as bumped arms moving past each other. Now, I crawl onto his lap, letting him wrap his arms around me, breathing in the scent of his aftershave again and placing my hands against his chest. Zach presses a kiss to the top of my head and sighs, his arms tightening around me.

"So what do we do now?" he asks me quietly.

"I don't know," I admit.

"Do you think we should talk about it?"

"Do you think you can form an opinion on anything?"

"Do you think you can stop snapping at me?"

I do, at least for the moment, and nuzzle into the crook of his neck, closing my eyes. "Yes, Zach. I think we should talk about it."

I feel him nod against me.

"You think we could at least have a cup of tea first?"

"Yeah. Tea sounds good."

But I don't move off his lap, and his arms don't loosen around me.

I don't know if we'll even manage to talk it through, or if we'll come out of this on the other side any better than we are right now, going into it, but I suppose then, at least, we'll both know where we stand, and we'll know we tried.

We'll talk about it, and we'll go make a cup of tea, but not right now. It'll wait, just a bit.

For now, just for a little while, we'll stay wrapped up in each other's arms, familiar and comfortable, and remember what it's like to just *be* together.

Chapter Twenty-seven

M aid of Honor's log, still day eight. Of course it's still day eight. *This day is. Never. Going. To. End. The living room is still car-*nage. *Stomach is grumbling, laptop is getting low on power. Headache now probably due to a lack of caffeine. The groom has texted me to check in because he's not heard from Kim. Have ignored him.*

Right now, Kim's taking a nap. Or at least, that's what she told Lucy and Addison. I think it's pretty convenient timing, given that I'm just finishing up work for the day. I should be relieved to be done with it for the week, but I'm scared of what's going to happen now I don't have the excuse to avoid everyone.

It's been a long week, for all of us.

(Have I mentioned that yet? I don't feel like I've mentioned it enough.)

Addison takes the opportunity to go out on the balcony for a little privacy to call her mum, now it's late enough over here for America to be awake. Lucy folds herself into the corner of the sofa to quietly go back to reading something on her iPad.

I fix myself a quick cup of tea, not having had one for a few hours. (Lucy snuck me one earlier, along with a sandwich; I hadn't risked leaving the bedroom for hours, having to wait until the rain cleared before I could seek refuge on the balcony to work for the day.)

I take my mug back to the living room and survey the damage.

I spot a couple of pieces of glass we missed when cleaning up last night. There's still a damp mark on the wall, but it doesn't seem to have stained. Looking at it, I really don't think she *meant* to smash the prosecco bottle like that. She did look pretty bloody surprised when it shattered against the wall.

I set my tea down and start to go around the room, collecting the little purple chocolates. I stack them up near the TV, then collect the broken bags, the scraps of netting. I take them out to the bin in the kitchen; by the time I get back, Addison's in from the balcony and she and Lucy are going around the living room to clean up too. Addison collects the centerpieces while Lucy gathers all the dried rose petals. I take care of the packets of Love Hearts.

"Sorry we didn't sort this out earlier," Addison tells me, shrugging one shoulder and giving me a small, sincere smile. "I was a little scared it'd cause another breakdown."

"How's she been?"

"How've *you* been?" Addison asks instead.

I shrug.

"Not so good," Lucy tells me, when I don't say anything. "She's just been really quiet all day. Sulking, I guess, you know?"

"You think she's going to ever talk to me again?" I ask, biting my lip. It's not like Kim and I have never fought in all the years we've been friends, but never like we did last night; this one makes me feel sick and sits heavy on my shoulders, threatening to crush me whenever I think about it too long. And she's been my best friend since we were five years old. I genuinely can't imagine life without her.

"You ask me," Addison scoffed, "*she's* the one who should be saying sorry."

"But you didn't say that," I joke, remembering our conversation this morning in the kitchen.

"Damn straight. Or, like . . . *not*."

I raise my eyebrows at her.

"Well. Damn straight, if it's your parents asking," she adds, muttering under her breath, pulling a cheeky, wide-eyed face with her lips pursed. She's standing close enough that she bumps her shoulder against mine and waggles her eyebrows.

I try so hard to ignore her, just on principle, but once I start laughing, a giggle sputters out of Lucy, and then Addison's laughing, too, and I don't actually think I've laughed so hard all week. We all seem to remember Kim, napping (or maybe not), and fall quiet at the same time—but as soon as we're trying not to laugh, of course it's all the more difficult *not* to, and I'm still wheezing with laughter, a stitch in my side, by the time we've finished cleaning up.

I sit with the girls for a while. When we hear movement from the bedroom, the sound of Kim getting up from her nap, I shut myself out on the balcony again, plugging in my headphones and trying to lose myself in some TikToks.

*

Maid of Honor's log. Still. Day. Freaking. Eight. I may live out here on the balcony forever now. Or at least for the next two days, until I can finally kick them all out of my apartment and have the place to myself again. Although currently unsure if I kick Kim out I'll ever see her again, the way today is going. Despite all of us being in each other's way all week, and currently being stuck under the same roof, it has been incredibly easy to avoid my best friend for the entire day.

Oh God, it's been *way* too easy to avoid her all day, and we've been trapped in the same apartment. What if this is just the beginning? What if we start avoiding each other in real life when this nightmarish, week-long sleepover is finally over, and just like that, we're not in each other's lives anymore?

Kim was the first person I came out to. She came with me on my first date and lurked at a table in the back of the coffee shop—a favor I returned on *her* first date to a Nando's. She's the person I dragged out to orchestra classes with me every Saturday morning when we were in school because I didn't want to go on my own, even though she'd sit reading or on her phone the whole time. She helped me dye my hair red when we were sixteen and got her belly button pierced with me when I got my first helix piercing. She's the person who came to a Jonas Brothers concert with me last year, because even as an adult I'm a die-hard fan, and who's always been on the other side of the phone to offer advice and reassurance when I'm having a relationship crisis (which is more often than I'd care to admit).

So what if she's been an utter bitch with all the wedding planning? I *know* that's not who she is.

I really, really don't want to lose her.

"Knock-knock?"

I jump, pulling out my earphones and twisting around as I'm joined on the balcony.

Pausing the video I was watching, I hug my phone to my chest as Kim steps outside.

"Brought you some tea," she says, rather unnecessarily, given that she's holding two mugs. She passes me one of them over and then slides the door shut before taking a seat. "Addy's making pasta for dinner. Chicken and pesto. She said she found some garlic bread in your freezer, too, if you don't mind us using it."

"Yeah, sounds . . . sounds good."

We both sit in silence for the longest of minutes. I watch clouds creep by, and some people pass on the pathways below. I listen to Kim as she keeps taking big breaths, ready to say something, and every time, letting it back out—quiet and shaky and defeated.

We cave at the same time.

"Kim, listen—"

"Liv, I didn't—"

We both fall silent, and both try again—still at the same time.

"I shouldn't have said—"

"I really didn't mean—"

Kim falters when I stop talking to let her finish, and her lips twitch before breaking into a nervous smile.

It's like a weight off my shoulders, seeing her smile: I know all is forgiven.

On her part, at least.

"I really am sorry," I say. "I know how stressed you've been about the wedding, especially with all . . . all *this* going on." I sweep my hand in an all-encompassing gesture out at the view. "I honestly didn't mean to upset you so much, saying it might all have to be, um . . . "

Kim crosses her legs and slumps in her chair. Her usual curls have turned into one big, frizzy mess. There's still a smudge of black under her eyes where she hasn't quite managed to scrub off yesterday's mascara, after all the crying. Her face is puffy and pale, her green eyes bloodshot.

But, at least, she's smiling, one corner of her mouth twisted up.

"No, you—you were totally right. I *have* been a bridezilla. And a total bitch too. Not just last night, or this week, either, but I . . . I think it's kind of hit me, lately, you know? Don't get me wrong, I love Jeremy, and I absolutely want to marry him—it's just . . . this is *it*, now. One guy, for the entire rest of my life. I'm the first of all our friends to settle down, and sometimes I think his sister and his parents don't even really like me or like I always have to try so hard to impress them, and it's all just felt like so much."

She takes a deep, shaky breath, and tells me quietly, "Jeremy said maybe it was a good thing. If it all got pushed back."

"Addison, she, um . . . I—I mean, Lucy said something about, uh . . . "

"Figured she'd tell you guys eventually, the way this week's going," Kim mutters. She rubs her knuckles into her forehead, eyes squeezing shut for a moment. "I was texting him about it yesterday. He said it'd be a relief if it got postponed because he knew how stressful it has all been, and it'd be good for us to have a break from all the wedding stuff, and . . . I guess it's just because I can't *talk* to him, really, or *see* him, you know?"

She turns on me, her eyes watering, and I'm honestly astonished she even has any tears left to cry at this point. Sniffling, she wipes her nose on the back of her hand.

"That must be hard," I say, sympathetic as any best friend can be. "Especially when you guys have barely spent any time away from each other since you got together."

"I just got so in my head after he said that yesterday, thinking, what if he meant *we'd* made a mistake, agreeing to get married? What if he regretted proposing to me, or he was changing his mind? What if the idea of spending the rest of his life with *me* was finally hitting him too?"

"Oh, Kim, I'm sure that's not what he meant."

I reach over, squeezing her arm, and Kim grasps my hand in hers, sniffling again. "Yeah, I—I know, but . . . I knew if I said it out loud yesterday it'd sound so stupid—or worse, I was worried you guys might all think that *was* what he meant, and . . . and then you brought up postponing the wedding and there was all that stuff the other day about the plus ones and I know you're mad at me for that, too, and I just—God, I'm such an *idiot*. And I've been so bloody horrible, especially to you."

"Just a little."

"I'm so sorry, Liv. I'm the worst best friend ever. I never should have—"

"Yeah," I mumble. "You shouldn't have."

"I *honestly* didn't mean to out you to Addison and Lucy like that last night either. I didn't mean anything I said, about you being bitter or growing old alone, or anything."

"I don't think you said anything about me growing old alone," I tell her, and Kim flushes before she realizes I've seen the funny side in it.

"I *am* sorry, Liv. I feel awful about it. Especially because Addison likes you, and it's obvious you like her, and—"

"Wait. *Wait.* She what?"

Kim's eyes light up and I just *know* she wants to gossip all about it, ask me a thousand questions, tell me a hundred and one things about Addison, but she reins it in quickly, saying instead, "You're *so* oblivious sometimes. It's been worse than that time I kept dropping hints I wanted the Chanel perfume for Christmas but you got me a blender instead."

"I thought you liked that blender."

"It's a wonderful blender, Liv, but that's not the point. Addy's been flirting with you *all* week, you know. What did you *think* she was doing, making a show of parading around in your T-shirt?"

Despite the tone of our conversation, I indulge in the gossiping for a second, thinking back. I immediately know Kim's talking about Tuesday morning, when Addison had run out of clean shirts so borrowed one of mine and came striding into the living room plucking at the shoulders of it, looking at it so critically and saying, "Hey, Livvy, you must have a really great set on you. Look at me! I'm drowning in this!"

She'd demonstrated the too-big neckline, letting the T-shirt hang off one shoulder, posing around the room.

And I'd said to her, "You know there are other shirts in the drawer. You could just find one that fits."

Now, I cringe, pulling a face at Kim. "I thought she was just being American."

She tries not to laugh, pressing a hand over her mouth. "No, *Livvy,* she wasn't."

I'm preoccupied thinking about all the other moments this week when I just thought Addison was being obnoxious, or friendly, but might actually have been trying to flirt and grab my attention—and there are enough of them that I feel like such an *idiot* for not noticing.

(To Kim's credit, it's no wonder I can't date anyone for longer than a couple of weeks, if I'm so bloody oblivious.)

I'm distracted by the solemn look returning to her face, though, and the puppy-dog eyes she gives me, looking so genuinely sad.

"I'm honestly so sorry, Liv. Even if you're not upset about me telling them, I—I *never* should've lost it like that at you. I was totally out of order. Especially this morning. That's why I was so upset today, you know. It wasn't anything about the wedding, not really. It was—you said you wished you'd never gotten involved, and . . . and I thought maybe I'd *really* ruined everything then, with us, and that you hated me. I'm so sorry."

I'm about to tell her, *It's okay*, and while it is, I still think she's got something to apologize for. So instead, I tell her, "Apology accepted. What're friends for, huh?"

"Will you still be my maid of honor? If there's ever a wedding, that is."

I squeeze her hand, smiling at her. "Of course I will—but on one condition."

Kim sits up straighter, blinking the tears out of her eyes. "Yes. Absolutely. Anything. *Anything.*"

"No more wedding planning parties?"

She laughs, and it's the first time I've heard her laugh like that in *months*. Like she really doesn't have a care in the world. "You got it, Liv. Promise—no more wedding planning parties. One was *definitely* enough."

I lift my mug of tea, holding it out. "Cheers to that."

Kim lifts her mug high. "To friendship."

"To bridezillas," I declare, and she laughs again, clinking her mug to mine.

APARTMENT #15 – ISLA

Chapter Twenty-eight

Danny's sucked into work for the evening after dinner—*again*. I can't hold it against him; judging by the deep frown etched on his face and the tired look in his eyes, he'd rather be doing anything but working right now. I watch a couple of old episodes of *Brooklyn Nine-Nine* but can tell it's distracting him by the way he keeps covering his ears and hunching over his computer, or when he laughs quietly and then shakes his head like he's chastising himself for getting sidetracked by Jake Peralta's antics, or a one-liner from Holt.

I turn the TV off, grab my headphones and a book, and head outside to the balcony. I settle into my large rattan chair, padded with cream and gold cushions. I probably spent way too much on this chair at the garden center last summer, and I *definitely* spent too much on the cushions at Anthropologie, but every time I sit out here in it, I'm reminded that it was worth every penny, just like the apartment itself. I put my phone and headphones on the gold-and-glass table, and light the candle I left out here a couple of days ago.

It's still light out, so I get to enjoy the purple dusk streaked with gold, silhouetting the other apartment blocks on the estate; it's pretty, so I grab a picture for my Instagram. I can see the tennis courts down the road from here, and wonder if they'll be closed by the time I'm allowed out of my apartment.

I wonder if there will even *be* anywhere to go, really, once the building is out of lockdown in a couple of days. Everything seems to be changing so fast right now. My dad told me I was lucky to get a food order when I did; the slots are filling up so quickly as the public panic is starting to rise, and you can't even get one two weeks in advance now. I keep getting emails from brands I'm signed up to reassuring me that it's business as usual except that their physical stores are now shut! But it's fine! You can still order from the website! Maybe only with a small delay and no more next-day delivery because they can't guarantee that anymore!

I know none of that should feel like a shock to me, since I'm working for a company where those sort of adjustments are our main focus right now but even so.

The reassurances are having the exact opposite effect. It's just making me feel absolutely terrified if I think about it too much. For the most part, I delete the emails and do my best to ignore the news.

Ignore it all you want, Isla, it's not going to change the fact it's happening.

I end up not really reading much of my book, and never even get around to putting my headphones in to listen to some music. I simply stay sat in my chair, unease at the uncertainty of the world gnawing at me. I hug my knees and book to my chest, staring out at the view and having a nice little existential crisis to ring in the weekend.

Maybe I should do some journaling. That would probably help.

Except, I can't even bring myself to unfold my limbs and get out of this chair. I feel like if I stop hugging myself, I might splinter into pieces.

I have no idea how long I'm out there, my mind running through a million and one potential disasters from losing my job to my relationship disintegrating to my family getting sick to not being able to take my book back to the library and what if they fine me for it . . . But eventually the door slides open behind me and I jump to find Danny standing there, smiling down at me.

It's dark by now. The lantern-style streetlights on the paths below us have turned on, and the motion-sensor light on my balcony has switched on, too, now he's come outside and activated it. It gives a yellow-orange glow to Danny's dark hair, and casts shadows across his face.

He's so beautiful. I love the way his hair curls at the ends, how long his eyelashes are. I love the way his eyes glitter in the soft lights, creasing around the corners as he smiles. I feel calmer just looking at him; the ache in my chest I'd been nursing vanishes, and I barely notice.

He hands me my favorite gray knitted cardigan, and sets two glasses of white wine on the table, before taking a seat on the bench.

"Thought you might be cold," he says, as I put down my book and unfurl myself to pull on the cardigan.

"Thanks. And what about this?" I ask, picking up one of the wines to take a sip.

He smiles again, shrugging. "Just thought I'd be cute."

I can't help but laugh. He *is* cute, with that dimple in his cheek and the way he raises his eyebrows, trying and failing to look cool, with his ski-slope nose and broad shoulders that his baggy sweat-shirt does *nothing* for, really.

"Well, mission accomplished," I inform him, and join him on the bench. He wraps an arm around me as I snuggle into his side and press a kiss to his jaw, where his stubble has started to turn into a beard.

He rubs it absently. "I haven't tried to grow out my beard since I did Movember a couple of years ago."

"You're going full werewolf," I joke, but he only grimaces. I kiss him there again. "Well, I think you'll look good."

"Let's see if you still think that when it grows in fully," he laughs, deliberately nuzzling his chin against my cheek so his soon-to-be-a-full-on-beard scratches over my skin. I laugh, wriggling away and trying not to spill my wine, but he draws me back toward him for a long kiss.

And. It. Is. *Divine.*

I can almost feel Danny smiling, and he strokes my hair. After a moment he says softly, "You know, it'd help if you *told* me what was going on sometimes, Isla. Instead of just assuming I know. Like with your workout and stuff, yesterday."

"You don't have to be a mind reader," I mutter. "Just a little more considerate. Like when I asked you to use your earphones for your meetings and stuff."

Danny nods. "I guess we both could've handled this week a little better. It's been kind of intense, you know? Not bad," he adds quickly, "just weird. Different!"

"It's okay. It's really fucking weird, Danny."

I hear his sigh of relief, just like when we were trying to work out our schedules for the week, and wonder if now's the right time to probe him about ex-girlfriends and previous relationships. Probably not.

Some other time, I decide. Or maybe after a couple more glasses of wine, at least.

"And for the record, I don't—I *never*—expected you to be perfect. I don't like you because you always shave your legs and get your eyebrows threaded," he says, teasingly, warmly. "And for the record, you fart in your sleep. Kind of a lot."

"Oh my *God*."

My face burns and I bury my face in his chest in absolute horror.

Danny laughs, though, drawing me closer to his side. "I just mean, I don't want you to . . . pretend to be some version of yourself you're not, I guess? I'm not. There's making an effort to dress up for a date, and then there's faking it all. I like you for you, Isla. The person. Not some—I don't know, some polished Instagram persona or curated Bumble profile that you think I'm interested in."

I peel my face away from his sweatshirt to look up at him, not sure how to respond to that. Is that really what I've been doing? Giving him a persona, instead of a person?

Danny kisses me, softly, sweetly. His lips still pressed to mine, he says, "I know we've got a long way to go, Isla, but can we agree to . . . talk, about stuff? To be ourselves, communicate a little better? Or try to, at least?"

My heart swells.

I nod, whispering, "Okay, deal," and kiss him again before settling back into his side, each of us nursing our glass of wine as we lapse into quiet.

To be brutally honest, I'm not *entirely* sure how I feel about being more upfront and honest with each other. This could open a whole new can of worms. (Well, probably *cans*, plural, judging by the way I blew up at him yesterday.)

Something tells me that you should probably wait until a little later on in a relationship to be so "warts and all" about things, and outright *telling* your partner exactly what it is they're doing to annoy you, and I'm not sure that it's the best thing to do when we're literally trapped here and can't do anything to avoid the other one if either of our feelings gets hurt.

But, maybe, he's got a point.

And I guess it's worth a shot, isn't it?

Honestly, it can't be worse than letting everything build up to breaking point, which was my approach at the start of this week.

Maybe it'll even stop us ending up like Zach and Serena down the hallway in a year's time, sniping at each other and having screaming matches—assuming we last beyond the end of this week, that is.

It's comforting how much he obviously wants to try to make things work.

What's important, I realize, is how much we *both* want to make this work. That's what's making all the difference here. Maybe neither of us is ready to say The L Word, but the fact we're both trying so hard proves how invested we are in this relationship, how much we mean to each other.

He's so quiet, I wonder if he's thinking the same thing as me. Instead of asking him, though, I twist around in my seat to face him better. I set down my wine, cupping his face in both of my hands to kiss him, shivering at the sensation of his tongue against mine.

And in spite of how badly I've handled things this week, I find myself wishing he didn't have to leave so soon.

APARTMENT #6 – ETHAN

Chapter Twenty-nine

It's automatic, the whole process of editing a video so that it's ready to upload on my channel. Cutting out the *um*s and *ah*s and the too-loud breaths, adjusting the white balance and the audio. It's not exactly mindless, but I'm so used to it by now it's not exactly mentally taxing either.

Needing a break, I walk away to get myself a coffee, and my mind turns back to Charlotte, and my pathetic attempts at a proposal speech. I got so in my head about it yesterday that I ended up vegging out on the sofa watching movies all afternoon, instead of doing literally *anything* productive; I've been trying to make up for that today. Now, I take off my glasses to rub my eyes, feeling a slight headache coming on from the glare of the computer screen.

I'm no good at putting words on paper, as was obvious after another ten pages of notes yesterday I quickly tore out, scrunched up, and dropped in the recycling bin in the kitchen. I considered asking some of our friends for advice, but the problem is that they're all *our* friends, mine *and* Charlotte's. After four years of being so devoted to each other, it was inevitable.

And I'm not sure I trust any of them to keep it to themselves while I figure it out, to be honest. There are a choice few people—like her sister Maisie, or like my best friend Jack from my old job—who know us both so well that I know their advice would be invaluable, but I also know they would only start dropping hints to Charlotte, too excited to stay schtum.

So I'm in this alone.

Well, except for Reddit.

I create a throwaway account and ask for advice in one of the forums I visit a lot, but while everyone's very supportive and encouraging, the clearest bit of advice I get is "just be yourself!" which honestly is not that helpful.

I'm no good at putting words on paper.

As I'm standing in the kitchen making myself a drink and thinking about the video I need to upload and schedule for tomorrow, I realize suddenly what I *am* good at.

Coffee in hand, I sit back down in front of my computer and switch on my camera. My vlogging setup is ready from the video I recorded first thing this morning, and I switch it all on mainly out of habit, even though I could probably get away with just my iMac's webcam for this particular video. Still, I turn on the light boxes and spend some time readjusting the curtains to reduce the glare, then settle back into my chair.

I hit record.

"Okay." I take a deep breath, looking at myself on the screen and nodding. My hair's standing up more than usual and my shirt is a little rumpled. I straighten my glasses and gulp. "Okay, Ethan, come on, you can do this."

I was never good at public speaking.

I used to do my best to get out of giving presentations at school. I got so nervous doing one to my tutorial group of a mere six students in university that I actually threw up. Whenever I meet strangers for the first time, I get so in my head trying to *not* make a bad impression, at the very least, that I think most of the time they think I'm just being standoffish and rude. (Lucky for me, Charlotte's a natural charmer, and good with people, and it's easy to ride on her coattails when we have to mingle with strangers at our friends' weddings and stuff.)

I started making video diaries years ago, after a suggestion from my therapist, who thought it would help with my social anxiety—and would at least help me get through the video interview stage of all the jobs I was applying for during my final year of university. And she was right: there was something about talking to the void and interacting with a handful of total strangers on the internet that was strangely comforting.

I was only supposed to try it out for a month, but I kept it going even after I stopped seeing the therapist, and once the video interviews for jobs were out of the way. I started putting more effort into the channel, investing in better equipment, devoting more time to learning how to edit properly. I thought about what I *actually* wanted to make videos about, and figured out what I actually liked doing, cross-referencing that with what got the best response from my gradually growing audience to decide what to make the focus of my channel. Eventually, I found my niche: video games and nerd culture.

There's still something about talking to the void and yet knowing *someone* is listening that I love.

Right now, I just hope it'll be enough to get my head straight.

I figure if I sit and talk at the camera for long enough, I can go back through it tomorrow, before Charlotte gets back, and find *something* articulate enough to rehearse saying to her.

"Right. Here goes."

My hands shake, and I wipe them on my jeans because they've started to sweat. I look into the camera lens, and go for it.

"Dear Charlotte . . . I've known you for two and a half years. I walked into you and almost knocked you on your butt, but you were the one who swept me off my feet. No—no, that's . . . that's shit. When we first met, I was supposed to be on a date with someone else. I've never been so glad to have been stood up in my life. I can still remember you picking popcorn out of your hair and popcorn falling out of your coat when I took you to dinner after the film. That was the first time I saw a movie alone, but now I've got you in my life, I know I'll never have to watch anything alone ag—*aaaaaaaaah*, God, that's even worse.

"Dear Charlotte. You're beautiful. I don't know if I tell you that enough, but it's true. You're beautiful when you don't blow-dry your hair and it just—" I wave my hands out at the sides of my head, mimicking it "—it just goes *out*, like that, and it looks bloody awful. You're beautiful when you're reading something really cute in a book and you have to put it down and breathe for a moment, and you do that thing where you hold your face like you have to physically contain yourself, you can't handle how cute it is that the characters are finally kissing, or whatever. You're beautiful even when—oh my *God*, this is negging, isn't it? I'm negging you. Fuck. Who ever tried to—*ugh*. No.

"Dear Charlotte. I've loved you since the moment I met you, and I don't believe I'll ever stop. I want to be ninety years old and sitting next to you rewatching the *Twilight* movies because you want to feel like a teenager again and there's absolutely nothing else on TV. I want you to sit through a *Lord of the Rings* marathon with me for the billionth time and still not have a clue who Sauron is, or why Gollum wants the ring, or which one's Merry and which one's Pippin. I—yeah, I'm still going to be a nerd when I'm ninety, if we're not all dead from this stupid virus by then and *wow*, nope, that took a turn, didn't it? Balls. I probably shouldn't . . . shouldn't be morbid, when I'm trying to ask you to . . . Yeah, that'll work great, huh? Super romantic. Let's elope before we all die. Jesus, Ethan."

I hunch forward, tugging at my hair, and let out a long, loud, exasperated groan.

At least it's going better than when I was trying to do this on paper.

I take a few breaths and sit back up, squaring my shoulders and trying again.

Once I've decided *what* I'm going to say, exactly, the worst will be over.

When she gets home on Sunday, I'll cook Charlotte her favorite meal (my so-called "famous" enchiladas, all gluten-free, of course), and crack open a bottle of the wine she likes so much. Not the "special occasion" wine, obviously, that would be too suspect. But the good wine. I'll say it's to celebrate her finally coming home.

I might even make dessert. Something fancy, like a cheesecake. Or maybe just some brownies—a gluten-free cheesecake seems a little too ambitious.

"And after dessert," I say out loud, reciting the plan to the camera so I don't forget it, "I'll reach across the table and take your hand, and tell you how beautiful you look, and how happy I am that you're back, and that I've missed you, and . . . and you'll say you missed me, too, and then I'll launch into this big speech, and tell you—well, I'll tell you *something*, because I'll have figured it out by then, and you'll probably start crying once you realize where it's going and what I'm doing, and then I'll keep hold of your hand and get down on one knee, and you'll probably barely even let me get the words out before you say yes and kiss me, and . . . *Jesus*, what am I going to say?"

I'm still there thirty-eight minutes later.

"Dear Charlotte," I sigh, and I smile just to think about her smile. "I love you. I think I could talk for hours—weeks—about why, and how much, but what other reason do I need? I don't have a ring, or some stupid, great big plan like something out of the movies and books you love, or rose petals to sprinkle on the floor or anything like that, but I fucking love you, and that's enough for me. So—marry me?"

*

"What's up guys, it's Ethan here. Mad Man Maddox back once again, and I still can't believe you guys let that stupid nickname catch on, but I kind of love it. Happy Friday night! You know, in case you're also going a little stir-crazy right now and need a reminder of what day it is . . . I'm joined tonight by a few beers and, obviously, *Call of Duty*. I was hoping to be playing everyone's favorite—*Animal Crossing: New Horizons*, but unfortunately, doesn't seem like I can broadcast live from my Switch, so you'll have to stick to my YouTube channel for that. Don't forget to subscribe at *emaddox*, and I'd say find me on Twitter, too, but to be honest I mainly just retweet TikTok videos so it's not even worth it."

It takes me a couple of minutes to get into the flow of my Twitch stream because I'm still thinking about the perfect way to propose to Charlotte, but I fall into the familiar rhythm of a video game and talking to some of the fans watching along, responding to the comments they're posting in the live chat.

For the first time all week, I forget that the world is a shitshow right now, how scary everything is, how out of sorts I've felt these last few days. At least for a little while, everything feels totally normal.

It feels like I can breathe again.

I spot Charlotte's name on the live chat and laugh.

"My girlfriend's watching along tonight too. You'll probably spot her in the chat. Everybody say hi, Charlotte. *Hi, Charlotte!*" I say for them, in a high-pitched, silly voice. "Usually she'd be sitting just out of sight on the sofa next to me and trying to tune me out, but this week unfortunately, she's at her parents' place. Yeah, our place is on lockdown, and she was just going home for the weekend since they live a couple hours' drive away. Had free reign of the apartment all week. How about that, huh? I'm kidding, obviously. Charl, it's been miserable without you."

I have to stop there, before I go on about just how much I miss her.

It's not like I don't care if anybody watching thinks I'm talking about her too much or anything. I'm more worried I'll run my mouth and say something I want to keep for the grand proposal.

Or worse, get so nervous I can't shut up, and then blurt the whole thing out.

As ten o'clock rolls around, I draw the stream to an end.

"Don't forget to check out my YouTube channel *emaddox* tomorrow morning for a new video, and I'll be back here next Tuesday with another livestream. But that's it from me for now, have a good night everybody—and to my girlfriend, Charlotte, if she's still watching and hasn't gotten so bored she's fallen asleep, goodnight, and I'll see you Sunday."

I wave to the camera, saying a cheerful, "See ya!" before turning everything off. I put the controller away, fix the blanket on the sofa the way Charlotte would, and log on to my computer. I send a tweet to thank everyone for joining me on Twitch, adding a link to my Patreon, and check through some notifications before remembering I haven't *actually* uploaded tomorrow's video yet.

Shit, I got so distracted by all the proposal stuff I forgot to finish editing it and upload it.

I'm up for another hour finishing the edits. It's not up to my usual standard, I know, but it's close enough, and I'll take that right now. While it's exporting, I work on a thumbnail, and by the time I've opened YouTube to create a new video, I'm barely able to keep my eyes open. The few beers I've had this evening have made me sleepy, and I drag the video to upload, on autopilot as I add the thumbnail I've just made and tap out a quick description, update some of my default tags.

4% done, 1 hour 13 minutes left . . .

Screw it, I think, pushing away from the desk. I'll leave it to upload overnight.

Right now, I need to go to bed.

I fall asleep dreaming of engagement rings.

Saturday

Chapter Thirty

> Do you think my life is chaotic?

LOL
obvs
what kind of question even is that?

> Nvm

it's a mess
but like
one I love very much, ofc

> But like
> Okay
> Not my life, but do you think *I* am chaotic? Like, ME?
> PERSONALLY?

oh, one hundred and eight percent

Lucy follows this up with a picture from a couple of weeks ago. It's one I sent our group chat, of a TV aerial on the house next door, with my bra hanging off it, after I'd left it on the bathroom windowsill and it blew outside. #BraGate had made us all giggle for days.

I can't even manage a faint smile reminiscing over it now.

Lucy follows up quickly, asking if I'm okay. It feels like too much to explain (especially since I'm still refusing to tell her that I'm quarantining with Honeypot Guy) and I'm not even sure *how* to answer that, so I tell her of course I'm okay and ask how she's coping, locked down with her future sister-in-law. I ask if everything's been resolved with the big argument they all had, after Kim apparently lost her shit and outed the maid of honor. She responds, but after a while I ignore the texts, the glow of my phone shining up at the ceiling as I lie on my back in Nate's bed, completely unable to sleep.

I feel like such an asshole right now, for taking up this lovely, comfy double bed, wide awake and likely not going to sleep for a few more hours yet, while poor Nate is stuck out there on the sofa for the sixth night in a row.

I reply to Lucy's texts for a while longer before she tells me she's going to sleep and we'll talk tomorrow. I scroll through Twitter for a couple of minutes before everyone there seems to have gone to bed too.

It's gone one in the morning when I give up trying to sleep, cocoon myself in the duvet, and shuffle out to the living room. The duvet drags behind me, the fabric whispering over the laminate flooring; it seems so loud in the silence of the apartment.

It's not just the apartment that's so quiet, though; it's *everything*. There's no sound of cars on the roads outside, no sirens, no shouting. I know this is a nicer neighborhood than where I live, but even so . . . It's disconcerting, like someone stuck the whole world on pause.

Nate's sprawled on the sofa, blankets half kicked off. He isn't exactly what I'd call a *tall* guy, particularly, but somehow he's managed to take up the entire three-seater sofa and has his feet hanging off the end of it. He's wearing pajamas but the T-shirt has ridden up, exposing his soft stomach. His arms are thrown out, one to the side and one above his head, and his mouth is hanging wide open.

It's the least composed I've seen him all week.

I shake him awake.

"Nate. Nate. Nate-Nathan-Nate. Honeypot. Wake up."

For a cute guy, he wakes up in the most unattractive way. He smacks his lips together, head rolling and eyes blinking, letting out a quiet little fart, and mumbling, "Whassamatter?" before he seems to remember some random girl is living in his apartment for the week, and now she's waking him up in the middle of the night. He sits up, rubbing his eyes and asking instead, "Immy? What's up?"

"You drool in your sleep, you know."

Automatically, his hand comes up to the line of dribble on his chin, and he scrubs it away. I wriggle my way into the gap he's made between himself and the arm of the sofa; the duvet's bigger than I thought, though, and he has to shuffle out of my way.

"You woke me up to tell me I drool in my sleep?"

"Yes."

He lets out a short, disbelieving laugh, before frowning curiously at me and saying, "Did you call me Honeypot?"

"Yes. And it suits you, so shut up."

"Okay."

"Do you really think I'm chaotic?"

His frown deepens, the amusement disappearing from his face now. "Oh. Still hung up on that, huh?"

"Just a little."

"What time is it?"

"One forty-three."

He sighs. God, how many times have I heard that sigh this week? So many that I know this isn't his annoyed sigh, or even the mildly irritated one, but an uncomfortable one.

"Okay, yeah. Fine. I think you're a chaotic kind of person. Not bad, not good, just straight-up chaotic. What I'm trying to say, is . . . You seem to have a lot going on. Which, you know, I didn't really mind when we matched on the app, because I was just looking for something casual, like I said. It just seemed like every day, there was a new batshit crazy thing you were stuck in the middle of. And I'm not being funny, but you did pretty much invite yourself over to my apartment in the middle of a global pandemic when you didn't even remember my name."

"When you put it like that . . . " I chew on my lower lip for a minute, then ask him, "Didn't you think they were funny, though?"

"Think what was funny?"

"My stories. Whatever batshit crazy thing I had going that day."

Nate shrugs one shoulder. It knocks against me. "Sure. I mean, yeah, you told a funny story, but mostly I just read the messages thinking, how the fuck does this much stuff happen to someone? I mean, you had an email threatening you and your housemates with bailiffs, then the next day you went to three different shops because you realized you had no toilet paper and you came back with a crate of wine instead. There was the neighborhood cat you left food out for, and then it got into the house and you couldn't get it to leave again . . . It just seemed like a lot of really wild stuff going on. I don't think I'd have believed it was all happening in real time if you hadn't sent pictures."

I blink at him. "You say that like that sort of thing's not normal."

"Do all your other friends do stuff like that?"

"Well, not . . . Like, not *exactly*, I guess. And for the record, I *did* buy toilet paper. Not just the wine."

"Good to know."

We both fall quiet, until Nate claps his hands softly to his thighs and says, "Vodka or tea?"

I don't remember the last time I turned down the offer of some vodka, but I give him a small smile. "Tea would be great. Thanks."

This time, when Nate gets back with two steaming mugs of tea, I'm hunched in the corner of the sofa, sticking my hands out of my self-made blanket burrito to take the mug off him; Nate doesn't even so much as *look* like he wants to admonish me for risking spilling tea on his lovely clean duvet.

He must be feeling sorry for me.

I'm used to people rolling their eyes at me, or being a little pissed off with me, and Lucy has *definitely* been disappointed in me more than once, but I don't remember the last time somebody felt *sorry* for me.

"You know," I mumble, "I think you managed to do in one day what my therapist has been trying to do for a year."

"Nobody ever called you chaotic before?"

"Not the way you did."

"Changing your whole perspective on yourself for a guy? And you called yourself a feminist in your bio."

He's teasing, though, so I cut him a mock glare.

"Should charge you for it," he muses, rubbing his chin melo-dramatically. "What do therapists charge these days?"

"One night of hot sex and the return of your Ramones T-shirt."

Nate laughs so hard he snorts, which makes me giggle, too, just a bit.

"So you, um, you see a therapist?"

"I thought loads of people did these days. I thought it was *hashtag-stylish*." I roll my eyes. "Of course I see a therapist. Like, half my friends do."

"Yeah, no, loads of mine do as well. Or did, at some point." Nate nods, slowly, thoughtfully, and I wait to see what he's going to ask me next. Probably wants to know *why* I see a therapist. Or what I think is so screwed up about me that makes my life so chaotic.

But what he says is, "It's not like it's easy, you know. This whole . . . *this*." He offers up a grand, and appropriately vague, sweeping ges-ture around the room. "I'm not saying some of my mates are even half as wild as you, but some of them seem to be . . . stuck too. And then some of them are off getting married and having babies and buying houses with south-facing gardens and it's like, way to show up the rest of us—but then they feel like they're the ones getting left behind when someone starts posting about their year traveling in Asia and volunteering to build schools in Africa."

"What?"

"What I *mean* is, everyone's just moving at different speeds. We all think we're on the same track and that we just missed the train, but the fact is, nobody's on the same track, and not everyone's even on a train."

I stare at him for a long moment, processing that, trying to get my head around it.

Maybe . . . Maybe he's got a *point*.

Lucy would be your average train, for sure. Maybe a nice one, with a fancy first-class carriage, and trolley service and nice comfy seats. And Nate, he'd be one of those boring seven-seater cars like all the dads used to drive when I was at school.

Which would make me, what? A hang glider? One of those duck buses that turn into a boat? A penny farthing?

Nate mistakes my silence for confusion. His face scrunches up and he grimaces, scratching his head.

"It sounded better coming from the vlogger I got it from. It sounded smart when he said it. But that's kind of my point, right? Or, his point, I guess, that I stole. What I'm trying to say is, just because you're not in the same place as other people, doesn't mean you have to make up for it by putting on this whole persona. When I said you were chaotic—"

"You meant it," I interrupt. "And I know what you were trying to say. I know. I get it from my friends all the time, but when they say it, it's like . . . expected? It's just, 'Oh, Imogen's off being Imogen again!' and we all get to laugh about it. You know my friend had to send me money so I could pay you back for some fucking underwear?"

Nate laughs, then seems to catch himself, like it's inappropriate.

"No, see, that's what I mean. Laugh away. I couldn't even afford *underwear*, Honeypot. I am stuck on lockdown in a total stranger's apartment, you're right, whose name I didn't even remember, totally broke, and this feels pretty average for me. Like, *that shouldn't be happening*, you know? I *am* chaotic."

"You're a goddamn hurricane," Nate tells me.

But he says it softly, almost reverently, and with a gentle smile that makes me blush and look away. A sniffle catches me off guard, and I blink away the tears that have suddenly filled my eyes. A couple break loose but before I can wriggle my other hand free from my blanket-burrito situation, Nate reaches over.

His palm cups my cheek, warm and gentle, his thumb brushing away the tear there.

I haven't made a secret of the fact that I think Nate's attractive or that I'd like to sleep with him again, but this feels different. This isn't getting tangled up in the bedsheets together, lips and hands everywhere. This feels *fragile*, and *raw*. I want to bury myself in his arms and kiss him and be held and have that be all it is.

I'm comfortable with guys. I'm comfortable with my body. I'm a tactile person and I hug all my friends. But the way Nate touches me now is so intimate without being romantic or sexual and it's so tender that I draw away, trying to process it. I think about the other night, when he kissed my cheek.

Being comfortable with guys and with sex is one thing, but this kind of intimacy feels completely foreign to me.

And God, I want it so badly. It's like not knowing how cold you are until you walk into a warm house, not realizing you were thirsty until there's a glass of water in front of you. I've always thought I was okay not doing the whole *serious relationship* thing but now, fuck, I'm *starved* for it.

Nate misunderstands why I've pulled away, though, because he clears his throat and changes the subject quickly.

"If you're broke," he says, "I mean, it's literally my job to manage projects in the finance world. I'm no stranger to a spreadsheet. I could, like . . . I mean, we've still got another day to go, right? Maybe we could take a look. See if you can get unbroke. Or, a little way there, at least. Work out budgets and payment plans to pay off your debts and stuff."

I gawp at him, my eyes filling with tears all over again.

And I suddenly feel so *stupid*, because maybe it could've been this easy all along. Maybe I could've just asked my parents or my friends to help me figure something out, instead of asking them to bail me out. Maybe if I'd just held up my hands and said, "I fucked up" every so often, instead of only ever making jokes about it.

My therapist has a lot to answer for if Nate can manage to turn my life around in a mere week.

"You'd do that for me? Even after I forgot your name?"

Nate laughs. "It'll cost you one Ramones T-shirt."

"You drive a hard bargain, Honeypot, but you've got yourself a deal."

And, to seal it, I lean over to kiss him.

He lifts a hand, though, pressing it to my shoulder, pushing me back gently, but firmly. His jaw clenches and he gulps, looking at me steadily. A smile ghosts across his lips.

"Immy . . . "

I can handle rejection. I'm a big girl.

But fuck, I'm emotional, and I *like* him, and I can't handle the rejection at all.

Too loudly, too brashly, I tell him, "If you're not attracted to me anymore because I'm a screwup or because you feel like you know me too well after spending a week together, it's okay. I get it. You can just *tell* me you're not interested. I can handle it."

Lies, lies, lies.

It's not like he wouldn't just come out and say it, either, because that's the kind of guy he is. Upfront. No-nonsense. But for some reason I feel the need to go on the offensive. The best kind of defense, right?

"That's not it."

I scoff.

"It's not," he insists. "Imogen, I—I really like you. That's the problem."

Oh, *great*, just when I thought it couldn't get worse.

"Ha, right. Yeah. Come on, Nate, you don't *like* me. You've just been stuck in this apartment with me for a week and I've been flirting with you all the time. And even if you did, the *problem* is, you don't *want* to like me. Because you're a serial monogamist and I'm not the kind of girl you want to take home to meet the family."

"What? No, that's—where did you . . . ?" Nate shakes his head, frowning, and then moves suddenly to grab my mug off me, placing both our drinks on the coffee table and then sitting with one knee tucked up on the sofa so that he's facing me. His expression is softer now, and he smiles. "Immy, believe me, I don't like you because I've had to put up with you for a week. I like you because you're . . . "

"Chaotic?"

"A hurricane," he says again. "You think I've turned your whole view of yourself upside down? What do you think you've been doing to me from the moment we matched? I like order and routine and structure and maybe that makes me boring—"

"It doesn't make you boring."

It does, a bit.

"But you make me want to *enjoy* it, even if it is boring, because it's my thing. You know?"

"I don't," I admit.

"You just really live your life—"

"Not very well, it seems."

"But you live it," Nate points out. "And it's yours. I think I forgot what that felt like, a little."

"Are you *sure* you didn't put some vodka in your tea?" I ask, scrutinizing his mug, but Nate laughs. He clasps my free hand, and with his other, strokes some of the hair back from my cheek.

"Imogen, I really like you. And not to sound either really cheesy or clingy as hell, but if things had been different and you hadn't bailed on me after one night, and we'd have gone on a few dates . . . If it counts for anything, I'd have been proud to have taken you home to meet my family."

I search his face, warmth spreading through my chest and my pulse racing wildly.

This time, it's *definitely* A Moment, and it's definitely happening for both of us. He looks a little nervous throughout his speech—vulnerable—the kind of thing that would normally put me off a guy. Now, with him, it's endearing. It's *everything*.

He's nervous it's A Moment only for him, the way I felt the other night.

But it's not, because he wants to date me, he wants to take me home to meet his family, and . . .

"Nate," I tell him softly, "I'd really like that."

This time, when I dive forward to kiss him, Nate meets me halfway, in a messy clash of lips and teeth and tongues, our hands grabbing at each other to pull the other closer, Nate eventually losing his balance enough to fall backward, pulling me down with him so we're lying on the sofa, breathless even from just a kiss. He cups my face in his hands, kissing my lips, my nose, my forehead, and I melt.

"Nate?"

"Yeah?"

"Kiss me again."

And oh, he does.

Chapter Thirty-one

I t's automatic, the way I check my phone before I'm even properly awake.

Wow, I think. *That's a lot of notifications.*

And then I think, *Shit, I overslept.*

Not that it *matters*, exactly, but I still groan and roll over, one arm flung out and falling through empty space, landing on Charlotte's side of the bed. Just one more night, I remind myself, one more night and then tomorrow she'll be home and life will go back to normal.

I yawn, stretching out and kicking the covers halfway down the bed, wriggling up against the pillows, and grabbing my phone again. I clear the notifications from my lock screen—I'll look through them properly on my computer later. It's not that unusual, I reason. My latest video will have gone up this morning, and all these comments and (I hope) new patrons on Patreon are a sign it's gone down well.

I've got a bunch of messages on WhatsApp, which does surprise me. One of the group chats must've kicked off this morning. I wonder who could have fucked up last night to cause so many messages.

I also, more worryingly, have a ton of missed calls from my best friend, Jack.

Grimacing, my stomach churning as I wonder what the hell is so wrong that he's *calling* me, I take my phone with me to the kitchen, putting the kettle on. I call him back as I reach for Charlotte's mug,

Beth Reekles

barely taking hold of it this time before I remember and let it go, just getting my own mug instead.

"Ethan, *finally*. I've been calling you for like an hour. Where the hell have you been?"

"Sleeping," I say, my voice thick and irritable, although I don't mean it to be. I knock my glasses out of the way to rub my eyes. "It's like, eleven o'clock. It's not *that* late."

It's pretty late, even by my freelancing schedule.

"Dude," Jack says, his voice so deadly serious it makes me feel cold. "What's going on? Is it your dad?"

Jack's dad had been in and out of hospital for the past six months with heart problems, and I'm not really sure a literal global pandemic is the low-stress environment they've been trying to maintain for him.

"Nah, it's not my dad," he says, "but we've got bigger problems. Or at least, you have. Have you checked your phone yet today?"

"Not really. Oh shit, please don't tell me I've, like, been canceled for my opinions on *Minecraft*."

"I think it's worse than that, mate. Just . . . go check your computer."

I forget about making myself a cup of tea and hurry to the living room, clicking the computer back to life. It pings with emails and more notifications, and I don't think I've *ever* seen that number on the YouTube bell so high.

I rack my brain, trying to think what in the hell is going on. I don't *think* I said anything that controversial in today's video or on the stream last night. I don't use Twitter enough for someone to have unearthed a tweet from me from, like, 2012, saying something rude.

Maybe I retweeted someone I didn't know was problematic?

Maybe I liked a video from someone who's been canceled?

I put Jack on speakerphone and put him next to the keyboard. My hands shake as I load my channel and I think I might throw up.

Immediately, I know something's wrong.

My subscriber count is up by seven thousand since last night.

So I'm not being canceled, but . . .

And then I see it.

Right there, in pride of place at the top of my channel, my most recent upload, posted right on schedule at nine o'clock this morning.

Dear Charlotte.

"Oh fuck," I whisper, loud enough that Jack hears it through the phone.

"Ethan?"

It's a miracle I can even click the video open, my hands are shaking that much. It's the thumbnail I made last night, the description for the video I'd planned. And then the video starts to play: me in yesterday's rumpled gray T-shirt and green flannel shirt, my hair a mess.

I hold out hope. Please, please, please, say I just named the file wrong because I had it on my mind, please, please . . .

But the me in the video says, "Dear Charlotte," and I see it's almost an hour long, and I die inside.

I hit pause and collapse over the desk. "*Fuuuuuuuuck.*"

"You saw it, huh?" Jack says. He's sympathetic, sorry, and he sighs. "Judging by the thumbnail and stuff, and the fact that you edited *none* of this, I'm guessing you really didn't mean to upload this. Which is what everyone else thinks, too, in the comments section. It's viral on Twitter, too, you know. There's a BuzzFeed article about it already and everything. You're going to be the new face of quarantine romance."

"This isn't happening," I groan. I keep my eyes squeezed shut and fist my hands tightly in my hair. "This is a fever dream, or I'm just still drunk. That's it, I'm drunk. I'm going to go back to bed, and when I wake up again, this won't be happening."

"I'm sorry, mate."

I moan. It turns into a weird noise that's part laugh, part sobbing.

"Is it too late to take it down?" I ask.

"You tell me. You're the expert. Take a look at that view count, Ethan."

Grudgingly, I peel my head up, cracking open one eye to take a look.

It's at half a million views. I cringe and refresh the page. Another forty-odd thousand gets added to the view count.

I want the world to swallow me whole.

My chest is tight and I'm on the verge of vomiting, and I'm sweating through my pajamas. I don't normally share a lot of my personal life on my channel, not to mention, this will totally mess with the rest of my feed, and, shit, and that's not even the worst part.

"You think she's seen it?" I croak.

Jack's hesitation is answer enough.

"Fuck," I say again. "I can't believe this. I can't believe I was so stupid. I was uploading it after the Twitch stream last night and . . . Oh my God. I hate myself so much. She's going to hate me. This is the worst."

"Since when were you planning on proposing, anyway? I thought you'd have told me something like that, mate. This isn't the cabin fever talking, is it? Like, you don't think this is just you going a little stir-crazy or anything?"

"Did you watch the video, Jack?"

"I watched the highlights reel on LadBible. It was you talking about how head over heels in love with your girlfriend you are, for *an hour*—so, no, I didn't watch it all."

"I love her. I want to spend the rest of my life with her."

"Good luck telling her that after you told the rest of the world first."

I cringe. "I've gotta call her, haven't I?"

"Yes, you do, mate. Let me know how it goes, okay?"

I groan in pure, utter despair, and Jack laughs before hanging up on me. Staring into space a few seconds longer, I know there is *no* pulling this back now, and how humiliating it all is, before snatching up my phone again and calling Charlotte.

It goes straight to voicemail.

I call her again.

And again.

After the eleventh time, I call Maisie.

The first time, it rings out, but the second time, she answers.

I barely even say "Hi" before I'm subjected to her laughing down the phone at me for eight minutes straight, quoting the worst bits of my video back at me before bursting into giggles again.

"I mean," she wheezes, "you actually *said* you wanted to marry her because of that time you both got the flu and she threw up on you. Do you know how goddamn weird that is, Ethan?"

"I didn't mean it like *that*."

"Dude, the whole *world* knows what you meant. You love her even having been around her in that kind of state. It's just a weird goddamn thing to say when you're trying to propose, you know? Like, you really . . . you really thought . . . "

She's laughing too hard again for me to get a straight sentence out of her.

"Maisie," I say, kneading my forehead with my knuckles, really glad I didn't FaceTime her to have to *see* her laughing at me like this. Somehow, the concept of hundreds of thousands of total strangers having seen the whole video is less painful than this. "Where is she? She's not answering her phone."

Maisie takes a few gasping breaths, finally clearing her throat and telling me in a haughty voice, "She said she needed some time to think. She's gone out."

"Out? Out where? Practically everywhere is shut."

"Just out. Look, Ethan, I'm sure you'll hear from her later, okay? It'll be all right."

"Yeah, I'll believe that when you stop laughing at me."

She just laughs at me all over again.

Chapter Thirty-two

While I'm having a rare lazy morning snuggling with Danny in bed, Maisie sends me the video before I see it for myself online somewhere. I recognize her sister's boyfriend in the video. Like Serena, he's a neighbor I follow on Instagram and smile and say hello to when I pass him in the hallway, but we're not especially close. I'm not even really that close with Maisie's sister, Charlotte, having only met her in person a couple of times.

I was vaguely aware that the boyfriend, Ethan, was a vlogger. I didn't know he was kind of a successful one. And I definitely didn't know he was going viral this morning until Maisie sent me the video.

I watch it avidly, cringeworthy as it is. Danny watches it with me too.

"That poor boy," I murmur, as he sighs and stammers at the screen, frowning to himself as he tries to figure out how to word his sentence about why he loves Charlotte in spite of her flaws, without sounding like he's insulting her. "He must be absolutely mortified."

"I dunno," Danny says. "Probably a publicity stunt."

I scoff. "Please. Who would embarrass themselves this much for a few extra followers?"

Danny chuckles, nuzzling his nose against my cheek and saying, "What, you're telling me you wouldn't be totally charmed if you received a proposal video like this?"

"I absolutely would not," I tell him. "The last thing I want is a public proposal."

Discussing how you want to be proposed to is probably not the sort of thing you do when you've only been dating for a month, but what really strikes me as weird is that it *doesn't* feel weird; and Danny obviously doesn't think so, either, because he doesn't try to change the subject.

"But how will you post about it on your Instagram?" he teases.

"Hopefully my future fiancé will know me well enough that he'll set up a camera to film this very sweet, very intimate moment between just the two of us, so I can share it with people later on."

Danny laughs. "So no marching band and skywriter in front of the Eiffel Tower. Got it."

"Is that really what you'd want to do?" I ask him. My nose scrunches up before I can stop it.

But his lips curve into a smile against my skin and he kisses my cheek before saying, "No. I think you're right. It should just be for the two of you. The wedding is when you share it with everybody else, but that proposal? That should be all about us. Or—or not—not, like—not *us*, like, like you and me, specifically, or—well, not *not* us, either, but . . . "

Danny is solid and charming and confident, so it is unbearably endearing when he gets flustered like this. It happens so rarely. Before this week, I'd only seen him like it once, and that was when he ran into an ex on one of our dates.

I laugh, nudging him with my shoulder. "It's okay. You can stop now."

Relieved, he lets out a long sigh and shuts up before he says something more embarrassing than Ethan in his *Dear Charlotte* video.

Chapter Thirty-three

I turn off all my notifications, except for calls. When Charlotte's ready to talk to me, she'll call. Probably when she gets home and finds out I haven't even taken the video down yet.

(I will, but right now I can't even bring myself to open the page back up long enough to delete it.)

In the meantime, I bury myself in my old university hoodie, the hood up and the strings pulled tight around my face, lying face-down on the sofa and slowly dying of the mortification. What does it even *matter* if I take the video down now? There are tweets about it. Snippets that have been reposted online. A damn *BuzzFeed article*. Everyone we know will have circulated it and I dread the next event we go to with mutual friends who will all be talking about it, and none of them are ever going to let me live it down.

Oh man, and how unprofessional is it? It's so *obviously* a mistake, so stupid. What if this costs me brand deals in the future? What if I end up having to go back to a nine-to-five, and *this* is the first thing they see when they google me? It's a disaster.

This could ruin my *life*. Not to mention it's most definitely ruined the proposal.

It was supposed to be *perfect*.

I was going to figure it all out, but now . . .

Oh, what's even the point?

My life is over and I'm locked in the apartment. I decide I can cut myself some slack; it's really not like there's much I can do right now *other* than wallow. Later, I'll pick myself up, delete the video, upload a new one explaining it was a mistake. I'll talk to Charlotte when she's ready, and hope she's not so humiliated she forgives me quickly, and once we've talked it through, I'll call my family back, or finally reply to their texts. And maybe, then, I'll stay away from the internet for a little while.

But right now, I groan into the sofa cushions again, and embrace the tightness in my chest, the sweating palms, the overwhelming sense of mortification that squirms through my whole body, and indulge in a pity party for one.

It's a while before I hear something outside. It sounds like someone yelling, and someone else shouting back at *them* to shut up.

I don't pay it much attention, until I hear them shout, unmistakably, "Mad Man Maddox, get your cute butt out here!"

No.

No.

Oh my God.

Chapter Thirty-four

I am absolutely, completely exhausted.

I study my reflection in the bathroom mirror. I look worse for wear for a lack of sleep, like I did on Wednesday morning. The bags under my eyes are even deeper, now, something I didn't think was possible. My eyes are bloodshot and puffy too—although this time it's from crying. I prod and poke at my face a few times, like I can turn it back to normal that way, before giving up and climbing into the shower.

I lean into the embrace of the hot water and steam, and let out a sigh I feel like I've been holding in for . . . not even just for a few days. For years, without even realizing it.

Zach and I spent all evening talking things through. We only argued a *few* times, and only shouted at each other once or twice. We kept talking well into the night. It must have been four in the morning before we fell asleep, both of us so tired we slept on top of the covers on the bed, side by side, and not even having changed into our pajamas.

I woke up this morning with his arm around me and my cheek pressed against his chest, and it made me want to cry, because I didn't know if we would ever really be back to normal again.

I guess, to be fair to Zach, my explosion on Wednesday morning *did* come out of nowhere. But he didn't argue with the fact that he *should* have his own opinions on what he wanted our future to look like, and that it was fair for me to expect that from him.

As it turns out, though, that's not the kind of thing you can figure out with a single late-night conversation. And it turns out that even now we've cleared the air and started talking, we're still pretty snappy with each other. Like we've been like that with each other for so long, it's a habit we can't suddenly break now. I'm not sure we ever truly will.

I did pluck up the courage to ask if he felt like he was settling.

And he *did* cry then, promising me that he always felt lucky to have me, and he was sorry if he made me feel like he *was* settling.

I was a big enough person to apologize and say I was sorry if I ever made him feel that way too.

We still have so much to work out—and Zach has a lot of decisions to make, some of which I'm not sure he ever really *will* have a strong opinion on—but, at least, I suppose, we're out the other side.

For better or worse. In sickness and in health.

Until lockdown lifts, do we part.

I sigh again and lean forward, pressing my forehead to the cool shower tiles. We still have to talk about what we'll do once we're allowed out of the building tomorrow. I feel like that's another painful conversation just waiting to happen.

Part of me regrets ever bringing any of this up at all. For not thinking, *Screw it, let the boy have pineapple on his pizza and forget about it*. Part of me wishes I were more like Zach, able to just not consider these things until . . . well, *until*.

And part of me wishes we'd done this a long, long time ago.

Either way, it's done now, and we've both said things we can never take back, and we both have to find a way to muddle through this somehow, whatever that means.

The thought of losing him, of him moving out, or maybe us selling the apartment and me having to move back home to my parents or, even worse, suddenly find myself living *alone*, is terrifying. The idea of Zach not being there, making me laugh, never surprising me with some random weekend away or spontaneous plans for a date night.

The idea that he might just vanish from my life completely, and that deep down I might *want* him to do that, is so overwhelming, that I start crying again.

I've composed myself by the time I'm out of the shower. My face is still puffy, and I still look run-down, but I feel better, at least. I wrap my towel around myself and am reaching for my moisturizer when the door flies open.

"Rena," Zach says, breathless, his blue eyes wide and bright. "Rena, you have *got* to come and see this."

Chapter Thirty-five

I lurch off the sofa so fast that I fall on my face, smacking my head on the floor and crying out. *That's gonna bruise.*

I half scramble, half crawl toward the balcony doors, throwing myself at them and dragging them open, falling against the railing and knocking one of Charlotte's spider plants off. There's a high-pitched yelp and the pot smashes on the ground. I don't even stop to worry about it, though; I'm too busy leaning over and blinking in shock.

I can't believe my eyes.

I mean, really. I actually take off my glasses and wipe them on my hoodie, jamming them back onto my face so frantically I only succeed in getting new finger smudges on them.

"Is it really you?" I shout down, still not believing it. This whole day has been like some warped fever dream—why shouldn't this be too?

Charlotte beams up at me and I've never been so glad we only live one floor up. She's far enough down that I can't see the hazel specks glittering in her eyes, but I can see her freckles. Her hair is wavy, not quite as tame as normal, pushed back from her face by her giant sunglasses. She's wearing a plain gray dress that must be Maisie's, because I don't recognize it, and her denim jacket. She's wearing her favorite ankle boots, with the small block heels.

"It's me!" she hollers, bouncing up on her toes. She braces one hand against her sunglasses and uses the other to wave up at me.

"What are you doing here?"

"I saw your video! Did you mean it, Ethan? Did you really mean all those things you said?"

I don't even hesitate to think about it before I open my mouth to reply.

Someone else interrupts before I finish getting the first syllable out, though, shouting from the main entrance, "Missy, I'm not going to tell you again. You can't be here if it's not essential."

"This *is* essential, you miserable bum!" Charlotte snaps back at him, and then grimaces. "Sorry, Mr. Harris, I didn't mean to call you a bum, or miserable. I promise I'll go in a minute, I know I can't stay . . . "

Chapter Thirty-six

Zach grabs me by the hand; I clutch my towel to me with the other and stumble after him, running to keep up as he drags me out onto the balcony with him. There are people shouting, but it's not because I've just come outside in my towel with my hair dripping wet.

Down below there's a ginger girl standing outside the building. I think she lives here. I'm sure I've seen her around before.

How did she get outside?

"What's going on?" I ask Zach.

"Remember that video we saw this morning?" he pants. "The one Matty saw and sent in the group chat?"

"That cringe-y proposal video?"

"Yeah," Zach says. "Ethan. I guess he must live downstairs, because that's his girlfriend."

"Wait—*that's* Dear Charlotte?"

We only skimmed through the video. It was blowing up online, so we couldn't *not* watch it a bit, but it was . . . well, safe to say, it was a bit weird to watch such a long, rambling proposal when Zach and I were on the verge of maybe breaking up.

"That's Dear Charlotte," he tells me, in pure, utter delight, and I whisper, "Oh my God," and we lean over the balcony together to watch.

Charlotte is yelling up, "Did you mean it? All those things you said in your video? Is that really how you feel about me?"

It's *definitely* weird to have what might just be one of the most beautiful, strangest proposals happening just a few stories below us when Zach and I are still trying to work out if we actually want to get married and want the same things from our life, but right there, in that moment, it doesn't matter.

All I know is that this is exactly the sort of thing I will miss sharing with him.

Chapter Thirty-seven

The sun is shining, the birds are singing, and I do not want to be anywhere else.

I snuggle against the pillows and sheets, wriggling a little closer into Nate's body. His skin is smooth and warm. I hook one leg over his, my foot skimming up and down his shin.

Nate, however, seems much more interested in the spreadsheet open on his laptop screen, where he has been working out a budget for me for the last half hour. I know I thought he was a stick in the mud, but I'm in no position to question his dedication to completing a project now that he's helping me out.

"How much did you say you spend each month on nights out?"

"Maybe like five hundred pounds?"

He whistles, long and low.

"What? I don't think that's so bad. Few rounds of drinks at the pub, few cocktails at a bar . . . If I go for a meal with anybody . . . Plus taxis there and back, sometimes. Entry fees at a club, sometimes. There's usually a bachelorette party or something for somebody too. Bachelorettes are *expensive*."

"Wedding season," he says, with sympathy, nodding. "I had that start last year. You know I spent, like, two grand just on presents and hotels and stuff?"

"The trick is to not book the hotel, and then have someone take

pity on you at the end of the night and let you kip on their floor.
Saves you *a lot* of money, believe me."

"Don't people get pissed off with you?"

"Not if you buy them enough drinks. Which is still cheaper than
the cost of a bed-and-breakfast in whatever rural village they've
decided to get married in."

Nate laughs. "Okay. Five hundred pounds. Any chance you could
make that more like two hundred?"

I almost have a heart attack at the prospect of all those nights I'd
have to cut short, or even miss out on entirely.

But, I guess, I would like to pay off my overdraft. And maybe my
credit cards.

"Fine," I tell him, "but only because you're so dang cute, Honeypot."

I reach up to cup his cheek in my hand, his stubble tickling my
palm, and I wriggle up the bed so I'm close enough to be able to kiss
him. I notice his lips start to curve up into a smile before my eyes
slide shut, and my heart does a little skip when he sucks lightly on
my bottom lip and deepens the kiss.

We're still kissing when there's some commotion outside, a girl
yelling, "Mad Man Maddox, get your cute butt out here!"

I don't realize what the noise is all about at first, but Nate pulls away
from me and sits bolt upright, recognizing the name immediately—
and I guess, the voice too.

"Oh my God," he tells me, eyes blown wide. "That's Charlotte."

"Wait—wait, Charlotte like from the video?"

He nods, scrambling out of the bed to peer out of the window,
trying to see. Earlier this morning he'd been browsing YouTube on
his iPad when I woke up, watching a video from some guy he follows
called Ethan. It was a really dorky, really sweet proposal to his girlfriend. I'm not totally sure he meant to upload it. When I'd opened
my own phone my friend Jaz had shared it in the group chat. It was
basically viral.

"Hang on," I bark at Nate. "You're telling me that vlogger *lives* in your *building*?"

"Yeah," he says, still peering out of the window, not getting the big deal. "Ethan. He's the guy I went to borrow clothes from, for you, on Monday."

"YOU'RE TELLING ME I BORROWED CHARLOTTE OF DEAR CHARLOTTE'S LEGGINGS?" I shriek, my voice about three octaves higher than normal.

He winces, and there's more shouting outside. A guy has joined in now. Ethan, I'm guessing.

And, oh my God, he's *here*, and *she's* here, and there is a viral moment happening right outside, right now, and I have to know if she says yes.

I fall over myself grabbing my underwear from by the bedroom door. The Ramones shirt is in the laundry basket but it's either that or the duvet right now, so I grab it and wrestle my arms through, bumping into the wall as I run out of the bedroom and throw open the balcony doors.

I lean over and there's a guy hanging over the railing of the balcony directly below Nate's apartment, and a girl standing beneath that. I was picturing someone blond and glamorous and tall and curvy, with a full face of makeup. I was picturing a literal celebrity, I realize now. But Charlotte is just . . . normal. She's plump and has a wavy ginger mane of chin-length hair and is currently yelling at Walter White, the caretaker who is not a serial killer. We think.

(Although, actually thinking about it, he probably does have enough cleaning products to dissolve a body in his bathtub if he wanted to.)

Nate joins me on the balcony, wearing a burgundy dressing gown. His arm wraps around my waist, hand curling around the railing on my other side. It's oddly intimate, but I kind of like it.

"This *is* essential, you miserable bum!" Charlotte is yelling at my buddy Walt, but it's promptly followed by, "Sorry, Mr. Harris, I didn't mean to call you a bum, or miserable. I promise I'll go in a minute, I know I can't stay."

Someone from an apartment above yells down, "What's going on? What's the shouting?"

Charlotte cups her hands around her mouth, craning her head back to shout a few floors farther up, "Do you mind? My boyfriend kind of just proposed to me online and I'm locked out of the building!"

Oh my God, she's talking to us. We're a live audience and *this is not a show*, and I forget any sense of public decency or decorum I might have otherwise had to scream down, "Oh my God, it's Dear Charlotte! Dear Charlotte, I've been wearing your clothes! You're famous!"

She laughs at that, and other apartments start pitching in, too, shouting down. Nate chuckles near my ear and says quietly, "Oh man. Ethan's going to be dying of embarrassment right now."

I don't get why, if he's the kind of guy with a decent following online he seems to be, but I take Nate's word for it. I give him a quick kiss before turning to watch the show unfold, and Nate tucks me a little tighter into his body, chin tucking over my shoulder as he watches too.

APARTMENT #22 – OLIVIA

Chapter Thirty-eight

*D*uties as maid of honor include but are not exclusive to: being
invested in any and all wedding-related matters; a knowledge
of princess-cut rings and what is an appropriate amount to spend on
them; current trends in the wedding industry, such as which song to
walk down the aisle to that is current but not too overdone.

I'm not sure a viral YouTube video exactly counts as a proposal
trend, but no offense to Kim, her engagement was *definitely* not as
good a story as vlogger Ethan Maddox and his mystery girlfriend,
Charlotte.

Addison saw it online this morning and made us all watch the
entire thing after breakfast. She squished herself between me and
Kim on the sofa, and I wasn't sure if she was trying to snuggle into
me or if she was just trying to get comfortable.

Kim gave me *a look*, but I still wasn't entirely convinced. Maybe
she's just a tactile kind of person, I thought.

I still wonder if I'm reading too much into it now that we're sat on
the balcony, and she's laughing that honking, loud laugh of hers at
something I just said about work, even though it really wasn't that
funny. She reaches over, her fingers brushing against my arm.

"Oh my God," she says, pretending to wipe a tear away. She grins
at me, but there's something . . . if I'm not wrong, there's something
coy about it. And I swear to *God*, she flutters her eyelashes. "Where
has Kim been hiding you all this time?"

I mumble, blushing.

It's not as though I'm a useless flirt, but something about Addison feels . . . different.

Charged.

I'm snapped out of it by shouting from somewhere down below. I get to my feet and lean over the balcony, Addison following suit. From five stories up it's hard to see much more than a redhead standing outside the building.

"Look," Addison points to one side. "Isn't that the caretaker?"

As if it could be anybody else in that luminous yellow hazmat suit.

"What's going on?" she wonders aloud, just as some guy a couple of floors below yells down to ask the same thing.

I can't quite make out the ginger girl's reply, but then another voice is added to the mix: some brunette hanging off the balcony just above her who shouts, "Oh my God, it's Dear Charlotte! Dear Charlotte, I've been wearing your clothes! You're famous!"

Loathe as I am to bring up any wedding-related conversation after Kim has finally stopped being a bridezilla and returned to being an actual human, I am left with, quite honestly, no choice.

I cannot, *cannot*, let this go unnoticed.

"Oh my God," I say, grabbing Addison's hand on the balcony and squeezing it tight. "It's her! It's Charlotte, from the video!"

"Shut the fuck up," Addison tells me, leaning farther out, her mouth agape.

I let out a high-pitched squeal before I can stop myself and shriek, "No way! Kim, Luce, get out here, it's the couple from that video!"

"And bring the rose petals!" Addison barks at them. She wraps her hands around my arm, leaning in close and tucking her chin over my shoulder as the girls hurry out to join us.

Maybe it's not a good idea to drag Kim into some kind of wedding drama, but if there is one thing I have learned in my time as maid of honor, it's that *nothing* is more important than celebrating romance.

And this viral-video-turned-real-life proposal is, quite probably, with no offense to Jeremy and Kim, the most romantic thing any of us will ever witness.

Chapter Thirty-nine

"Oh my God," Danny murmurs. "Isla! Isla, are you seeing this?"

He springs up from my favorite rattan chair to lean over the balcony, both hands clapped over his mouth, his eyes shining, utterly enchanted—despite his cynicism that it was all some publicity stunt.

I'm already up and videoing, zooming in and focusing the camera on Maisie's slightly shorter, slightly chubbier twin, Charlotte. I can't see their balcony or Ethan from here, but I can hear him calling back to her, "Is it really you?"

It's London Lane's own personal rom-com, I think, unfolding right before our eyes.

And as embarrassing as this probably is for Ethan, it *is* very sweet.

She's yelling at Mr. Harris when Zach calls down, "What's going on? What's the shouting?"

Charlotte asks him politely to shut the hell up, but someone else from an apartment downstairs is shouting down—something about how she's wearing Charlotte's clothes—and another girl upstairs calls for people to come and join her.

I see Zach lean far out over the balcony, his body twisted so he's looking up toward the top of the building. He cups his hands around his mouth to shout, "Shut up! Let them talk!"

And since everybody else is participating, I can't help myself either. I shove the phone into Danny's hands, jumping up and down and waving my arms wildly, while Charlotte's attention is directed up at all of us instead of at her boyfriend.

"Charlotte!" I cry. "Charlotte, it's me! Hi! Maisie told me you were on your way. I'm recording it all!"

She's smiling so wide, and her face is flushed, and she's not even really gotten to talk to Ethan about his weird, awkward, online proposal yet. She looks like she's on cloud nine.

I glance at Danny, expecting to find him still focused on the scene below, but instead he's looking at me, beaming, eyes creased around the corners.

And I know, I just *know*, that in that instant, he's thinking exactly the same thing as me. Momentarily, he's oblivious to the scene playing out below us, with only one thing on his mind.

I love you.

There's more commotion below, though, and we tear our eyes away from each other. Let Charlotte and Ethan have their moment, I think, stealing another glance at Danny. I can tell him later.

Chapter Forty

My face is burning, and I'm glad I can't see anybody else on the other balconies right now. Charlotte's face is pink and flushed, too, but she's got this great big, goofy grin on her face and giggles when she looks back at me.

She's waiting for an answer.

"I forgot what you said," I admit.

"Did you mean it?" she repeats herself. "All those things you said in your video? Is that really how you feel about me?"

I don't remember most of what I said in the video, to be quite honest, but I *do* know I meant every word. So I yell back down to her, "Yes! All of it!"

"Then yes!" she shouts up to me, jumping again.

"Yes what?"

"Yes, I'll marry you, you moron! I love you!"

"I love you too!" I shout, but I'm not even sure she can hear me over the chorus of cheers and excitable shrieks that erupt from all the other balconies on this side of the building. A cascade of rose petals flutter down from one of the apartments above. A couple of them land in Charlotte's hair and she giggles at them, blowing a kiss to whoever threw them and then looking at me with a smile so big, so goddamn ecstatic, it melts my heart.

She said yes.

She—said—*yes*.

Sunday

Chapter Forty-one

It's already light out. It's early but already bright, sunlight pouring through those rubbish venetian blinds and encasing the room in a hazy glow. Birds are singing. I hear a few cars pass by, and the steady, heavy breathing of Nate beside me. There's a cold foot against mine, and an arm tucked under my neck, wrapped around me. The mattress creaks as I shift, stretching and yawning.

I knock him in the arm with my elbow when I try to lift my arms, and Nate grumbles in his sleep, rolling onto his back. He scrubs the back of a hand over his mouth while I rub the sleep out of my eyes.

"Sorry," I whisper, my voice thick with sleep.

He doesn't answer, though, because he's still fast asleep. I consider waking him up but as soon as my hand reaches across the bed to shake him, I stop myself.

It's Sunday.

It's Sunday and the lockdown is over and *we can go outside* and— and I can go home.

I draw my hand back toward me. No, I think. I'm not going to wake him up.

My bare feet make almost no noise when they touch the floor, and I ease myself gradually off the bed. Nate is still flat out, and I'm as quiet as I can be as I collect up my things. My newly purchased ASOS order is bundled in one of Nate's dresser drawers and I open it slowly, quietly, to get my things. I pull on a pair of the yoga pants, find my bra on the floor by the wardrobe, and wriggle into one of the T-shirts.

Nate had seemed like a great prospect for a one-night stand. He'd been easy to talk to, could take a joke, but he was still a pretty sensible-sounding guy. And both of us had been upfront: we weren't looking for a relationship.

Don't get me wrong, I love guys.

But that's sort of the point. Why tie myself down to just one of them?

I don't know when this went from being trapped in the apartment of my one-night stand and casual sex to actually *liking* the guy, but . . .

It's kind of nice.

Extra nice that he's been trying to help me and not be too judgemental about the haphazard (read: somewhat-shitty) state of my life since yesterday, doing things like helping me make a budget and setting up a standing order to pay off a little on my credit cards each month, and helping me write an email to the landlord about some of the things in my house share he should be fixing for us—all the things I told him I'd been putting off, because it was intimidating and I didn't even know where to start.

Extra *extra* nice that we had sex again after our talk on Friday night, and a few times since, and that it's really *good* sex.

Not so nice that he's very adamant I am not allowed to keep his Ramones T-shirt as I've become particularly attached to it this week. We've been using it as a kind of bartering tool. Our own personal in-joke.

"You can have the shirt if you cook dinner and do the washing up afterward."

"I'll give you the Ramones top if you clean the bathroom and let me do the living room instead."

I'm still not *totally* sure when the cuddling had become such a thing, though. I'm not usually a cuddler. Mostly, really, because I was always too busy getting up and sneaking out of the guy's place, or getting up to get dressed so he knew he had to leave.

It was never like there was any point in *pretending*. I wanted to spend the *night* with the guy—whoever he was—not a morning in bed pretending we were a couple, and this was what we did. I had places to go, people to see. Sometimes, I just had to get to work. I didn't want to waste my time like that—and neither did he, not really.

Apparently, though, I am a cuddler. At least when it comes to Nate.

Now that Sunday is here, I'm . . . pretty disappointed, actually, that my one-night stand is finally at an end. I'm disappointed that I'll have to go home, and that my time with Nate is up.

But, you know. All good things must come to an end, and all that jazz.

Where's my coat? I haven't needed it all week . . . Oh! Right, it's on the hook in the hallway. And my bag . . . Shit, where *did* I put my bag? I was packing it up yesterday afternoon, collecting my crap from where I'd strewn it around Nate's apartment, and then . . . Ooh! Yes, got it. I left it next to the sofa.

Okay, phone, keys, purse . . . Check, check, check.

I pull on my coat, grab my bag, and slip out of the front door. It clicks shut behind me.

The hallways are silent. I guess nobody else is awake yet. I mean, they can't be; if they were, wouldn't they all be clamoring to get out, just to see something other than the four walls of their apartment for a change? I know I'm desperate for that.

I half expect to find the caretaker downstairs standing guard, the doors chained shut, laughing at me for thinking I might finally be free. The doors are right there. Just waiting for me . . .

I'm right in front of them.

"Going somewhere?"

I jump, feeling like I've just been caught doing something genuinely, properly wrong, and cringe, turning slowly. "Heeeeeeeey, Walter White. How's it going?"

He's still wearing his mask and gloves, which I think doesn't bode very well, but then the bit of his face I *can* see crinkles in what has got to be a smile, and he laughs. Look at that—he's capable of human emotion after all.

"Saw you sneaking down the stairs on the security cameras. Should've guessed if anyone was going to be first out, it'd be you."

He unhooks the giant ring of keys from his belt and waves for me to back up. When I realize he's unlocking the doors, I start singing that "Pomp and Circumstance" tune, the graduation-type one, and I stand as straight as I can to salute him the whole time.

"If I'd known we were doing an unlocking ceremony, I'd have worn my glad rags," I tell him. Walt takes his key out, retreating down the hallway to a "safe distance" so I can leave. I look back at him with a grin. "Next time, maybe?"

His smile vanishes. "Please, God, no."

Whoa, *and* he has a sense of humor. Who knew?

"Go on," he says, waving me off and heading back to his own apartment on the ground floor. "Get out of here, Ramones."

I press a palm to one of the doors, holding my breath, and it gives way.

Oh, sweet, sweet, freedom. Hello, world. Good-bye, building. Halle-fricking-lujah.

I push the door open the rest of the way, and teeter outside in my heels, bag swinging from my arm, and take a deep breath.

*

I knock on the door. There's a minute or so before it opens, but I can hear movement on the other side.

When it opens, Nate looks pissed off.

"Ooh," I say, grinning, "looks like someone *is* a grouch in the mornings, after all. Just as well I brought breakfast then, huh?"

I hold up the Starbucks cups and the brown paper bag of McDonald's breakfast, grinning at him.

The scowl on Nate's face vanishes, relief taking over instead, and he laughs, stepping back to let me inside. "Jesus, Immy, I thought you'd pulled your escape act again. Just leaving without a good-bye."

I guess I can't blame him for jumping to that conclusion.

Feigning offense, I gasp, "*Me*? Now, really, Honeypot, would *I* do a thing like that?"

Nate pulls me toward him, kissing me softly, and takes the drinks and breakfast from me so I can get rid of my shoes and coat and dump my bag. We eat on the balcony, talking quietly as the rest of the world starts to wake up, coming to life around us. A plane goes by overhead. People leave the building below us, walking along the paths; some have their car keys in hand, others walk off the little complex and in the direction of the shops. An elderly man goes and sits on a bench in the common area, his face tilted toward the sky, eyes closed. Another guy comes to join him after a while, coming from the next block of apartments over.

After we're finished eating and our coffee cups are empty, a sense of finality settles on my shoulders.

It's Sunday. And it's time I went home.

I say as much, and Nate nods, following me into the apartment while I collect up my things again.

He stops me after I put my coat on to kiss me again, and why, *why* does he have to be so good at kissing? Why does he have to make my insides melt like that, and make my heart race this way? Why does he have to do that thing where he kisses me right at the corner of my mouth like he's teasing me before really *kissing* me, in a way that makes my brain stop working? It's not fair.

It was good for one night, but for a week? It's just uncalled for. Because now I'm hooked, and he's making it harder to remember why I should leave.

He's wearing the Ramones top, as if to make a point. I run my hands over it, over his chest, and narrow my eyes at him. "You know, that looks *much* better on me."

"Next time, maybe. We can draw up a rota."

"Oh-ho, *next* time? You sound awfully sure of yourself there, mister."

He blushes.

Fuck, even that's cute.

How *dare* he.

"Just, you know," he says. "I thought, maybe, when this all blows over, maybe we could . . . "

"Do this again?"

"Maybe I'll even take you out to dinner first," he says, lifting his chin, his eyes sparkling, even though he's still blushing.

"Gosh, I'm swooning."

"It was just—we don't have to."

I pat his arm, stepping back. "It was good knowing you, Norman, and I liked our little chat in the middle of the night on Friday night, but now I'm free, this whole *Beauty and the Beast* fantasy is over, and I'm going to head back to my quaint little village and forget all about you."

Nate laughs, understanding my humor well enough after being stuck with me for a whole week to know I don't mean a word of it.

"I'll call you when I get home," I suggest. "I know you'll be missing me already by then. You won't remember how you ever lived without me in your life."

"Oh, I believe that," he says softly.

I let him walk me to the door. I put my shoes on. There's another note under the door, this time reminding residents of the building that the lockdown has been lifted and while they continue to urge caution, we are now able to go outside again.

Hallelujah.

My stomach twists again. Even Nate looks sad to see me go, even though I barged into his life, pretty uninvited, messing up his apartment and getting in the way of his life all week.

I lean forward to kiss his cheek. "See ya round, Honeypot."

*

I'm halfway down the path to leave, when I hear a familiar voice.

Oh boy, I think, here we go. The jig is officially up.

I glance around to spot Lucy saying good-bye to some girl. She starts off around the side of the building, not having noticed me at all.

I *could* have got away with this, scot-free, without her being any the wiser.

But, I think, squaring my shoulders and sticking out my chin, I *am* trying to turn over a bit of a new leaf, here. And I obviously want to tell her all about my week, so it's not like she won't ever find out.

Plus, I could really do with a ride home.

You know, since I'm trying to actually actively *budget* my Ubers now.

I run after her (well, as best as I can in my heels). A pair of underwear flies out of my handbag and I have to turn back to snatch them up.

"Oi! Lucy Kingsley!" I holler, and she jumps, turning around, head twisting side to side before she notices me.

"Oh my God," she says, eyes bugging.

"You absolute *bitch*," I declare, none too quietly, as I stride toward her. "How *dare* you not tell me where you've been all week. How *dare* you be in the same goddamn building as me, and not even mention it."

She laughs, hugging me back when I engulf her in my arms.

"I don't believe it," she says. "What the hell are you *doing* here? Did you come to welcome me back to the real world?" And then something dawns on her, and her face turns serious; her mouth falls open, and her eyes narrow at me. "Hang on. Hang on, why are you all dressed up? Oh my *God*, Immy. Don't tell me. Don't even tell me."

"Honeypot kind of lives here," I admit. "And I kind of thought I shouldn't tell you because you'd only—"

"I'd only worry," she finishes with a terse sigh, but she quickly laughs. Lucy rolls her eyes. "Tell me what kind of best friend I'd be if I didn't worry that you had to shack up with a random one-night stand for a whole week. He could be anybody! He could have been a serial killer!"

"Speaking of, that caretaker . . . "

"So weird, right? Did you see his hazmat suit?"

"Yes! He looked like—"

"Like Walter White!" she finishes, and we both burst into giggles. Lucy's grin fades slightly and she sighs at me again. "Honestly, Immy. What are you like? I can't believe you hid this from me all week. I have to know *everything*. Especially why you're sporting a big old hickey, right here."

She jabs at a spot on my throat where Nate left a love bite on Saturday, and I'm a bit mortified to find I'm blushing, and it's not like I get embarrassed easily. Lucy's eyes light up immediately, and she gasps, clapping both hands to her face.

"You *like* him!" she accuses.

I don't deny it, and she squeals.

"I need to know absolutely everything. I don't remember the last time I saw you going all goo-goo eyed over a boy. I cannot *believe* you've been here all week! Bloody hell. Where have you been all this time?"

"Number Fourteen," I say.

Lucy shakes her head. "Of all the gin joints . . . " She takes a look at my bag, overflowing with scrunched-up clothes, and my shoes. "You're not walking home, are you?"

I shrug with a faux-forlorn look at the main road, already knowing she's going to offer to drive me home now I've run into her. "I was going to see if the buses are still running."

Lucy huffs at me, turning away and striding toward her car. "Get in, Immy. I'll drive you home."

"Have I mentioned lately how much I *love* you?"

"You can keep saying it, but you still owe me money."

"But I do. I love you *so much*."

Lucy just laughs, and once we're in her car we barely stop to catch our breath as we spill every detail of the last week at each other.

My phone buzzes on my lap when we're halfway back to my place. Lucy glances at it. "Who's that?"

And right there on the screen, in the text notification that's just appeared, is the honeypot emoji, followed by the words:

You were right—I'm missing you already x

Chapter Forty-two

It's automatic, the way I roll over, my arm reaching out for Charlotte. I jolt awake, remembering, and snatch up my phone. I just got a text message—that's what woke me up.

It's her.

Charlotte's text is just letting me know she's on her way back home now, and she'll see me soon. She adds some kissy-face emojis and a string of *X*s and *O*s. I rub the sleep out of my eyes with one hand, already texting back with the other to say I can't wait to see her.

I can't.

She's *coming home*.

I don't even care how needy and clingy I seem, if it makes me a loser or anything like that. None of that matters, because Charlotte is on her way home, and *she said yes*.

Fuck, I can't believe I'm engaged.

I can't believe she drove all the way here to tell me she'd seen the video, and to tell me *yes*. I can't believe practically everyone in the damn building came out to witness it.

Well, I guess I wanted some iconic, unforgettable proposal.

After I reply to Charlotte, I scroll quickly through the barrage of notifications that have pinged through overnight. New Patreon patrons, new subscribers, a few creators *I* like who've tagged me on Twitter saying how much they love *Dear Charlotte*. I risk opening up YouTube, and see hundreds of new comments waiting for me to scroll through. A quick glance reassures me they're overwhelmingly positive, which is a relief.

I open my email, thinking I'll clear a few things out of my inbox, delete the most recent junk mail, and a couple of emails catch my eye. One from a company selling photography and video I initially assume is junk, another from a nerdy subscription box company with the subject *Collab*.

And I was worried accidentally uploading the wrong video would ruin my career. At least *some* brands don't think so.

I know I should already be bolstered enough by the simple, brilliant fact that I'm engaged now, but the response online, those emails, the tweets from people I admire, definitely gives me a considerable boost.

I set my phone back down and get up, kicking the sheets to the bottom of the bed and stretching, then grabbing up my glasses. I make my way to the kitchen before correcting my routine, taking a shower first instead.

Charlotte's not going to be here for a couple of hours, and it's not like any of this should be a big deal, but it *is*. Once I'm dressed, I head out—out for the first time in days, beyond the balcony, a shopping list ready on my phone.

There's nobody around when I go downstairs, which is in itself a little unnerving; after the last week, I think I was half expecting to see Mr. Harris here signing people in and out, giving out face masks and hand sanitizer. I grab the door handle hesitantly, almost surprised when it's not locked.

I'm pretty sure I'll have forgotten what a luxury this feels like in a week. But for now, nothing can bring me down. I'm *outside*. I'm engaged! I'm a goddamn viral sensation. I'm unstoppable. I could swear everything looks brighter, smells sharper, but I'm not sure if that's because I haven't left my apartment in so long or because I'm in such a good mood.

Maybe the way I'd planned to propose didn't go exactly the way I wanted it to, but I still want to make this weekend special for her, as much as I can. I end up filling the cart with a few extras: some chocolate chip cookies, fresh from the bakery I know she likes; smoked salmon; eggs; and an avocado so I can make her a fancy breakfast tomorrow. I stop by the booze aisle, reaching for a bottle of prosecco before catching myself, and grabbing a Moët & Chandon with wild abandon.

It's not like extra special champagne can spoil the surprise now, right?

It's a long walk home, and I probably (definitely) shouldn't have gone so overboard. It's warm out today, and between that, the weight of the shopping, and the fact that I'm not exactly what you'd call *athletically inclined*, I need another shower by the time I get back.

I spend some time trying to tame my hair, even though it's a fairly useless effort. It stands up and out and across in a puffy mess. One of these days, I'll bother to spend some money—and time—investing in some hair products that might make my hair a little less . . . well. Just *less*.

Giving up on my hair, I notice a bruise on my forehead where I fell off the sofa yesterday. That's going to look *great* in the selfies I know Charlotte will want to take, I think, grimacing.

I raid the makeup she left behind, experimenting with dabbing on some concealer. I accidentally use some highlighter the first time, though, ending up with a sparkly forehead.

"Maddox, you look like a fucking unicorn," I mutter at myself in the mirror, turning at an angle to see the bump on my head, now shining in the daylight. I scrub it off and try again, pleased when I'm a little more successful this time—even if it does look a bit orange-y.

I potter around the apartment, but I already tidied and cleaned it up yesterday afternoon. There's not really anything else to do.

I check on Find My Friends, but Charlotte's still a while away.

Agitated, I sit on the sofa to play video games, but I can't even focus on *Animal Crossing* for more than five minutes. My knees are bouncing and I feel sick with excitement. I go through some of my notifications; the proposal video is still gaining traction.

Charlotte giggled over the phone to me yesterday when I apologized and said I'd take it down. "Don't be silly! People love it. It's *really* cute, Ethan. I don't mind if you want to leave it up."

Now, I move to my computer, pulling up the YouTube Studio page, hovering over the trash icon beside the *Dear Charlotte* video ready to delete it.

I can still hear Charlotte's giggle echoing in my ears, see the way she grinned up at me from the grass outside.

The only reason I was so devastated the video got out was because it ruined all my (not very) carefully laid proposal plans. And Charlotte's right—people *do* seem to really love it. I've noticed, maybe, like, a couple hundred or so trolls or mean comments— which is basically nothing, in the context of the number of views and comments the video has.

I move the mouse away from the Delete button, and turn on my camera instead.

I clear my throat, smooth back my hair, and start talking.

*

"Hey, guys. It's me—Ethan. Some of you probably don't know me that well, and have never heard of my channel before, but . . . well, I guess you know me *pretty* damn well by this point, after watching me lay my soul bare over the girl I love. If you're new here: thanks! It's great to have you! I'll link a couple of my most popular playlists down in the description if you want to check those out, and if you like it, be sure to subscribe and find me on Twitch for more, and you can find a link to my Patreon there, too, if you'd like to help me keep creating.

"But . . . " I pause here, rubbing the back of my neck and giving an awkward laugh before looking up at the camera again. "I guess

I just wanted to address that last video. Obviously, it wasn't what I was planning to upload yesterday. My girlfriend, Charlotte, got stuck staying with her parents all week because our building was locked down for this whole virus sitch, and in case it wasn't completely bloody obvious in my video, I really missed her, and I guess that got me thinking about our future and stuff.

"I'm not . . . not good with words, usually, but talking to a camera is something I'm pretty comfortable with." My hands flap back and forth between me and the screen, as if to demonstrate. "I figured if I sat there and talked at my camera long enough, I'd know what I wanted to say to her when I proposed. Except, obviously, that plan went all to shit, because I accidentally uploaded the wrong video. And I know some people think it was some kind of publicity stunt, or just a bid to go viral, or whatever, but I can *promise* you—I was mortified. I was half-asleep—and a little tipsy—when I uploaded the video, and it was a total accident.

"A happy accident, though, because . . . well, I know a lot of you guys are wondering . . .

"She said yes! So, uh, yeah. Thanks for, uh, watching, and for all the well wishes. I really appreciate it, and so does Charlotte. It's really sweet of you guys. But, hey, that's it from me for now! And sorry this isn't my usual kind of video, either, but I figured after the last one, I'd better update you all. And," I add finally, clasping my hands lightly together, my index fingers pointing together toward the camera while the rest of my fingers fold over each other, "regular programming will resume on my channel from here on out. I don't expect to turn into a wedding planning channel, but, hey, who am I kidding? I'll probably be so damn excited I'll be telling you guys everything anyway.

"Thanks for watching, I've been Ethan Maddox, and you've been awesome."

*

I sit back and hit upload before I can second-guess myself. It's not even edited to cut out the *um*s or the long pauses, and the audio and lighting and color grading probably aren't too great, either, but I can't bring myself to care in the way I usually do.

It's really *not* what I'd normally post, but if I'm going to leave the *Dear Charlotte* video up (even if just for a little while), I'd better follow up and address it.

Especially since the whole internet is clamouring to know what happened.

I title the video *She said yes*, and aside from the default message pushing viewers to subscribe, and links to some of my playlists and other social media, I leave the description blank.

Jack messages me within five minutes of the video going live to tell me I'm a sap, and good God that was sickly sweet, and he loves me and he's waiting for an equally great viral video for me to ask him to be my best man.

I laugh at the text, but now he's mentioned it that might actually be a really fun idea.

And I mean, *obviously*, he's going to be my best man. I'll bet Charlotte's already asked Maisie to be her maid of honor. I get a message from Nate a few minutes later too—berating me for "doing too good a job" and setting unrealistic expectations for him, when he finally does find a girl he wants to settle down with. (It makes me wonder how the week with his one-night stand has gone; I'll have to ask him.)

I do have another video. Maisie's friend Isla, who lives in Number Fifteen upstairs, recorded the whole thing on her phone yesterday from her balcony. The audio quality isn't great, and the footage is shaky, but I have it saved on my computer and know I'll treasure it regardless.

I definitely have no plans to upload that one, though. That's just for me and Charlotte.

Speaking of . . .

I check Find My Friends again.

She's only a few minutes away.

I jump back out of my seat, pacing the apartment to burn off my renewed nervous energy. I go out on to the balcony, leaning over it and bouncing on the balls of my feet, watching her little dot move closer and closer on the map, and then finally:

"Oi!" I shout down from the balcony, spotting a shock of ginger hair and a familiar bag. "Future Mrs. Maddox!"

Charlotte's head immediately twists in my direction, and her face splits into a smile.

And just like that, I'm gone, clattering out of the apartment and not even wearing a pair of socks, barreling down the stairs and almost falling flat on my face again, throwing the door open just as Charlotte arrives outside.

She looks startled to see me, but I only catch the look on her face for a split second before I've wrapped her in my arms, pulling her flush against me, getting a whiff of her coconut shampoo, and I'm kissing her, and it feels so goddamn *good* to kiss her, and I'm not sure I've ever been this in love with her.

Charlotte lets out a startled squeak against my lips, but it quickly turns into a giggle. Her bag hits the ground and her arms wrap around my neck, like she can pull herself even closer to me. Her lips curve into a smile as she kisses me.

"Hey, you," she murmurs.

"God, I missed you."

She giggles again as she kisses me once more. "You don't say?"

We break apart for air when someone clears their throat.

It's Mr. Harris, raising an eyebrow at us and trying not to look too smiley at our soppy display.

"You kids want to take that inside? Or farther outside? Six feet, remember? You're blocking the way."

We both look around and see an older couple dithering on the stairs, not sure if they're allowed to scoot past us. I give them a sheepish smile, while Charlotte doesn't even blush. I pick up her bag and we stand to the side to let them out, before going inside to our own apartment. I wrap an arm around her waist, like I can't get enough of her—because, well, I can't.

"Hang on," I tell her, stopping her as she gets to our door. I might not be *athletically inclined*, but I can manage to scoop her up, bridal style, to carry her two feet through the door before setting her back down. Charlotte can't stop laughing, or smiling, and I love it. I love her, so much.

"Watch it, or I'm going to start expecting this sort of treatment all the time."

"Well, you know, I'm only doing it for the YouTube views," I joke back, and then she's folding herself into my arms to kiss me again, and I have never been so happy to screw something up so badly in my life.

Chapter Forty-three

"So this is . . . "

"Weird, right? And . . . "

"Totally crazy?"

Danny laughs, looking a little relieved that I'm on the same page—but, mostly, excited. "Abso-fucking-lutely."

My heart is beating fast, but I can't stop smiling. This *is* crazy. I must be crazy for even suggesting it; and Danny must be crazy for agreeing to go along with it. A week of total isolation from the rest of the world has driven us both utterly and completely bonkers.

It's the only explanation for it.

Why else would we be agreeing to move in together for the fore-seeable future, after only dating for a month—well, five weeks now?

Definitely, definitely crazy.

Danny was slow to get his things together this morning, and I could sense his hesitation. Finally, he asked me when I thought we'd see each other next. The general guidance to the public has gotten a lot stricter in the last week, leaving us faced with the idea of spending the next several weeks apart.

I feel like Danny and I have got to know so much more about each other this last week, so much faster than we might have done otherwise; and he'd told me that he thought the same thing. How else would I have known he brushes his teeth after breakfast (while I brush mine before) or that he folds his boxers so precisely after they've gone through the laundry, or that he likes rewatching old Trevor Noah videos for a quick distraction from work when he's getting stressed over something? I didn't even bother putting on *makeup* yesterday. And I managed to poop this morning without freaking out about the fact that Danny was in the apartment.

I've liked having Danny around. Well. All things considered, *overall*, I've liked it.

So when he asked when we'd see each other next, I'd said quietly, "I don't know," and he'd said, "Yeah. It's weird, isn't it? I'm—I'm going to miss you, Isla, a lot."

And then I'd been staring at him and thinking how bloody handsome he was and how I was most definitely *in love with him*, and how much more difficult it would be for us to keep our new relationship going if we couldn't see each other or really spend any time together, and he'd been looking at me like he was thinking the same thing, and . . .

Well, here we are.

Being utterly crazy.

And moving in together. At least, sort of, for now.

I can only imagine what all my friends and my family are going to say when I tell them. Although Maisie said it wasn't the most ridiculous thing she'd heard this week; I guess I do have some serious competition there.

I *know* it's wild, and a huge step we might not be ready for . . .

But, I guess, on the other hand, if it doesn't work out, then we'll know sooner rather than later.

And I just like him so darn much.

I love him.

I love him!

"Just a month," Danny says, trying to be serious, his lips pressed into a firm line even though his eyes are glittering at me.

"Thirty-day trial period," I confirm. "Like Amazon Prime."

He laughs. "I'll be sure to mention that in my epic proposal speech viral video."

"The one you'll have the skywriters for, in front of the Eiffel Tower, right?"

Danny cups my face in his hands before peppering it with kisses, leaving me giggling and blushing, and swooning when his lips close over mine. His beard tickles my cheek, but I kind of don't hate it. It's actually a really cute look on him. It makes him look older; it's quite distinguished, actually. I rest my hands against his chest, broad and firm, loving the way the rest of the world stops existing when he kisses me. I feel almost light-headed, delirious, but in the best way possible.

I could spend a *lifetime* kissing this guy.

When we break apart, his arms are still wrapped around me, and he nuzzles his nose against mine. "And you're *definitely* sure about this?"

"Only if you are."

"As long as you still promise to cook dinner a couple nights a week."

I laugh. "What, like my special cinnamon chicken last night didn't put you off for life?"

Like it was *my* fault he'd decided to tidy up my kitchen to make it a little more cooking friendly (talking about the "flow" of it, like I had *any* clue what he meant) and rearranged the handful of spices I owned, meaning I'd accidentally added a generous dash of cinnamon to our fajitas last night, instead of chili powder.

Danny makes an exaggerated gagging noise at the mere memory of my dinner disaster, but hugs me closer anyway, kissing the side of my head. "Don't worry. By the end of this month, I'll have you cooking like a pro."

I don't actually *hate* the idea of spending time in the kitchen with Danny, and him teaching me how to cook. I get a sudden image of us being middle-aged, in some big, cozy kitchen, cooking some big family meal side by side, and bury my face in his chest before he can see me blushing.

Because I am *really* running away with myself here.

But can you blame me?

He's *perfect*.

Maybe *perfect* is a bit of a stretch, but he's as close as any guy could ever get, I figure. I'm starting to see what Ethan meant in his video, where he talked about all of Charlotte's flaws, and loving her not just in spite of them but including them.

There's still so much I have to learn about Danny. I know not all of it will be perfect. Rather than scaring me, though, it just makes me excited to spend more time with him.

"Okay," he says, and lets me go to step away, picking up his phone, wallet, and car keys, then putting on his coat. "I'll be back in like, an hour? Maybe two, if the queue at the supermarket's bad. Text me if you think of anything else you want me to pick up."

I nod, promising to, and follow him downstairs. I'm only wearing a pair of my yoga pants, one of his hoodies, and my slippers—but don't really care.

Danny has seen me looking a *complete* mess this week, and he doesn't even mind.

It's so refreshing to be able to completely relax around a boy, to not have to feel like I'm still making a good impression so early on in the relationship, or easing out of being the "perfect girlfriend" to, like, actual human being, who has morning breath and gets angry about silly little things and needs to use the bathroom.

He's going home to pick up some more of his things, to move in for—well, who knows how long? We agreed we'd try it for a month, but on the understanding that if it's going well, he'll stay beyond that.

And he's going to go grocery shopping, because he has a car and I don't, and because—well, *duh*. He is the cook, out of the two of us, as proven by my culinary catastrophe of cinnamon chicken.

We kiss good-bye again, and I'm *so* relieved it's only for a couple of hours. I think I might actually have cried a little if I'd had to say a proper good-bye.

I decided yesterday I wouldn't tell him how I feel, just yet. I didn't want him to think I was just swept up in the rush of the romantic proposal we watched, or that I was only saying it because I knew we might not see each other for a while. I think we were on the same page about that too.

But, who knows? Maybe in a couple of weeks, even in a few days, I won't be able to keep it to myself any longer, and I'll want to tell him.

I mean, if this past week of living together hasn't scared him off, I think, he's not going to go running for the hills because I say "I love you."

It's a beautiful feeling. My whole body feels like it's full of fizz, like if I jumped I might just float away. Like I could spin around and sing my heart out and smile forever.

I stay outside for a couple of minutes after Danny's driven off, enjoying the feeling of starting to fall in love, and the sunshine, and the fact that I'm *out of the building* for the first time in over a week, and it's blissful. I can't wait to go for a run later.

God, it's going to be so good.

Chapter Forty-four

I know Zach's strengths don't lie in big-picture planning—God knows I know that, after this week—but I'm still so confused. With the quarantine on the building finally lifted, we're allowed out again. Which is why Zach is . . .

Which is why Zach is packing a bag.

He looks through the wardrobe, picking out another shirt and folding it up carefully, smoothing it out before placing it into his bag.

It's just a couple of weeks, I remind myself, watching him.

It's . . . for the best.

It's for the best, we both decided. It was actually Zach's decision—for a change. He'll go stay with Matty and Alex for a couple of weeks, in their guest room. Just to give us both space and give *him* the chance to really think about what he wants.

We talked some more yesterday, but once he'd told me, in an unusually firm and serious manner, that he'd decided to go and spend some time with his brother, neither of us had been in the mood to hash things out. We'd ended up cuddling under a blanket on the sofa and watching a movie instead.

I don't think I'd care that much if he told me he was really against getting married. If he thought it wasn't worth the money and the extravagance, and he didn't *get* the whole ceremony when it just boiled down to a contract, and couldn't we just get one of those instead. I could live with that. If he said he didn't want to stay in the city—well, that would be okay, I guess. We could find a compromise and work that out. I couldn't compromise so much on kids, though—that doesn't seem to have so much gray area.

It's not like I want to break up with him. Really, it's not.

I love Zach. And maybe it took this huge fight for me to really remember that, but I *do*. I want to be with him.

I just want him to figure out what *he* wants.

At least now, though, Zach gets that. And he knows he needs some space to work it all out.

"Have you seen my black jeans?" he asks, rifling through a drawer. "The ones with—"

"They're on the radiator in the hall. You spilled pesto on them the other night, remember?"

He snaps his fingers at me, nodding, and goes to get them, folding them carefully and adding them to his bag. I watch him packing, going through a mental checklist in my head.

"Got your laptop charger?"

"Yeah."

"And your prescription sunglasses?"

"*Yes.*"

"And your nasal spray? You know your hay fever's going to be way worse out at Matty's place."

"*Yeah*—uh, no. Shoot, I forgot that. Thanks."

He rifles through the top drawer of the dresser looking for it.

"You left it on the balcony."

"Thanks."

I wander out of the bedroom after him, lingering in the lounge and spotting all the places his stuff is missing. His Kindle's vanished from the coffee table, along with his laptop and headphones. The apartment's going to feel so empty without him around, I realize now, even if it's not for long—and even if I'm desperate for a little space too.

I scrape my hands back through my hair, my stomach tying itself into knots.

God, I really don't want us to have to break up.

And if I could, I'd tell him not to go, I'd tell him none of this mattered and that we could forget all about it. But . . . well, it *does* matter. Maybe not right now, maybe not in a year, but at some point, it's all going to matter, and it's not something I can just forget about. We can't just move on; for better or worse, we need to figure out how to move *through* this.

Zach skirts past me, saying offhandedly, "What if we got a *small* dog, though? Like, a cat-sized one. I could forgo the golden retriever for a little dog."

"Oh, and you'd walk it all the time and pick up the poops?"

"More than I'd be cleaning out cat litter," he scoffs, nose wrinkling. "And one that wouldn't *shed*."

I'm about to argue with him over how much more work dogs must be, but stop myself. *He's trying*, I remind myself. And it's not like I don't like dogs, or anything.

I can't help the way I purse my lips, frowning at him. "Just please promise me you're not going to do something ridiculous like adopt a dog while you're gone."

"I would *never*," he says, looking affronted, holding a hand to his chest. When I raise my eyebrows at him, he averts his eyes, mouth twisting up on one side as he mumbles, "You know we're not allowed pets in this building, anyway."

I've never been so glad for the rule; I honestly wouldn't put it past Zach to do something like find some adorable little cat-sized mutt at a dog shelter, bringing it back with him and holding it up next to his face, giving me his own set of puppy-dog eyes and winning me over with this adorable little monster, like it'll help fix all the cracks in our relationship instead of making things worse.

He would *absolutely* do something like that.

And then I'd have ended up getting horribly attached to the dog and it would've been some crazy custody battle situation to try and figure out which of us got to keep the dog if we *did* end up breaking up. Like we didn't have enough shit to work through already.

I hate that I'm thinking like we're already broken up. Like it's guaranteed that we will.

I think I'm just . . . trying to mentally, emotionally, prepare myself for it.

Because after this week, it feels more like an inevitability than anything else. But I need to be *sure*, and I need Zach to be sure too. Even if our one major decision as a couple is to break up, I need us to at least do this much together.

I need to know we tried. Or that, maybe, there was simply no amount of trying that could fix us.

Zach finishes gathering up all of his stuff. He carries his duffel bag and backpack into the hallway, setting them down with a sigh and then looking at me, his eyes wide and sad, his mouth downturned. His hair is a mess.

"Well," he says.

"Yeah," I whisper.

I don't want him to go.

I don't want this to be over.

"It's just a couple of weeks," he says, like he's reading my mind.

I nod, afraid that if I open my mouth, my voice will wobble and I'll start crying.

Is this how it ends?

Zach sighs again, and steps toward me, enveloping my stiff body in a warm hug. I bury my face in his shoulder, inhaling the scent of his cologne like I might never smell it again, which I know is silly even as I do it. He kisses the top of my head then steps back, holding me at arm's length.

"I love you. You know that, right?"

I nod, sniffling. Shit, I *am* crying. Brilliant. "Yeah. Yeah, I know. I love you too."

"I can still call Matty, if you want. Get him to come pick me up."

I shake my head. "Take the car, Zach."

"No. No, you might need it. It's fine. I can take the bus into work."

"Don't be so silly. I can walk to the shops from here, and it's not like I'm driving into the office right now or anything. You'll need the car to get back for work."

It's going to be a long commute for him, but Zach was adamant that he'd leave, rather than me going back to my parents' place. He's always been sweet like that. Selfless. Wanting to make life easier for everyone else—like the way he wants to leave me the car, even though it makes sense for him to take it. *Damn him*, and his big heart.

I get the car keys off the hook near the door, pressing them into his hand. "Take the car, Zach."

He's ready to argue, but sees me smiling at him, and shakes his head, giving in. I grab his backpack, and the two of us step out of the apartment to really *go somewhere* for the first time in a week. Mr. Harris, the caretaker who's been keeping us all under careful lock and key all week, barks at us to "Keep your distance, folks. Six feet, remember? Not having this bloody place being shut down again already."

We hang back a little from the older lady who's roughly our parents' age leaving the building. She tries to hold the door for us before we all realize that'll compromise the whole social distancing rule, so there's an awkward back and forth before she gives us an apologetic shrug and lets the door go.

Outside, we stand out of the way on a patch of grass, facing each other again.

"Can I . . ." Zach cuts himself off, biting his lip and frowning down at the floor. I wait, and eventually he takes a deep breath and tries again, "Can I call you, later?"

"I—I think . . . I think maybe it's best you don't, Zach. Not tonight, anyway. But maybe . . . maybe we can talk in a few days? Check in?"

"I promise I'm going to take this seriously," he tells me, and he looks more sincere than I've ever seen him. There's a gravity about him I'm not used to. "I'm really going to think about all of this. Us. Our future. If we have one, what I want it to look like. I want us to make this work, Serena."

"Me too. I just don't want it to work in a way either of us are just . . . settling for, or don't really want."

He nods. "Yeah. Yeah, I know. Well, I'll—I'll call you, um, in . . . I'll call you soon. And I'll see you in a couple of weeks."

Even if it's just to move out for good, seems to go unsaid, but we both know that might end up being the reality of it.

I step toward Zach to hug him again, and kiss his cheek before we part. "Drive safe."

We both hesitate for a moment, but then Zach gives me a last smile, and heads off to the car park around the side of the building, and it's suddenly hard to breathe.

Watching him go, I don't feel as sad as I did upstairs, I realize. I'm scared, sure, but, if anything, I feel . . . at the very least, peaceful. This is the right thing, for both of us, even if this is it for us.

"Hey, Serena!"

I turn around, spotting Isla from down the hall waving to me from a little way off. She walks toward me, careful to keep a distance. She's in her slippers and a boy's hoodie, and folds her arms over her chest. She's not wearing makeup—which, I realize, is the first time I've ever seen her *not* all done up. Even when we were getting our shopping the other day, she was all dressed up with a full face of makeup. Without it, I see she's got freckles, and a couple of spots on her chin, and she gives me a sympathetic smile, nodding her head in Zach's direction.

"Was that Zach just leaving?"

"Um, yeah. He's going to stay with his brother for a little while. Just, um . . ."

"I—I heard you guys arguing, earlier this week," she tells me, her cheeks flushing as she admits it. "Did you sort it all out?"

Oh God, I *hate* that the neighbors all heard us arguing. I was scared she might have, but when she hadn't mentioned it on Wednesday— *or* made any reference to it on her Instagram—I thought we might've gotten away with it.

I really hope they don't think it was only about the pineapple pizza.

"We're . . . working through some stuff, you know."

She nods, her smile brightening a little. "I'm glad to hear it. I hope it's—well, I hope you two work through it."

"Thanks."

"I'll get Zach's things back to you as soon as I've washed them. Thanks again for letting me borrow them. And if . . . if you ever want someone to talk to," she adds, blushing, looking a bit unsure of herself, "we can always sit out here with a drink one day. If you wanted an impartial opinion, or whatever."

"Uh . . ."

I don't know if Isla's just after some gossip, or what, but she looks so sweet when she offers that I realize maybe she's just a little lonely—and even though we can, like, actually *leave* the building now, it's not like we can really go very far or socialize much; the rules have all changed so drastically in this last week we've been in lockdown.

I guess it wouldn't hurt to have another friend to hang out with, or talk to about some of this stuff. Especially someone *actually* impartial, like she is. (Plus, I'd love to know more about this guy she's been talking about on her Instagram all week. I had no idea she had a *serious* boyfriend.)

I guess I'd like to know that someone's found their relationship is worth fighting for, this week.

So I smile, and say, "Sure. Yeah, I'd really like that."

At the very least, it might take my mind off Zach.

I miss him already.

Chapter Forty-five

*M*aid of Honor's log, *day WHO CARES IT'S FINALLY OVER OHMIGOD I AM FREE AT LAST HALLE-FREAKING-LUJAH SOUND THOSE CHURCH BELLS I AM FREE THEY ARE LEAVING.*

I'm trying very hard not to get in the way of everyone, but it's difficult.

I want to sing and dance and bounce around my apartment cheering at the top of my lungs, chivvying them all out so I can finally have my space back and get some normality back in my life.

The apartment has been chaotic all week—between the wedding stuff, the air bed, all the extra blankets and pillows where Lucy and I were staying in the living room, everyone's things, and the fact that there are, in case I hadn't mentioned it enough yet, *four people* in my little apartment, it would've been impossible to keep it under control, hard as we all tried.

But right now, it's like a bomb went off in here. The place is a wreck. The clean lines, the modern minimalism I cultivated so carefully on moving in, is a thing of the past. It makes that Tracey Emin bed look like something out of the John Lewis catalog.

It looks even messier than after Kim had ripped up the wedding favors and centerpieces and smashed the prosecco bottle—which is *really* saying something.

The air bed is half-deflated, standing propped up and sagging against one wall. My laundry basket is in the middle of the room, overflowing with this week's sheets and blankets. As I watch, Lucy starts rummaging through it, looking for her other bra and muttering to herself. There's a cluster of mugs on the coffee table—some of them empty, one of them still steaming hot, others half-drunk and forgotten. The boxes of wedding favors and centerpieces are pushed underneath the dining table, although Kim has promised to take them with her, now that Jeremy's coming to pick her up.

It shouldn't be this difficult for three girls to pack their bags.

And yet.

Here we are, having all been awake for hours, and they're still packing.

Addison was convinced she couldn't find her phone anywhere, and it was only after we all went deathly silent and called it, listening carefully for the telltale buzz, that we found it had somehow ended up in the bottom of Lucy's immaculately packed bag, which Addison promptly upended onto the sofa (hence the currently missing bra). Kim has been running back and forth, suddenly remembering something else of hers that either she brought, or that Jeremy packed and dropped off for her, that is now floating around my apartment somewhere.

The entire morning has been punctuated with shouts of:

"Liv, is this yours? I don't remember mine having this mark on it."

"Ads, will you *move*? You can't possibly need all this space. I'm trying to pack here."

"Has anybody seen my other slipper?"

"Luce, where did you say you saw my skirt? *Yes*, I'm sure I didn't pack it already, I . . . Oh, no, I did. Never mind."

I've been trying to hang at the edge of the room, surveying the carnage. There's not a lot I can do to help, after all. This is absolutely one of those "too many cooks" situations.

But God, if I could help, I would. If I could shove all their things into a bin bag and toss them out onto the curb to restore the sanctuary of my apartment, I absolutely would.

Which I know is completely overdramatic, but I never realized what an introvert I really was until this week—and not just because Lucy suggested one night that we all do the Myers-Briggs test. It's been *exhausting*, in every way possible.

It was bad enough before the fight with Kim, but since we cleared the air, I've spent the last two days hyperaware of my every interaction with Addison.

I'm still not totally convinced she *is* flirting with me.

Or that if she is, it's just because she's simply a flirty sort of person.

Either way, I've had the great joy of spending the last two days overanalyzing *everything* she does, and *everything* I've said to her, which has been just *delightful*.

I hate everything.

I hate Kim for pointing it out, and I hate Lucy for agreeing with her.

Friday night, once we'd all gone to bed, I'd whispered through the dark to Lucy, "Kim reckons Addison's been flirting with me all week. Which is ridiculous, right?"

"Ridiculous that it took her pointing it out to you for you to realize," Lucy said, which was the most aggressive stance she'd taken on anything all week. "She's been trying to make you laugh all week. Anytime she cracks a joke, she looks at you to see if you're going to laugh. Why do you think she kept doing her impression of Trump?"

I propped myself up on one elbow to peer through the darkness at Lucy, whose face was illuminated slightly by the glow of her phone. "You're telling me that her talking like Trump is her way of flirting with me?"

"She wanted to get your attention. It's all she's been doing all week."

"I still think that's just because she's—"

"American?"

"I was going to say exuberant."

"That too."

It didn't help that Lucy and Kim started to give me a pointed look or nudge whenever Addison said or did something that they counted as flirtatious; it was completely cringeworthy, because neither of them was exactly subtle about it, and I was also pretty sure that Kim had mentioned our conversation to Addison, to encourage her not to be put off by my lack of responsiveness. ("It's not that she doesn't like you," I could imagine her saying, "it's just her resting bitch face.")

Even without the complication of Addison flirting (or not) with me—I can't wait for them to leave. I can't wait to scrub the apartment clean and get the laundry done. I can't wait to take out the overflowing recycling bin. I can't wait to sit down on the sofa in absolute peace and quiet, and not have to worry about playing hostess, or being conscious of anybody else, or have to hold a conversation or discuss what to watch on TV.

Oh God, I have never been so excited to be *alone* again.

At this point, I don't care if the whole bloody *country's* in lockdown and I might not be able to hang out with anybody again for a couple of months. This past week has been *more* than enough socializing to see me through the next year.

*

I see them all to the main door of the building, one at a time.

Lucy is the first to leave—the most organized, her bags are packed first, and though she offers to stay after the others are gone to help me clean up, I tell her not to be silly and to get herself off home. Neither of us are big huggers, but we stand outside the building awkwardly, smiling at each other, before she clicks her tongue and sighs, smiling, stepping forward to give me a light, one-armed hug, which I return.

"Thanks so much for the last week," she says, for the billionth time.

"I really appreciate it. I know I wouldn't have been able to handle it if it was the other way around. It's been really nice, though."

"Apart from the whole fight and Kim losing her shit?"

Lucy laughs, biting her lip, as if to try to stop herself. "Yeah. Yeah, apart from that."

"Well—drive safe."

We do the awkward dithering thing again, but don't hug this time. Once was *plenty*. She turns back once she's halfway down the path toward the car park to give me another smile and a little wave, which I take as my cue to go back inside.

Jeremy shows up not long after, so I walk Kim down to where he's idling along the side of the road. He jumps out, all but running to hug and kiss Kim hello. It's sweet, how much he's obviously missed her.

Sweet, but I still clear my throat to interrupt them, gesturing as best I can with my stack of boxes of wedding favors. "Not to interrupt the reunion, but you think you could open the boot?"

He does, blushing, and starts taking boxes off me to load into the car.

I tell him he owes me one, for suggesting it'd be a good thing to postpone the wedding, and feeding into Kim's insecurities and our whole argument. Jeremy looks abashed, but I can't stay mad at him. He's a total sweetheart.

Once we've stacked the last box in the car, Kim gives me a warm, tight, and sudden hug. "Ooh, thanks for this week, Liv. You're the best. And I'm still really sorry about . . . er . . . "

"Water under the bridge," I tell her.

"Please," she deadpans, giving me a serious look and clasping my hands, "*never* let me forget it. Next time I start acting like a bridezilla, bring it up. Never let me do that again."

I laugh. "Code word: lockdown."

"I love it."

It almost seems worth it now: Kim has totally mellowed out (at least for the foreseeable future) about the state of her wedding. She was even the one who grabbed some of the petals from the wedding favors to throw off the balcony when Charlotte showed up to respond to her boyfriend's online proposal yesterday. *And* she even said that it'd all work itself out, and maybe it wasn't such a bad thing if the wedding got postponed a little after all.

"Let me know how it goes with the caterers, and the venue," I say, though. Whatever else, I *am* still maid of honor. "Give me a shout if there's anything I can help out with. Making calls, sending emails, whatever."

"No." Kim's still holding my hands, and squeezes them now, smiling at me. "You have done *more* than your fair share of being my maid of honor, believe me. I'll sort it all out."

She gives me another hug before we part ways for her to climb into the car, where I notice Jeremy picks up her hand to kiss it. Through the open window, she calls, "I'll text you later. Bye, Liv!"

And then, at long last, it's Addison's turn to leave.

By the time I've waved the lovebirds off and gone back to my apartment, it's somehow miraculously back to looking vaguely like *my apartment*. The mess is gone, and Addison's stuff—which had still been *everywhere* until maybe ten minutes ago—is now packed up into her bag, and she's waiting near the door with her coat on, car keys dangling on the end of her finger.

She runs her free hand through her hair, shaking out the long waves, and cracks a smile at me, head tilting to the side slightly. "Don't look so surprised, Livvy. I know you're *dying* to get your apartment all back to yourself."

I try to smile, but just end up biting my lip and grimacing. "That obvious?"

"You were going behind us fluffing cushions and picking up empty cups last Friday, and we'd only been here a couple hours. Kim said you're kind of, uh . . . "

"High strung?"

"Reserved," she corrects me. "And bitch, please. Miss Kimberly is in *no* position to call anybody high strung," she adds with a cackling laugh. "She just said you're normally kinda shy, that's all. Private."

I dread to think what else Kim might've said about me, but I say, "You're not wrong. I have been really looking forward to being able to hear myself think again. It's been a long week."

"Oh, tell me about it. But, hey, if I could stay in lockdown hanging out with some awesome people and not having to work, I'd totally do it. So? Come on, Hostess with the Mostest, Butler Extraordinaire, you gonna escort me to my car too?"

I don't know why I'm suddenly so apprehensive for her to leave, but I swallow the lump in my throat and nod, opening the door again and walking the same route for the third time, down all the stairs and out of the building.

Neither of us says anything—which is only so noticeable because Addison's been a goddamn chatterbox all week; and it's not like I can't hold a conversation.

I'm suddenly glad for the note under our doors earlier this week imploring us not to use the lifts unless absolutely necessary, in an attempt to reduce the risk of infection, because there's suddenly a weird tension in the air and I don't think I could cope being in a confined space with her right now.

Am I overreacting? Is it just me, or does she notice it too?

I dither once we're outside the building, ready to say good-bye, but Addison keeps on walking, so I end up following her around to the little car park, where her yellow Mini Cooper is in one of the visitors' spaces.

I can't help but laugh when I see it. It's ostentatious and seems like *exactly* the car for Addison.

As if reading my mind, she grins at me as she tosses her bag into the back seat. "Cute, right? I couldn't resist. It's, like, not even the size of the cab in the truck I had when I was seventeen, I swear. It's so *quaint*."

"It's so *yellow*."

She closes the door and then steps back toward me, crossing her arms, one hip jutting out. Her eyes catch the sunlight, and her mouth twitches like she's trying not to smile. "So?"

"So what?"

"*So*," she says, "are you going to do this, or are you going to keep playing hard to get and make me do it?"

Oh my God.

I flush, but only manage to mutter, "I'm not playing hard to get."

"Fine." Addison tosses her head and fixes me with an amused look. "Livvy, when all this pandemic shit blows over, you wanna get a drink?"

My entire face is on fire.

My heart is pounding and my palms are sweating. Mostly, I think, because despite my first impressions of her, I really *would* like that. And I'm stunned that, even though she's had to put up with me just being myself, not even, like, the *best* version of me, for an entire week, she's *still* interested.

"Yeah. Yeah, I'd, um . . . " I clear my throat, not sure when my mouth suddenly became so dry. Addison is not what I'd call "my type," but hey, it's not like "my type" has worked out for me so far, right? And there's *something* in the air between us right now, something that has my heart racing and a smile playing at the corners of my lips.

So I suck in a sharp breath and get a sudden burst of courage to say, "I'd really like that, *Addy*. But maybe in the meantime, we can jump on the bandwagon and do one of those Zoom dates everyone's posting about."

She laughs, beaming at me. "Just say when. You've got my number."

"Yeah. I'll—I'll text you, then, I guess."

"You do that."

We stand there grinning at each other for a moment, before I surge forward, leaning up to kiss her. Just quickly, but *oh my God*, and when I step back, Addison's the one blushing, and all my nerves have disappeared.

She fiddles with her car keys and then says, "You know, since it's probably gonna be a while before we get to do a date IRL,"—oh, Jesus, she actually *said* "IRL," am I sure about this?—"I think we should probably do that again."

Whether she's the kind of person who says IRL or not—I absolutely, wholeheartedly, agree.

And I kiss her again.

ACKNOWLEDGMENTS

It's probably pretty obvious what inspired a book about being suddenly stuck inside 'on lockdown' due to a very contagious disease, so we don't need to talk about that too much here. But I will say that from March 2020, a couple of weeks before writing this book, I found myself on lockdown, on my own, in my little flat. Some of us, in a *Shaun-of-the-Dead* level of optimism, thought we'd give it a couple of weeks, bake some banana bread, and wait for it all to blow over.

Originally, this book—*Lockdown on London Lane*, as I titled it at first—was A Project. It was intended to keep me busy, give me focus for a few weeks when there seemed no end in sight for the lockdown. I decided to upload it on Wattpad to give me that sense of community I was missing, and because, well, maybe there were other people around who, like me, found the news too depressing to even contemplate watching, and needed a light-hearted distraction that didn't feel "doom and gloom."

So I hope that's what this is. A light-hearted distraction, from whatever might be going on.

There are a lot of people to thank for this book, so let's get started.

First up, I need to thank my friends. Ellie, Hannah, and Emily (the very same Cactus Updates crew from the dedication) for the brilliant virtual get-togethers; Lauren and Jen, always there to lift me up; Katie and Amy both for always being there on the other side of Messenger, putting up with me when I was being a needy extrovert stuck by myself. Aimee, because even if we haven't seen each other in months, you never fail to make me laugh. I feel like all my friends put up with a lot from me during lockdown, so thanks for always being there. I love you.

Massive thank-you to my family, as well. Mum and Dad; Gransha (my biggest fan, always); Auntie Sally and Uncle Jason. It was hard to be away from you guys for so long in the midst of all the madness, but the regular FaceTimes and virtual Happy Birthday singalongs every so often made that distance feel like nothing at all. And, of course, my brilliant sister, Katie, who deserves a special shoutout after having to live with me for almost an entire month before Christmas in our own sort of lockdown.

And then there are the people without whom this book would absolutely not have been possible. My wonderful agent, Clare, who is always championing me, along with the rest of the wonderful team at Darley Anderson. The entire team at Wattpad—specifically thanks to Caitlin, I-Yana, Deanna, and Paisley!—and the whole community on the Wattpad platform who kept me scrolling through comments for hours each week when I was uploading this in 2020. Bec and the team at Sphere, whose enthusiasm for this book was a much-needed boost in a really weird time!

This book is filled with a lot of characters, which feels apt given how many people go into helping create it behind the scenes. I hope you fall in love with the cast of this book as much as I did, and I hope you enjoy their adventures, whether you're reading this while at home on the sofa or out in the world on an adventure of your own!